BUM RAP IN BRANSON

Foreword

What ever happened to Jim Stafford? I wound up in Branson Mo. I moved to Branson in 1990, got my own theater and never looked back. I have a wife Ann, and two children; Shea, 10 and G.G. 6. I am 59. What's that like? Like never having to send the grandkids home. My wife and children are also in my show. Talk about a Mom and Pop operation. I love it.

So, one day I get this e-mail from a guy who says he's a writer and that Branson is the setting of his next book, and he'd like to talk to me. I call him up and he says he wants to put me in his book, which is a murder mystery, and he wants me to be a suspect in the murder. I say, "Did I do it? He says, "When I finish the book we'll both know." I said, "Go for it."

I'm glad I did because along to way I got to know Glenn Meganck (aka J.R. Ripley) and his family...nice people.

When Glenn finished the book, he sent me a copy and I really had fun with it. If you like mysteries that are funny and have thrills, spills, twists, turns and an ending you only thought you guessed, you'll like it too.

I think you'll also enjoy reading about Branson. You might even want to come see the place and take in some shows. Mine for instance...I really kill 'em.

Jim Stafford
Branson, Missouri

Praise for the author and his works:

"An entertaining outing...Tony and Rock remain an engagingly laid-back sleuthing duo." *Booklist*

"... Ripley comes up with a mixture of innovation, some wry commentary of the fads of the day...a grab bag of fun and excitement." *Midwest Book Review*

"Ripley pens exciting book of sex, murder, local color."
Oklahoma Tribune

"Ripley combines a fast pace with graphic descriptions...The Body From Ipanema reads like a TV thriller..." *I Love A Mystery*

"...Action-packed plot. Recommended." *Library Journal*

"Mystery fans will enjoy the clever plot, loopy characters, and sardonic humor." *Booklist*

"The action moves right along, dialogue spurts from the mouths of as eccentric a group as you could wish for." *I Love A Mystery*

"Wacky characters, liquid prose, frequent humor, and a decidedly light plot place this [Skulls of Sedona] in the fun, breeze-to-read category." *Library Journal*

"Skulls Of Sedona is quick and light-hearted and likely to give you a pretty good vibe." *Miami Herald*

"He always seems to write with a sort of tongue-in-cheek attitude...He has that touch of the bizarre, the outre, the silly...Always entertaining to read."
Oklahoma Tribune

"Written in a totally off-the-cuff, bare bones fashion...has a cutting sense of humor."
Midwest Book Review

"The story is light-hearted, sexy, funny and entertaining. Well-plotted, it rises to an amazing finale. The characters are well-drawn, interesting and believable." *The Tribune*

"...A mix of mystery, murder and mayhem."
The Chattooga Press

"...A thriller laced with a good dose of humor...it's perfect for an afternoon at the beach." *Island Reporter*

"If his books are as good as his songs, I reckon I need to get my act down to the library." *Nightflying*

"Trenet is a well-developed, likable character, and the novel offers an absorbing mystery set in the exotic playground of the rich and famous. An entertaining new series..." Booklist

"!!!!Exceptional" Today's Books, a Public News Service

"It would be hard not to like MURDER IN ST. BARTS. The dialogue, the humor, and the sarcasm give us all something to enjoy." I Love A Mystery

"It's A Young, Young World, by Glenn Meganck. . .fast-paced, wryly told, deftly written adventure laced with a very special insight into today's youth-centric culture. Highly recommended." Midwest Book Review

To all the new friends I've made in Branson...

BUM RAP IN BRANSON

J.R. RIPLEY

Beachfront Publishing

Beachfront Publishing, POB 811922, Boca Raton, FL 33481. Correspond with Beachfront via email at:
    info@beachfrontentertainment.com

    First edition January 2004

    Library of Congress Cataloging-in-Publication Data

Ripley, J. R. date
  Bum Rap In Branson / J. R. Ripley.
  p. cm.
  ISBN: 1-892339-89-7
  1. Kozol, Tony (fictitious character) – Fiction. 2. Rap musicians – Crimes against – Fiction. 3. Kewpie dolls – Fiction. 4. Guitarists – Fiction. 5. Branson (Mo.) – Fiction.
  I. Title: Bum Rap In Branson, a Tony Kozol mystery.

PS 3568.I635 B86 2004
813'.54-dc22   2003062816

    Printed in U.S.A.   10987654321

MAR 22 2004

BUM RAP IN BRANSON

Chapter 1

"Where the deuces is Butch?" hollered B.A.D.

"He ducked out for a bite."

That was Cyndi Parker, B.A.D.'s personal assistant. She'd poured herself into a thin pair of purple and black striped stretch jeans with a white Spandex tube-top. Glittering sequins accentuated areas of her chest which needed no accentuating. Cyndi Parker had one of those curvy, voluptuous bodies that was always getting her in trouble and men in more.

B.A.D. scowled. He was surrounded by incompetence and lassitude and footing the bill for each and every one of the malingerers now lurking about on the freshly painted, black stage floor. "That dude don't need a bite. He's so big, somebody ought to take a big ole bite outta him."

He drummed the fingertips of one hand against the other. They looked like a couple of big, brown tarantulas practicing Kung Fu fighting. The wispy tufts of hair on the backs of his hands only added to the illusion. "Dang. We open in a month and this whole darn stage has got to be extended. There's no room for all the dancers. I want this thing big. BIG!"

B.A.D. raised his hands high over his head. "We're trying to put on the biggest, baddest show the world has ever seen. Don't any of you people get it?"

B.A.D. turned and stopped outside the door to the large, private apartment attached to the back of the theater. "This is a B.A.D. Spike show." His hands gripped the doorframe. "It's got to be big. It's got to *be* B.A.D." His eyes circled the room, shooting bolts of fire at each and every one of the dozen or so employees unfortunate enough to be within his field of vision. "You all got that?"

Lowered heads muttered nervous, anxious-to-please replies.

"Cyn!"

"Yes, B.A.D.?" She was standing in the corner near the red velvet curtain, furiously jotting notes on her clipboard.

"Tell Butch to get his behind in here the minute he gets back." B.A.D. slammed the door and retreated.

The apartment was B.A.D.'s temporary living quarters. It contained a full kitchen, bath, two bedrooms and a living area where he entertained.

He was building a big house, 7,500 square feet worth, up above Table Rock Lake. The way things were going, it was gonna end up costing him nearly twice what he'd initially contracted. People were sucking him dry. This whole stinking enterprise was sucking up all his money, but it was going to pay off in spades.

B.A.D. rubbed his hands together. He just knew it.

B.A.D. Spike was gonna rule again.

Anything was possible if you just wanted it bad enough. And he did. He wanted success bad. That's why he called himself B.A.D.

Bad and Dangerous.

That was him. That was how he told himself he was going to live and he had. Still did.

Yeah, you just have to want it bad enough.

Attitude. It was all about attitude. And B.A.D. wasn't afraid to give attitude. Heck, he exuded the stuff. And he had to spend money to make money. It was an old adage, but true.

He was going to impress these people. With his money, his presence, his show.

B.A.D. stripped off his shirt and turned on the hot water. Going back to the living room to crank up the stereo, he caught sight of a tall figure of a man dressed in a tan suit and cowboy boots, complete with white cowboy hat coming in through the back door. "What the deuces are you doing here, man?" His voice rose two and a third notches. "And how'd you get in anyway?"

Merel Pearce grinned. "I own this place, remember?" He was chewing on a fat cigar.

B.A.D. scowled. "You might *own* it, but while I hold the lease, I decide who comes and goes." His eyes lighted on the key dangling from between Pearce's fingers. "Gimme that key."

Merel Pearce shrugged his broad-set shoulders and tossed the key over onto the red leather sofa.

This only made B.A.D. all the madder. "I've got the shower running, so why don't you just run on out of here your own self, Merel?"

"Now, now, Donald, don't get yourself all in a huff. It ain't good for the complexion."

B.A.D. was in Merel's face in two giant steps. Tall as Merel was, B.A.D. was taller. "Don't call me Donald. I've already told you that."

"Why not? It's your name, ain't it? Donald Milquist? That's what your birth certificate says."

"At least I've got a birth certificate," retorted B.A.D. Merel snapped. "What's that supposed to mean?"

"Figure it out, smart guy. Now, if you don't mind, clear out. I've got things to do." B.A.D. snatched the key off the couch and dumped it in the drawer of his desk.

"In a minute. In a minute. I hear things ain't going so well. Not too late to get out. I'd be happy to tear up the lease. Let you go. I'm a generous guy."

B.A.D. laughed. "Generous? Right, man! That's you, Mister Generosity." He was shaking his head. "I'm paying you top dollar for this joint and you know it."

"I wouldn't be leasing it to you at all if I hadn't outgrown it. My new place seats twenty-eight hundred. But," Merel drawled, "I guess a little old place like this will be enough for you. More than enough."

"You don't know nothin', Pearce. My opening show is booked solid. Once word gets out, folks will be coming from hundreds of miles away. Every night of the week. I'll be booked solid into next year."

"*If* you open."

"What's that supposed to mean?"

"I hear you've got troubles. Work's going slow. Problems with the stage. . ."

"Well, you heard wrong. Everything is right on

schedule."

"I also hear you want to do some remodeling. I won't allow it. You rent this place 'as is' and it stays that way."

B.A.D. smiled a big, toothy grin. "Already talked with my lawyers. All's I'm doing are leasehold improvements. I can demolish that stage and rebuild it if I want to." His grin grew even larger. "And I want to."

"I'm warning you, *Donald*, don't mess with me or my theater."

"Oooh, I'm so scared. You know, where I come from, a good old boy like you wouldn't last a day."

Merel's countenance darkened. "And where I come from, a boy like you would be pickin' cotton."

B.A.D. grabbed the handle of the door so fast and hard that the knob came off in his hand, but not before the door flew open. "Get out."

Pearce tugged on his bolo tie, looked the rapper up and down and strode slowly out the door to his pickup.

"Come back and see the show opening night," chided B.A.D. "I'll save you a seat in the VIP section. It's gonna be killer!"

He waited until Pearce and his pickup were out of sight then gripped the edge of the door with his fingertips and slammed it shut, mouthing a string of expletives as he did so.

B.A.D. propped a leather armchair up against the door to keep it from swinging open. He made a note to himself to talk to Cyn about getting it fixed. He waved a hand in front of his nose. The living room stank of Merel's foul cigar.

The water was still running and B.A.D. cursed. More money wasted, this time literally down the drain.

Nonetheless, he let it run a little longer. He had a call to make and this was more important.

He flipped through his address book, then dialed. "Hi. Listen, you got to get over here." He took in an earful of why this wasn't possible. "I know, but you've got to help me. Please?"

B.A.D. frowned as he listened to the response. "Well, just get here as soon as you can then. Yeah, I'll be waiting for you."

He laid down the receiver and headed for the shower, hoping the hot water hadn't run out. If it had, it would be just perfect. Everything seemed to be going against him.

Nothing was going the way he'd expected. If it weren't for bad luck, he'd have no luck at all. Wasn't that a song or something?

He'd been in Branson six precious months already. Six months of burning money and still he wasn't open for business. He tipped back his head and let the water soak into his tense muscles.

Fame. Fortune. Where had they gone? Six years ago, he'd still been on top of his game—on top of the world. Oh, well, he'd had a good run.

"I suppose I ought to be grateful," he muttered to the insensate Italian tiled walls. Grammy award winner for Best solo rap performance, best rhythm and blues song and best long form video, all in the early nineties. He even won the Billboard Magazine Music Award for #1 rap artist, an American Music Award, and the Soul Train Award.

He'd made commercials for Pepsi and Nike. Helped kids all over the country. Visited city schools, especially in San Francisco, where he'd been born and raised. Giving something back to the community. That was what it was all about.

Mattel even made a B.A.D. Spike doll—discontinued now— in a white suit with gold trim and big faux gold buttons. Man, that had been a gas. To this day, he kept one of the little characters on his dressing table. He called it Lil' B.A.D.

But in the course of the decade, B.A.D. Spike's star had dimmed greatly and now, he had to face it—he was washed up.

Standing in the shower—washed up. B.A.D. laughed at the irony. The hell with them all. He'd come back like a specter from the dead. B.A.D. would rise again. Just like the South, according to that pain in his backside, Merel Pearce.

He heard a commotion in the apartment. "Somebody out there?"

A second later, a voice replied. "It's only me, Cyndi. I'm looking for the checkbook. Syscomp says they won't install the new computers without a check."

B.A.D. cursed under his breath. "Fine. It's in the desk. Help yourself." Couldn't they wait until the job was done? So much for trusting your fellow man.

"Thanks."

As he dried himself off, he heard the apartment door being closed. "Yeah, help yourself. Why not? They all help themselves to my money." He tossed a T-shirt on over his sweat pants. "What little of it I've got left."

He slammed his feet into a pair of loose, plush slippers. His stomach growled. "Lawyers, guns and money." He stomped to the kitchen. "Now, I *know* that's a song."

Chapter 2

"I can't stand small planes." Rock stopped, oblivious to the exiting mob pushing past him, and began dusting himself off. Salty cracker crumbs fell from his black slacks to his shoes. He stamped his feet to shake them loose.

Rock Bottom, a giant of a man and a gifted bass player, sporting his usual buzz cut, wasn't about to let even an angry mob get in his way, let alone this relatively docile bunch of plane-tossed tourists. He was dressed in black, as always, like his hero, the Big Man himself, the Man In Black, Johnny Cash.

"It wasn't a small plane. You're a big guy." Tony was shorter than his friend with a bushy brown head of hair that never stayed in one place—sort of a metaphor for his life as an itinerant musician, always on the road for one job or another, working with one act or another. Country, classical, New Age, whatever paid the bills.

Tony spotted the sign to the baggage claim area and headed that way, lugging his guitar case in one hand. It held his prized Martin D-28, one of the few things he had of any value. It had once been his father's. Tony's dad had been a frustrated musician, working as an office manager, when what he'd wanted to do was to be a jazz guitarist. Tony was determined not to make the same mistake. Life was worth more than that.

As for Rock's gripes, Tony was used to them and didn't let them get to him anymore. "And would you hurry, please? We're running late on account of you. We've already missed the opening ceremony. Nanci won't be happy."

Rock pulled his shirt out like a tent stuck on the side of a steep mountain. "Ooh, the opening ceremony. Be still my fluttering heart. Besides, Nanci will get over it. I think she likes me."

"Sure," said Tony. "Keep the dream alive." Nanci Dement, a well-known folksinger, had hired Rock and Tony to accompany her in concert for a series of shows she was doing in Branson in conjunction with Kewpiecon, the annual celebration of Kewpie dolls and the life and works of Rose O'Neill, the creator of the Kewpie doll.

Tony figured Nanci liked Rock about as much as she liked toe fungus. Rock was a good guy, a great guy, but Tony couldn't see his pal being Nanci Dement's type. No, she was more the lover of the studious, pensive and moody poet type. Rock was more the beer in one fist, bass in the other type. A sweet heart, but not a complex heart.

Tony marched on. The distance between himself and Rock was growing.

"Listen, Tony," replied Rock, hurrying to keep up, his bass case slamming against his leg, "any plane without a jet engine attached is a small plane and that thing we came in on only had propellers. Propellers are ancient, like dinosaurs. And what do you mean 'on account of me'?"

Tony laughed. "I think you're blurring a few eras. Besides, old is what we're here for." He'd stopped at the baggage carousel. "And we had to catch a late flight today, instead of yesterday like we were supposed to on account of you."

"I told you. I had an appointment."

"You had a date," Tony said.

Rock looked shocked. "How did you know that?"

"Linda's cousin Joan works at Club Cristoff. She saw you there." Tony snatched his bag from between two businessmen who acted like they owned the spot. "Said you were at the club until closing, in fact."

"Hey, she was a neurosurgeon. I always wanted to date a lady doctor. What can I say?"

"You can say you're sorry. You can say, 'Tony, I'll never do anything so irresponsible ever, ever again.'" Tony pushed past a couple of kids and watched the bags roll along.

"Yeah, right," said Rock, catching his red bag on the first pass as it came tumbling down.

"Besides, I thought you had the hots for Nanci?"

Rock shrugged and deftly changed the subject. "So, about these Kewpie dolls—I never even heard of them until Nanci hired us for this show. Did you?"

Tony hoisted his own piece, a green duffel bag, over

his shoulder and marched off towards rental car country. "My Aunt Louise had a Kewpie. She got it when she was a little girl. She showed it to me when I told her about the gig we were going to be doing." Tony had been raised by his aunt and uncle after his own parents had died in a tragic boating accident.

"Aunt Louise has this delicate looking little pinkish Kewpie wrapped in tissue paper in a box up in her bedroom closet. I'll show it to you when we get back to Florida."

"Sure. You know I'm a big fan of pop culture." Rock searched his pockets for a stick of gum. He pushed the pack towards Tony, with a raked eyebrow, but Tony declined.

"Speaking of Aunt Louise, I told her I'd try to see what those old Kewpie dolls are worth. Who knows? Maybe she's sitting on a fortune."

Rock laughed. "Now you're dreaming."

They picked up their economy car, spent a moment bickering over directions from Springfield to Branson—neither had bothered listening to the rental agent's instructions—came to an agreement and headed south.

"Just once I wish we could rent a bigger car," said Rock, squirming around, looking for that perfect position. With his size and weight distribution there was none.

Tony's hands gripped the plastic wheel. "Since we had to cover our own expenses on this gig, consider yourself lucky to have a car at all. We could be on a bus."

"I think Nanci should be picking up all the expenses," griped Rock.

"Tell Nanci that," dared Tony. Nanci Dement was successful by folkie standards, but hardly rich. Tony and Rock had worked for big names before and been swaddled in luxury. This was not to be one of those times.

Some gigs worked out well, and they came home with money in their pockets; others were busts commercially and they barely broke even. Oh well, thought Tony, it kept the creditors at bay. Tony had failed as a lawyer through no fault of his own, and a restauranteur through no fault of his own and he wasn't about to fail as a musician. It was just about all he had left.

Tony hoped this gig for these Kewpie doll people wasn't going to end up in the latter category. It had been two solid months since they'd had a paycheck and what with shelling out for expenses on this trip, it didn't leave much money left to cover the rent. If something went wrong and Nanci didn't pay them, he'd lose his condo and he was on the brink of losing it anyway. If it wasn't for Rock moving in and helping with expenses, he'd have lost it long ago.

He'd have to move in with Aunt Louise. Not that shacking up with his aunt was so bad, but he was a grown man after all and cherished his independence. Something which, if he moved back home with his Aunt Louise, would be lost.

Aunt Louise was well-meaning but, with all she'd been through with her husband, his Uncle Jonathan, being incarcerated and losing everything, she had become demanding and needy. He didn't mind it on an outpatient basis but he did not, definitely did not, want to take it on twenty-four/seven.

"I just might tell Nanci," Rock said bravely, in

response to Tony's challenge. Though he knew he never would. He rapped his knuckles against the dash revealing a row of blue tattooed numbers. Years before, Rock had had the spaces between his knuckles tattooed, numbers one through five on each hand. He told Tony it had helped him learn to play the bass, knowing which finger was which using the Nashville numbering system.

They headed up and down Highway 65 as it cut a path through the Ozarks. One pile of rubble in the mountains through which the road had been cut looked more like an Aztec ruin than a plundered work of Nature. Tony expected to see Quetzalcoatl, the feathered serpent god, prancing around on top the mound announcing the day's sacrifices.

For what seemed like forever, their car got stuck behind a wheezing semi in one lane and some class act in a pickup with Arizona plates who was hauling about a thirty-foot boat on a run-down trailer in the other. There was an obnoxious sign affixed to the back of the boat that read: BOOZE OR GAS, NOBODY RIDES FOR FREE.

"Now there's a real winner," said Tony.

Rock shrugged. "That's America, Tony. You've got to take the good with the bad."

"Sure, but when we left Ocean Palm and landed in Springfield I was hoping the good would outdo the bad."

"It does." Rock rolled down his window. "Smell that good mountain air. Reminds me of home." Rock was from a small town in Arkansas. His folks still lived there. Tony figured Rock was about the wildest thing to come out of that town.

Fumes from the semi belched in their faces. The red ape with the boat turned off the highway and, with some effort, Tony was able to coax their little Focus up the next ridge, even managing to beat out the semi.

Eventually they came to Highway 76, exited, hung a right and found themselves snaking along a street lined with theaters, tourist shops and places to banish your hunger, no matter what size your appetite or how exotic or ordinary your tastes.

"This reminds me," said Tony, "of International Drive in Orlando."

"Sort of," replied Rock, "but this is nicer, especially with all the hills. Reminds me of home."

"There are an awful lot of cars though, and all these RV's, too." Tony was trying to see past the one that was rolling along slowly in front of them now. "I wonder where the hotel is?"

"Never mind that, I'm starved. Let's get something to eat."

"Don't you want to check-in first? Get our bearings?"

"No," Rock grabbed Tony's right arm and he lost control of the car. "There's a place!"

"Don't do that!" The two-door Focus barely held the road. Tony's foot stamped on the brake.

"Sorry. But look, there's a Chinese buffet just ahead."

Tony exhaled loudly. For a best friend, Rock had a lot of annoying habits. "Fine." Kozol eased into the parking lot. The billboard-sized sign read: MONGOL'S, WHERE HOARDING IS A GOOD THING — ALL YOU CAN EAT. $6.95.

"At least the price is right." Tony rolled up the

window and locked up the car.

The place was packed.

"Must be good," figured Rock.

"It's cheap," noted Tony.

They were escorted to a booth with no view of the street but one heck of a stunning view of the glistening and steamy, double row stainless steel buffet. The guys each ordered up tall glasses of iced tea and filled their lunch plates to the edges.

"Would you just look at that," grumbled Rock, twirling a fork full of lo mein like he was hauling up a buried treasure on the end of a rope.

"What?" Tony turned his head.

Rock pointed across the room with his fork. A strand of lo mein dangled over the edge of the table and mounted an escape to the floor—a noodle on the run. "That guy over there. Look at all that food. He's piled it up a foot high. Skinny guy like that. Where is he gonna put it all?"

"Maybe he's sharing a plate." Tony noted that Rock's own mountain of food was about a foot taller than the other man's.

"With who? Girl Scout Troop number 29?" Rock was shaking his head. "Nope, he's sitting alone. Look."

Sure enough, the fellow took a seat by himself at a small table in the corner facing the door. "Hey, wait a sec." Tony snapped his fingers. "Do you know who that is?"

The fellow in question had short dark hair with just a stately touch of grey. He was wearing loose blue jeans and a denim jacket with a white T-shirt. There was an embroidered American flag on the back of the jacket.

Rock shook his head no.

"That's Jim Stafford, he's a big star. I remember seeing him when I was younger. It was on the old Smothers' Brothers Comedy Hour."

"Really?" Rock leaned in for a closer look. "Cool. Let's go say hi." He wiped his big hands off on a paper napkin then crumpled it up.

"No, let's not bother him. Folks don't like to be bothered by strangers when they're eating."

"Nonsense," replied Rock. He ran his tongue over his lips to get the sauce off. "He's a star, so you said. And stars are used to it. Fans are always coming up to them. It's all part of the gig. He won't mind one bit, Tony. Besides, could lead to some work."

"We've got a job."

"Could always use another."

"Rock—" Tony snatched at his friend's thick arm and missed. Muttering all the way, Tony hurried after his companion who even now loomed over the hapless entertainer looking like he was going to gush like a human geyser any moment. Jim Stafford—assuming that really was Jim Stafford—was about to be slathered in Rock Bottom gush. Not a pretty sight at all.

"Jim Stafford?"

The man slowly lowered his fork, which at that moment held an inordinately large piece of chicken-fried steak steeped in Mongolian barbeque sauce, raised his head and looked at Rock through the inquisitive yet suspicious slits of his blue eyes. "Can I help you, son?"

Rock thrust out his hand. "My name is Rock Bottom and I'm one of your biggest fans." He handed over one of his business cards: Rock Bottom, Master Of The Bass.

Tony rolled his eyes and made scoffing sounds behind Rock's back.

"And this is my friend, Tony Kozol."

Tony said hi.

"Pleased to meet you, boys." The fellow turned his attention to his plate, lifted his fork to take a mouthful, noticed that the two men were still there and said again, "Can I help you?" He made a show of looking at his wristwatch.

Tony tugged Rock's arm.

"I was wondering if I might get an autograph. And take your picture?" Rock started digging around in his black jacket for a scrap of paper and a pen. "I know I've got something in here somewhere to write on. And I've got an instamatic in the car."

"Come on, Rock. We're bothering the nice man."

"Don't be silly, Tony, Jim doesn't mind at all. Do you, Jim?"

"I am kind of in the middle of some—"

"In fact," Rock ran on at the mouth, "if you give me a moment, I'll run out to the car and fetch my camera and—"

Stafford dropped his fork. It clattered across his plate and bounced off his boot. He shot up. "You!"

Rock backed up.

Stafford pushed past him. In five big paces, Stafford was at the door. A thick black man in an ill-fitting brown mustard suit was speaking with the hostess.

The fellow smiled and, even from a distance, Tony could see that smile was as false as a zirconian diamond. "Hi-ya, Stafford. Care to join me for lunch?"

"I wouldn't join you for your last supper," snapped Stafford.

"Suit yourself." The man nodded to the hostess and she led him to an empty booth.

Jim Stafford tagged after them. "Why don't you and your employer give it up, Butch? Nobody wants you here. Can't you see?"

"What? You don't want me here?" Butch was looking at the waitress. She shrugged noncommittally. "You see, Stafford? She don't mind. Why should you? I'll have the buffet and a Diet Pepsi, ma'am."

"We don't want your type around here. We run a clean town and mean to keep it that way. Why don't you tell *Donald* to take his *bad* behind back to New York?"

Butch said cooly. "He likes it here. He likes the fine people."

Tony whispered, "I wonder who Donald is?"

"Who knows?" said Rock. "Quiet, Tony, I want to hear this."

"Well, the people ain't gonna like him," predicted Stafford. "Right, miss?"

The waitress's mouth fell open and she hurried off.

Butch shrugged and sipped his cola. "We'll see."

"We'll see is right," muttered Stafford. He turned and stomped out only to return half a minute later, drop a twenty on his table, polish off his ice tea and stomp out again.

"Darn," whispered Rock, "I wish I had my camera now."

"Forget it," Tony answered. "We didn't come over a thousand miles to Branson, Missouri to take pictures of celebrities. We've got a show to do."

Rock's lip turned up. "This looks far more interesting to me."

Though he agreed, Tony kept this dangerous opinion to himself. It was always hard enough keeping Rock on course when they were on the road and, if he gave his friend even the least bit of encouragement, Rock would be off on a tangent of no return. And if that happened, who knew what would happen next.

And they most desperately needed this gig and the money it would provide.

The rest of the meal was uneventful, if overspiced, and the boys found the Ramada Inn up the road on the left without any trouble.

The office was down the hill from the rooms, a freestanding, squat, log cabin-styled affair. They checked in and, as they drove up to their room, Rock declared, "Look!"

Tony eased into a tight parking space overlooking the pool and glanced over his shoulder. "At what?"

"The windows," said Rock, his voice filled with awe. "Look at those wild windows. I can't believe it."

Tony pulled the key from the ignition. He thought he heard an audible sigh of relief from the small, yet game, little car. "Let me get out of here and see what you're looking at and if I can believe it."

Rock was already out the door, camera in hand. "I have got to get pictures. This is perfect!"

Tony climbed out. The Ramada stood three stories high. All the rooms opened to the outdoors with those big, typical hotel glass windows running from side to side and top to bottom. He held a hand up over his eyes to cut down on the glare which sliced across the sky and bounced hotly off his exposed forehead.

"Is this too cool or what?"

"It's too cool," agreed Tony. He crossed the parking lot for a closer look. Nearly half of the dozens of guestrooms in sight had their blinds open and the rooms, at least the windows, were decorated with Kewpie dolls and Kewpie memorabilia.

"You know," said Rock, scratching his head, "this could make a great photo spread. I'll bet I wouldn't have any trouble at all placing this story in a few magazines."

"Story?"

"Yeah." Rock looked sheepish. "I was thinking I might be able to pick up a couple extra bucks as a photographer or something."

Tony started to protest, but stopped. "That's not a bad idea, Rock. You just might have stumbled onto something." Maybe they'd make some decent money on this assignment after all. Get paid for the gig and make a little cash on the side selling a story and/or some photos. Tony didn't believe for a minute that they'd manage to get in the door let alone sell to any magazines, but some of the local Florida papers might bite. If they could come up with something decent.

They got a little closer. Rock was snapping away. Tony pulled a notepad from his pocket and began taking notes. He kept a notebook with him at all times for writing down song ideas. They climbed to the first floor and slowly walked past the rooms.

"The effort that must have gone into these displays is incredible," Rock said, his eye never leaving the viewfinder.

"I'll say," agreed Tony. Some of the windows had

simple table top displays through which he could see all the way to the very backs of the hotel rooms. Others had curtains hung behind the window display tables for privacy, he suspected.

The tables ran the gamut from the very simple to the most complex and extreme display settings of Kewpie dolls and other creations that he didn't even know the names of. There were entire villages set up in some of the rooms. Placards in the corners of the windows proudly declared which chapter of R.O.S.E. the room in question was decorated by.

Tony jotted the information down in his notebook. R.O.S.E. He frowned. Tony had no idea what any of this was all about. The gig had come up suddenly and, besides the paycheck, it had meant nothing to him. "I thought this was going to be some simple doll show."

"Tony, these folks look like they take their dolls very serious." Rock pressed his finger against the window of the next room. "See?"

Tony peered inside. An elderly couple sat side by side on the farther of the two twin beds, calmly reading a shared newspaper that the man held open. They smiled in turn as the boys stared unblinkingly into their room. They wore matching pink Kewpie air-brushed tees.

Tony felt like a Peeping Tom and part of him wanted to turn and leave but another part of him couldn't stop looking. "Holy cow." The display of dolls in the room was awesome. There were dolls and accessories and collectibles of all kinds, from ashtrays to T-shirts spread out everywhere. Barely an inch of unoccupied space remained. The couples' suitcases sat atop one another in the far corner under the sink—tucked away, he expected, so that the bags wouldn't spoil the fairy world they had carefully created.

An idyllic display in the window featured several naked Kewpie dolls, some played with animals; ducks, dogs and cats. Others stood blissfully by. All were gathered around a natural looking waterfall and pond in the center of the grass covered table. The grass was fake. The water was real. And there were real goldfish swimming in lazy circles. A fat one broke through the surface then retreated. "I don't believe it."

"Believe it, Tony."

"Get a picture."

"Already did." Rock snapped a picture of the couple inside.

"Rock," chirruped Tony, "don't do that."

"Do what?" Rock waved to the couple and smiled. They waved back. "See? They don't mind. What do you think they go to all this trouble for? Themselves? They want us to look at all this. They want us to admire their collection. They're proud of it."

"I suppose. I just feel a little weird peeking in strangers' motel rooms is all."

"Hey, get used to it," said Rock. "It could be fun."

Tony made some quick notes on the cherubic little nude dolls with the funny little topknots of hair on their otherwise round and simple heads. There was something appealing and endearing about the little things. No wonder his Aunt Louise had held on to hers all these years.

"Let's find our room, get changed and get registered for this Kewpiecon thing. And let Nanci know we're here. We've already missed the opening ceremony.

Hope she isn't too upset at having to perform solo."

"Nanci's a pro. I'm sure she managed just fine." Rock looked at the paper slip the keycard had come sleeved in. "Two-fourteen. Up the stairs and over a few doors."

"Maybe, but I hope she doesn't deduct it from our pay." They climbed to the second floor. A heavy-set, bearded man with a mop of reddish hair was pulling the door shut on the corner room. His face registered surprise as threw the ends of his mauve scarf over his shoulder. He wore a gray herringbone jacket.

Rock recognized him. This was the ape that had been in front of them coming down from Springfield tugging his boat behind.

"Afternoon," said Rock.

The stranger bowed his head and turned the corner. They heard his heavy steps falling down the stairwell.

"What's with that guy?" said Rock.

"Who knows? Did you see the look on his face?"

"Yeah, looked like the guilty type to me. Maybe he's having a hot affair. Two married lovers meeting once a year under the mask of Kewpiecon—sharing their passion for each other."

"Right. Two lovers, mad about each other and Kewpie dolls. Must you be so lurid?"

Rock shrugged Tony's comments off. "It gives a guy something to do."

Chapter 3

Tony stuck out his hand. "Hi, Tony Kozol. And this is Rock Bottom."

"Hello." This somewhat lackluster response came from a rotund little middle-aged woman in flats with mousey brown hair and a face to match.

"We're here doing a concert with Nanci, Nanci Dement." The woman's eyes looked dead. "For Kewpiecon."

"I see."

"So," said Tony, realizing that he was going to need a pair of dental pliers if he wanted to pry any information out of this woman, "I understand you are the president of R.O.S.E.?" At least he'd figured out what the acronym ROSE stood for—his finely-honed, super-sleuthing abilities combined with the banner he'd seen for the Rose O'Neill Society of Enthusiasts—had done the trick.

Tony and Rock had caught the last minutes of the R.O.S.E. meeting in the conference room down the hill in a separate building from the hotel's rooms figuring they might catch up to their temporary employer, Nanci Dement, there. But they'd had no luck.

It was the usual boring meeting, election of officers, reading of minutes. All in the over-capacity and under-cooled room. Ho-hum time and the guys were grateful that they'd missed the lion's share. But the fellow sitting on Tony's left had said something to his wife on his left about Virginia Plat being the out-going president and that's what this woman's name tag read.

"We don't say R-O-S-E, honey. We just say ROSE."

"Sorry. But you are the president, aren't you?"

"Yes, though Susie will be taking over next month."

From her speech, Tony judged Ms. Plat as being from the central states, maybe Michigan or Ohio. "Do you think you could spare a few minutes to give me some background on your organization?" Tony had decided to assist Rock on his quest to sell a story on the side. A little extra cash couldn't hurt. And they'd stand a better chance of succeeding if they worked together.

The woman looked unsure. She glanced over her shoulder. "What sort of information?"

"What your goals are, something about the size of your membership—"

"What year you have to go back to in your time machine to get your hair done up like that," whispered Rock naughtily in Tony's ear.

Tony reddened. But he had the presence of mind to keep his eyes on Ms. Plat when what he wanted to do was swat Rock in the nose.

"I'm afraid we have a directors' meeting now," replied Ms. Plat.

"Sure. I understand." Tony glared at Rock as if Ms. Plat's dropping off his hook had been Rock's fault. "If you could tell me what time would be convenient?"

Ms. Plat played with a Kewpie pin on the bosom of her chartreuse blouse. "I don't know—"

"It's going to be a very flattering article," pressed Tony.

"Sure," added Rock. "That's what we're here for. We're here to flatter. Flatter, flatter, flatter." He showed more teeth. They were big, flat and white. "There will be lots of pictures. Tons of them." His lips stretched and reached their limit. It was an awe-inspiring display, one Tony would never get used to.

A seventy-something gentleman at the table set up in front of the facing chairs was calling the directors together.

"Why don't you come by the trade show later? Perhaps we can talk there."

"The trade show? Where's the trade show?" But Ms. Plat had already marched off and an old woman in a wheelchair was scooting along beside her, tugging on her sleeve and talking animatedly.

Tony turned to Rock. "Where's the trade show?"

Rock shrugged. "I told you we should have registered first."

"Then we would have missed this meeting."

"Oh, yeah, like this has been a golden opportunity."

"Hey, you never know."

"Says you," Rock retorted. "Me, I *always* know."

Tony rolled his eyes. He'd gotten good at eye rolling since teaming up with Rock. He and the big guy had joined forces back in Austin playing for Clint Cash and the Cowhands and been together ever since. Tony wasn't sure if the relationship had improved his lot in life any, in fact, there was much to be said for the opposite, but he had grown quite fond of Rock along the way. And didn't know what he would do without the big guy. Life would be far less interesting, that was for sure.

A small stenciled sign on a wooden stake pushed into the lawn pointed to the registration area but when the boys got there it was closed. Rock yanked on the handle even though the room was obviously dark and empty.

The red-headed man with the gray herringbone coat was heading up the walk.

"Ask him where we register," said Rock.

"You ask him."

Rock apparently thought better of it. He pressed his face against the glass. "I can see some papers in there and some bags. Maybe somebody will be coming by soon."

A lanky woman with snow white hair and a matching cane with a black rubber nub stopped and called out. "They're closed. Registration's up in Becky's room." Her cane pointed the way and then she pressed on.

"Follow that invalid," said Rock.

Tony hoped the woman hadn't heard. Rock was not known for his tact.

The woman with the cane was quicker than they would have expected and soon left Rock and Tony in a cloud of lingering perfume, something laced with gardenias.

Still, they found a handwritten sheet of white paper taped to a hotel room door which, in uneven black marker, read *Registration Inside*.

The door was open wide and Rock stepped on in.

"Shouldn't we knock first?" Tony asked, looking around the empty room nervously.

"It's open, for crying out loud, Tony," Rock replied in exasperation. "Would you look at this place? It's like stepping into an antique doll shop." He waved a hand in front of his nose. "Smells like one, too."

Tony nodded. And Rock was the bull. Danger lurked everywhere. The table in front of the window held an assortment of tiny porcelain Kewpie dolls. The bedspread was covered with books like *Scootles in Kewpieville, a Rose O'Neill color book* and *Kewpie Kutouts*. The Scootles character seemed to have more hair and a more mature face. Tony extracted his notepad from his pocket and made a note of this.

Rock picked up the over-sized *Kewpie Kutouts* book and was riffling through it. "Rock," whispered Tony, "please, be careful. That book looks ancient. It's probably valuable."

"I am, I am." Rock laid the book open on the bed and pulled out his camera, a tiny digital one that he'd picked up in Brazil. Rock didn't have the first idea how to use it—not that he'd admit this—and the instructions were in Portugese. "I'm just going to get a couple of shots of this."

The bathroom door opened. A matronly looking woman with a Kewpiecon '74 T-shirt and peach-colored slacks came out. A not unexpected look of shock sprung up on her face. She had one of those name tag-on-a-rope thingies hanging around her neck.

Her name was Evie.

Tony stepped back, moving towards the door.

"Hi, there," said Rock. He waved his camera in the woman's direction. The flash went off and the poor old dear squinted. She didn't look like she'd even seen the sun since '74, let alone had a flare go off in her face lately.

"Hey!" she cried.

Rock was not the kind of thing you wanted to find standing in your room unexpectedly.

"Oops. Sorry," muttered Rock, dropping his camera to his side.

The woman was looking at the open Kewpie book on the bed. She crossed the room, gently closed the book and folded her hands across her generous belly. "Can I help you, young men?"

Rock shot out his hand. "I'm Rock Bottom and this is my partner, Tony Kozol. We're here for Kewpiecon."

"Actually, we're working with Nanci Dement. I play guitar, Rock plays bass."

The woman looked unimpressed.

"We're also on assignment. Doing a story on Kewpie dolls."

"A story?" She looked almost interested.

"It's going to be in magazines," Rock added. "National magazines."

"Really? What magazines?"

"We don't really know yet," explained Tony. "Our agency sends us out on the stories and then it's up to them to sell the stories wherever they can."

"What agency is that?"

Rock's mouth popped open. Tony was staring at him. "The, uh, David Bowie Agency."

She scratched her head. "Sounds familiar." Though this seemed to do nothing to impress her. "The books are quite delicate. The dolls, too. Folks here will appreciate it if you are very careful with how you handle their valuables."

Even Rock reddened this time. "This is Becky's room, isn't it?"

The woman nodded once. "Becky's out."

"Do you have our registration badges and our schedules? Nanci said they'd be here."

"You boys are signed up for Kewpiecon?" Evie seemed surprised.

"Yes, Nanci sent in the paperwork last month." Though the boys had only been offered the gig two days before. Apparently, they had not been Nanci's first choice. Tony tried not to dwell on this unwelcome fact. Rock was fingering a doll and Tony pulled him away from the bed.

"That's different." Evie's personality took a turn for the better. "Come on over here," she replied. "I can take care of you." She pulled out a shoebox of bulging registration envelopes resting on the seat of the chair tucked under the front table. "Last names again?"

Rock and Tony repeated their names. They were handed number ten envelopes which Evie explained held their badges, schedule of events and banquet tickets. She then handed each of them a cloth bag with Kewpiecon-in-Branson emblazoned on one side and a sketch of a cherubic Kewpie face on the other.

"Enjoy yourselves," said Evie, pointedly walking them to the door.

Tony was running down the schedule of events. He stopped just inside the door. "Can you tell us where the trade show is?"

Evie reached into Tony's bag and pulled out a simple, hand-drawn then photocopied map. "This here is Highway76. Turn left and just keep going until you get here. The theater is on the left." Her wizened and bent thumb jabbed a spot on the map marked with a star. "That's the old Merel Pearce Mongrel Theater. But it's not there anymore. I've been told he's got a new place out by Tom E. Landry's theater."

"So what exactly is the name of the place we're looking for?" Rock asked.

Evie scratched the side of her head. Pink flesh revealed itself through thin, gray hairs. "I think it's some goofy thing like Spikes or something."

"Spikes?"

"Or something. Don't worry. You can't miss it. We've got a little sign out front shaped like a Kewpie doll. The trade show isn't in the main theater though. You men park in the lot and then go around to the side. There's a big room there that gets rented out for special events. That's where you'll find the trade show." She pushed Tony out the door. Evie was stronger than she looked. "Can't miss it."

Tony was about to raise another question when Evie gently closed the door in his face. They still didn't know where Nanci was.

"Well," said Tony, "I hope you're happy."

"What did I do?"

"You and your manners. First you've got us barging into somebody's room without knocking and then you go playing around with a priceless, rare book like you were browsing through the bargain bin at a South Beach bookstore."

"I was only trying to do my job."

"Try doing it with a little more tact. If things keep going this way, nobody is going to talk to us and what kind of story will we get then? Besides, your job is to play the bass. Don't forget that."

Rock bowed. "Yes, Your Majesty. Yes, Your Highness."

"Oh, just get in the car," said Tony, marching off. "And what was all that nonsense about the David Bowie Agency?"

"It was the first thing that popped into my head," said Rock. He scratched his thick skull. "I mean, it was either that or the Ziggy Stardust Agency."

Chapter 4

"B.A.D. Spike's CRIB?" Tony was reading the sign atop the big white and gold trimmed theater. Two giant fake spikes that had to be thirty feet tall rose from the ground on each side of the marquee out front.

"Looks like Paul Bunyan drove them in with his giant hammer," commented Rock as they pulled up.

The Texas-sized spikes were golden yellow. *Grand Opening Next Week* read the sign in-between them. The letters overhead reading B.A.D. Spike's CRIB, all in two foot tall capital letters, flashed from red to white to blue every thirty seconds or so.

"What kind of a name is that for a theater? What is this guy thinking?"

Rock shrugged. "I kinda like it."

"You think this is the right place?"

"There's the Kewpie sign out front."

Tony waited for oncoming traffic on Highway 76 to

let up then darted across the road and into the parking lot.

"Pretty odd place for a bunch of doll collectors to be having a trade show." Tony wondered if Evie had sent them off on a wild goose chase and, almost as importantly, whether she'd done so on purpose. "Do you think this place belongs to *the* B.A.D. Spike? I mean, I haven't heard *that* name in ages. Another one of those 'where are they now?' guys you expect to show up on a VH1 special."

Rock looked bemused. "How would I know? Maybe this one's some Hee Haw knock-off with a corncob pipe and too big bib overalls."

"We'll find out soon enough."

"Look," Rock pointed, "there's a bunch of cars over there by that open side door. Let's go check it out."

Tony parked and they headed up the hill to the door. Branson was full of its geographic ups and downs. Tony's legs were more accustomed to the flats of South Florida and by the time they'd reached the side door, he was very nearly out of breath and shoe leather. One of these days, he swore, he really was going to start that exercise program. "Don't you want to get a couple of shots of the theater and that crazy sign with those spikes?"

"What for?" snapped Rock. "We're here for Kewpies, Tony, not gaudy landmarks. Let's get to work. I can smell the byline already."

"Fine. But keep your eyes open for Nanci. The sooner she knows we've arrived, the better."

The trade room was divided into two sections. The hall they entered contained row after row of long, narrow tables, behind which sat or stood various vendors with their Rose O'Neill related goodies. A second room was more of an exhibit-only area—look don't touch—with many more fine collectibles arranged inside locked glass cases. Tony supposed if you had enough money even these were for sale, though he could see no price tags. Maybe it was one of those 'if you have to ask' kind of things. A small, temporary stage had been installed in the far corner of the main room. Tony figured that's where they'd be performing.

There were all sorts of Kewpies, some naked, some clothed. One was dressed like an Indian, carrying a tomahawk in one hand, with an amulet of some sort around his neck.

There were books on Rose O'Neill and by Rose O'Neill. There were Kewpie cups and saucers, a Kewpie windmill and more. A charming four inch Kewpie police officer, complete with hat and nightstick stood on the top shelf, as if keeping a Kewpie eye on things.

Rock snapped up some pictures while Tony diligently made notes. This was going to be one great story.

"Look, there's Jim Stafford again."

Rock turned. The entertainer was slowly walking from table to table with a lovely little blonde girl holding his hand. "You think that's his daughter? Maybe I could get a shot of the two of them together?"

"No, Rock," Tony said, putting his foot down. "If he's here with his daughter looking at the dolls, you've got to leave them alone. Let's get on with this. I'd like you to get a shot of that shelf of stuff over there. Looks interesting."

Rock grunted.

Tony stooped to tie his shoe. "And don't forget to write down what you're shooting, so we can piece it all together later." This article writing was tougher than it looked. Tony stood.

Rock was gone.

He had trapped poor Mr. Stafford and his daughter and was arranging them like a couple of pieces of two-legged fruit against one of the walls. "There. Just like that. Now, smile!"

"Rock!"

The camera clicked and whirred in quick succession.

"Hello, again." Jim stuck his hand out in Tony's direction. "Nice to see you."

"Mr. Stafford, I am so sorry about this." Tony planted his feet and pulled Rock's elbow. "We don't mean to intrude." Rock wasn't budging. And Tony wasn't big enough to force the issue.

Stafford smiled. "It's all right, son. I'm glad to see you, to tell the truth. I feel bad about what happened back there at the buffet. You see, it's all a big—"

"You needn't explain anything to us," Tony said.

"I'd feel better if you would let me explain." He slapped the side of his skull. "But what am I thinking? Where are my manners?" He turned sideways. "This here's my daughter, G—" He frowned. "Now where'd she go?"

"She's over there, Jim." Rock pointed to a long table where Mr. Stafford's daughter held a boxed Scootles doll, her face filled with little girl longing. The young child set the Scootles down carefully, then lifted a Kewpie in a yellowed box with a cellophane front to her nose.

The woman at the table looked uncomfortable with this action on the girl's part. Probably worried Jim's daughter would poke her nose right through the cellophane wrapping. Ka-ching! Down would go the price on that little dollie. Of course, Jim would probably be on the hook for it, so maybe this would work in the seller's favor.

"About this afternoon—let me make it up to you boys."

"Really, that's not necessary, Mr. Stafford." Tony was making not so subtle faces at Rock to leave.

"I know, I know, but I want to. And call me Jim. How about a couple of tickets to tonight's show? If you boys aren't busy?"

Rock's face lit up. "You mean your show?"

"Sure."

"That really isn't—"

Rock cut him off quickly. "Why, we'd love to, Jim. Thanks."

Stafford smiled. "Great. You all come by the theater, anytime after seven. I'll leave two tickets in your name. Rock Bottom, right?"

Rock had a high-beam look of triumph on his face. "That's right, Jim."

"I'll take care of everything." He waved and maneuvered his way through the small crowd, heading for his daughter.

"Nice guy," said Rock. He picked a Kewpie magnet off the nearest table, seemed to consider the thing, then replaced it.

"Did you have to put him on the spot like that?"

"What do you mean? I didn't put him on the spot for anything."

"You took his picture *and* finagled free show tickets out of him."

"You heard Jim. He offered us those tickets. I didn't ask for them."

"Yeah, well." Tony stuck his notebook in his pocket. "Maybe, but it was probably just so he could get rid of us—of you. Besides, did you ever think that we might not be able to go to his show? That we just might have a show of our own to do?"

Rock looked dejected and Tony felt badly. "Oh, come on. Buck up." He slapped the big guy on the shoulder. "I think I spotted Nanci over there. Let's check it out. Maybe we'll have some free time tonight, after all." Like if she fires us, he thought grimly.

B.A.D. pushed Cyndi off his lap, pulled open the fridge and dragged out the turkey and half a loaf of bread. "You want anything, honey?"

"No, thanks." She pulled her tube top up from around her waist.

"I'm famished." B.A.D. pulled a long knife from the block and carved up some breast and built himself a sandwich, light on the mayo. The back door rattled and he jumped. "When the deuces is that locksmith gonna get here?" he spat, his mouth full of whole wheat and bird.

"I tried to call him back. All I got was the answering service. So it probably won't be before tomorrow."

"Wonderful." B.A.D. sighed and looked at his watch. "Oh, well. Things will get done, I suppose. Folks around here are good about that. Did you hear what Butch said?"

Cyndi nodded but B.A.D. answered her anyway.

"He said the fellows are gonna start work on expanding the stage tomorrow. According to the engineer, they're gonna have to tear up a back section and put in some extra supports to carry the load. But the job should go quickly. The contractor promised he'd be done in plenty of time for next month's opening even if he's got to have his crew working nights and through the weekends."

He rubbed his hands together. "Now that's what I call action. I wish I could get that much juice from everybody else around here." He grinned slyly. "Excepting yourself, of course, honey."

She leapt from the sofa and gave him a kiss. One of her hands was sliding over his body, looking for trouble. She found it. "You let me know what else I can do for you."

He patted her behind. "Right now you can get yourself out of here."

Cyndi looked hurt. "Why? What for?"

"I've got an appointment." He picked up Cyndi's purse from the counter and handed it to her.

His assistant's green eyes narrowed. "With who?"

"Never you mind. Go on now." B.A.D. slapped her behind.

Cyndi grabbed her purse. She didn't look happy.

"Oh, don't go looking at me like that, honey. This is business. That's all."

A loud sigh escaped her lips. "All right. But what am I supposed to do?"

"I don't know. Go see a late show or something at the Imax." He reached into his wallet and pulled out a bunch of bills.

Cyndi reached for them without asking. She leaned

up and planted a kiss on the tip of B.A.D.'s nose, then looked at the chair holding the door shut. "You want to let me out and then push the chair back?"

"Go on out the front. Have you got your phone with you?"

Cyndi nodded.

"I'll call you when my meeting is over." B.A.D. walked Cyndi up through the quiet theater and out the front door. A waft of cold air sent shivers up his arms.

He locked up.

Chapter 5

The silver flying saucer shot overhead, hovered and then headed back in their direction. Rock pulled out his tiny camera, took aim and snapped off two quick shots.

"Rock!" Tony hissed in horror. "Didn't you hear that guy? He said no flash photography once the lights went out."

"Ooops."

Tony sank down in his chair. The smiling young man on stage earlier in the tuxedo had specifically warned the audience about flash photography and videotaping during this black-out portion of Jim Stafford's show. Why couldn't he have a normal partner? Why couldn't he have a normal bestfriend?

At least they weren't thrown out and the rest of the show went without a hitch. The theater was full. They were lucky to be there. Nanci had been a little miffed that they'd missed the opening ceremony but had forgiven them. Rock insisted this was because she had the hots for him. Tony figured it was more likely that she would have a tough time replacing them at the last minute. She had insisted on a run through of tomorrow's performance and then given them the night off.

The boys had had pretty good seats; center row near the aisle about a third of the way up from the stage. They had found themselves laughing hysterically and they weren't alone. Stafford packed them in and kept them smiling.

During intermission, a large screen had dropped down on stage and an unseen camera panned the audience. Unsuspecting guests suddenly found themselves part of the show when computer generated gag lines appeared beneath their on-screen faces. A perfectly ordinary looking grandpa of a man sitting two seats over from Rock found himself on the screen with an accompanying caption stating that he was in the witness protection program. The audience howled.

"Good thing Jim Stafford's fans have a sense of humor." Rock nudged Tony. "Some of these folks might want to kill him."

With the show over, everyone headed for the doors or the gift shop. Tony and Rock made their way down to the side of the stage where Rock proceeded to accost one of the ushers. He tapped the elderly usher on the shoulder as he collected 3-D glasses in a big plastic bin by the rear exit.

"Excuse me," he began, "but we're friends of Jim's and we'd like to go backstage and say hello to him, if that's all right?" Rock flashed his best smile, trying hard to close the sale.

The usher looked doubtful.

Tony stood by silently. If he'd known what Rock was up to, he'd have gone out the front exit.

"In fact," added Rock, "Jim was kind enough to give us free tickets to tonight's show." He waved the ticket stubs under the usher's nose as if they proved anything. "We sure would like to thank him."

Rock's smile looked awfully practiced and artificial as a politician's on the reelection trail to Tony but the usher apparently bought it because he said, "You boys will have to wait here a moment. I'll check." He disappeared behind the red curtains.

A moment later he returned and said with a shrug, "Sorry, Mr. Stafford has gone for the night."

Rock looked at his pocketwatch. "Wow, that was quick. The show hasn't been over five minutes. Are you sure he's not back there?" He pulled up the edge of the curtain.

"Let it go, Rock." Tony grabbed Rock's hand and pulled him out the door. "Thank you, anyway, sir."

"Goodnight, boys." The usher waved and, as they were now the last to leave from this part of the theater, he closed the door behind them.

Rock stopped in the parking lot. "You think Jim's really gone or that he doesn't want to see us?" He was staring moodily up at the theater. There were lights on upstairs.

"It doesn't matter. Let it go, Rock."

Tony pulled his cell phone from his pocket and powered it back up. He'd turned it off during the show. Tony listened to his messages. There were three; two from Nina, his sometime girlfriend back home and one from Nanci. It was too late and he was too tired to deal with either of them.

Jim pulled into the lot. It was awfully dark in contrast to the lights out along the main road. He swerved around a small, dark shape and stopped to get a look at it. It was a doll. He picked it up and tossed it in the backseat. He'd deal with it later.

Two other cars, one up near Highway 76 and the other way in the back, sat quiet and apparently unoccupied. The big parking lot was otherwise deserted. Jim parked near the entrance, in between two handicapped spaces, locked up and headed for the main doors.

The main lights were out. A row of small white bulbs strung along the facing lobby wall gave off a yellowish glow just above the floor. He knocked, not really expecting an answer. Jim pulled on the nearest door. It was locked.

"Oh, this is just great," he muttered. "I don't know what I'm doing here anyway. Waste of time. I could be home relaxing."

Frustrated, Jim yanked on the next door, nearly pulling out his shoulder. "Dang," he muttered. "That's gonna ruin my tennis game for a week." He yanked even harder on the following door handle and, to his surprise, it flew open. "Whoa!" He stepped back to keep the door from hitting him in the face.

Jim laughed to chase away his fear. The door flying open had spooked him a little. He wasn't fond of dark places to begin with. He was used to bright lights, big crowds.

Being all alone in an empty building was not his most favorite thing in the world. But this was Branson.

Nothing to worry about.

Jim put one foot over the threshold. "Donald?" His word was swallowed up by the empty theater. A lingering aroma of popcorn and coffee set his stomach to growling. He'd only had a light dinner before the show. There was also the distinct odor of fresh paint. In the dim light, Jim paced the lobby. Photographs of B.A.D. Spike filled the walls, along with copies of all his hit records, nine to be exact.

There were a couple of B.A.D.'s old stage outfits arranged within tall glass cases set up on black platforms. One of the costumes was all mirrors, little square ones that someone must have painstakingly sewn or glued on by hand. Incredible. Even the accompanying boots and beret were adorned with the little mirrors. Jim rolled his eyes at that one. Not that his own costumes weren't just as outlandish. Not to mention the chicken suit he sometimes wore in his own show.

A sound from the depths of the theater made Jim start—a low, scraping sound. He held his breath and listened for a moment, but the sound was not repeated. Jim tiptoed to the doors leading into the main theater. The heavy doors were wide open. He slowly peered around the corner.

There wasn't enough light to see his hands in front of his nose, let alone anything else. Row after row of seats lay still like rows of bony-crested dinosaur crocodiles just waiting for him to wade out to them. And then, gulp! He'd be gone. No way he was going to let those bone-plated dinocrocs trick him.

Jim's hand fumbled for a light switch on the nearest wall. There was none. He really ought to carry a flashlight, something that would fit in his pocket. He'd tell his wife to pick him up one at the Walmart.

His pupils adjusted to the light some. He could make out a faint glow coming from beneath the distant curtain. "Donald?"

His voice bounced back in his face. "Donald, are you out there?" He stepped further into the room. "It's me, Jim."

He heard that scraping sound again—it seemed closer this time, maybe behind him. He shouted and hurried down the sloping ramp towards the stage. His heart pounded in his chest like it was trying to get out. Getting out was the only thing on Jim's mind, too.

Jim reached the stage and clambered up, banging his knees and tearing his pants on some raw boards. He glanced over his shoulder. The theater was deadly still. He took a couple of deep breaths, struggling to regain his composure. A distant click only set him off again.

Jim headed to the back of the dark stage, working his way to Donald's apartment. If this was B.A.D.'s idea of a joke, he was going to kill him. His feet creaked across the floor, giving his location away to any lurking monsters or madmen. Jim hurried to the curtain, thrashed around, found an opening and ducked behind.

He bumped into a stepladder and it came crashing down at his feet. Jim shouted, louder this time. He whirled, looking for a way out. It was even darker here than it had been out in the empty seats.

"Donald," he said loudly, "where are you, man?" Keeping his hands before him so he wouldn't knock into anything else, Jim made his way across the dark stage. He had reached a wall and was about to turn around and head back in the other direction when his hands closed around a door handle. It was cool to the touch. "Thank goodness."

Jim twisted the handle. "Donald? Donald, are you in there?"

The lights came on.

Jim was blinded. He threw a hand in front of his eyes. "Donald!"

Donald stood in the entry to the kitchen, one hand on the light switch, the other on the counter.

"I swear, you've got some nerve. What were you trying to do, scare me half to death?" Jim dropped his arm. "You start smoking?" He waved a hand in irritation. "Place stinks of cigars.

"And what's with the get-up?" B.A.D.'s t-shirt was splotchy and sweat-stained. "Ain't you got running water here, yet? Don't be letting yourself go, Donald."

B.A.D.'s hand fell from the light switch to the kitchen counter. "Jim, I—" He stopped.

"You what?" Jim tapped his foot. "And what was so important that you had to drag me out here tonight? Still all worked up about your opening? You worry too much, you know that?"

B.A.D. opened his lips to speak. A trickle of blood, not words, tumbled from his mouth.

"Donald!"

B.A.D.'s knees buckled. He fell to the ground like he was a marionette whose puppeteer had cut his strings without the least forewarning. He hit the tile with a horrible thud that sent a vibration along the floor and a shiver up Jim's spine.

Jim raced to Donald's side. His back was wet and

bloody. His t-shirt torn. Jim dropped to his knees and rolled B.A.D. gently over.

"Donald!" he cried. "Donald! What's happened?" A bloody knife and a blood-stained kitchen towel lay on the floor beside them.

"Doll. . ." B.A.D.'s eyelids fluttered then went still.

Jim nervously shook B.A.D.. The backdoor burst open, flinging the chair that had held it shut flying across the room. A police officer stepped inside. Her eyes fanned the room. There was a gun in her hand. She leveled it at Jim.

Jim hobbled backwards on his knees, away from the body. "I didn't do it!" he cried. He threw his arms in the air, palms forward. His hands were trembling.

"Don't move!"

Jim opened his mouth. Nothing came out. He looked from Donald to the police officer. Donald looked dead and the officer didn't look amused. The gun was trained on him. The sight of which was just about enough to kill him, even if the bullet missed.

Jim swallowed.

Hard.

He was in trouble this time.

Chapter 6

The ringing in his ears wouldn't stop.

Rock groaned and buried his head in his pillow. For a second, he thought it was the alarm clock and that some fool previous guest had set it for this ungodly hour. Then he recognized the distinctive ring of his cell phone.

With a conscious effort not to open his eyes, hoping beyond hope that he'd be able to get back to sleep somehow when this was all over, Rock dropped an arm over the side of the bed and reached for his trousers. He'd left them lying on the floor beside the night table the evening before, too tired to put them away.

After a few frustrating tries, he succeeded in retrieving his phone from the back pocket. "Hello?" He listened a moment, chewed his lip. "Very funny." Rock hung up.

Tony sat up. "Who was it, Rock?"

"Some idiot. Said he was Jim Stafford. Moron." Rock checked the clock on the night table. Eight o'clock. He scratched his neck and yawned, an inhuman sound akin to that of a cow giving birth.

"We should get an early start. Take advantage of our time here. We've only got a couple more days. With the show, we won't have much time to write a story on Kewpies."

"Yes, Mother."

"There's a breakfast thing with the Kewpiecon registrants. We don't want to miss that."

Rock rolled his eyes. "Yes, we don't want to miss that." The big guy went to the bathroom and turned on the shower.

"Your phone's ringing again."

"Ignore it."

Tony dug around in the covers and found Rock's phone. "Hello?"

Rock came out wrapped in a bath towel, head dripping. "Who was it?"

"Your idiot again."

Rock shook himself. "Gonna have to get a new number if this keeps up."

Tony dressed quickly, tossing on a pair of blue jeans and a Neil Young t-shirt. Rock dressed in black. No surprise there.

The Kewpiecon breakfast was being held at the Ramada's restaurant. A young hostess with ponytails guided the boys to a banquet room where the meeting was already in order. The mousey Virginia Plat, outgoing ROSE president, was speaking. A podium had been set up on the head table and she was leaning into the microphone.

Tony's eyes searched the room. There were better than a hundred people present. Nanci was nowhere in sight. A waitress bustled past carrying a tray of water glasses. Tony moved out of the way and the boys found a couple of seats at a table along the back wall. He pulled out his notebook and jotted down some statistics that Ms. Plat was spouting.

Ms. Plat stopped after a moment and introduced some lanky, middle-aged fellow with thick black-rimmed glasses who proceeded to bring the audience up to speed on the ROSE website. His name was Rick Elf.

Tony made a note of his name and the URL. Both could be helpful in the future, in case he found out later that they needed some follow-up information when they got back to Ocean Palm and sat down to finish off the story. And no doubt they would.

Tony shot Rock a look. The big guy's phone was ringing again. Rock's hand dove into his pants and the ringing stopped. Tony looked more embarrassed than Rock.

A waifish waitress came by and asked if they wanted the eggs or the pancakes. Tony opted for the pancakes and some tea. Rock insisted on an omelette with mushroom and cheese, plus the pancakes. He was a big guy, after all.

In a matter of moments, a steaming pile of maple-scented heaven came to the table tempting his taste buds and his waistline. A mound of butter the size of a snowball stood melting in the center of the thick stack of buttermilk flapjacks. Summoning all his willpower, Tony pushed half the sweet butter aside and spread the rest around, mixing it up with the maple syrup. That was going to save twenty future pushups right there.

The meeting broke up just about the time Tony was forcing down his last pancake. Rock's omelette had only just arrived. Served him right for asking for something off-menu. He'd polished off his own stack of flapjacks as an appetizer.

Tony shut his quickly filling notebook and watched Rock eat. "So who called this time?"

Rock shrugged, his mouth full of egg. He pulled out his phone and handed it to Tony.

Tony looked at the number on the display. "Don't recognize the number." He pushed the Send button.

"Branson Police Department."

"Sorry, wrong number." Tony ended the call.

Rock looked at him rather oddly. "What was that all about?"

"I hit the Send button and got the Branson Police Department."

"Branson Police Department?" Rock cleared his palate with a mouthful of ice cold milk. "Got to be a joke."

The phone, lying on the table between them, rang again.

"Answer it," said Rock.

"You answer it," said Tony. "It's your telephone."

Rock growled and picked it up. "Hello? Now, listen you—" His big , square jaw dropped. "Huh?" He pulled the phone away from his ear and stared at it.

Tony heard tiny sounds coming from the other end. "Who is it?"

Rock ignored Tony's question. "Is this really you?" His eyes narrowed. "All right. But this better not be some kind of joke." He dropped the phone in his pocket and pushed his chair away.

"What is it?" demanded Tony. "What is going on?"

Rock wiped his napkin over his lips. "That was Jim Stafford. He's in jail. He's been arrested on suspicion of murder!"

Chapter 7

"This is nuts," Tony said.

"I'm telling you," Rock insisted, "it was Jim's voice on the phone. It's pretty distinctive. I recognized it for sure."

"And he's been arrested for murder and he wants to see us?" Tony looked dubious. "Sounds like a sick joke to me and we've got work to do. We don't have time for jokes."

"Sir?"

"Yes?"

"I'm Officer Robinson. How exactly can I help you?" She had a Missourian accent, thick and sweet as molasses. And she was very easy on the eyes with flowing brown hair with blonde highlights and eyes that sparkled like green diamonds. Her eyebrows were luxuriant and perfectly shaped, as if Michelangelo had gone into the follicle business.

Tony had been expecting a little country police station and instead they had discovered a modern brick complex housing city offices and the police department. What he hadn't been expecting was such a good-looking officer of the law. His phone rang. "Excuse me." He pulled it out and answered quickly. "Yes?"

"What's happening?"

"Hello, Nanci." Tony cursed himself for not looking at the caller I.D. He did not want to talk to his boss now.

"Where are you guys? I wanted to run through a new number before the show."

"We, uh, went out for a drive. Taking a look around. Had a flat. I'll call you the minute we get back."

The folksinger told him it had better be soon in no uncertain terms.

"Oh, it will. I promise."

The uniformed officer cast an impatient look in Tony's direction. "Look, Nanci, I have to go help Rock with the tire. Talk to you later. Bye!" Tony snapped his phone shut and stuffed it back in pocket. He waved to the officer. "Sorry about that."

The officer nodded. "How can I help you?" She had a pleasant face that came alive when she smiled, Tony suspected, but she was all serious now. There were dark circles under her eyes.

"My name is Tony Kozol. That's Rock Bottom." Rock, who'd been snooping around the cavernous lobby, lumbered over.

Officer Robinson folded her arms across her chest. "Okay."

Rock blurted, "I got a call from Jim Stafford, saying

he was here." He lowered his voice. "That he was in jail for murder."

Officer Robinson nodded once more. "Come with me." She opened the door to a narrow hallway and led them to a small office. "Have a seat."

Tony helped himself to the chair across from Robinson's desk.

Robinson picked up her telephone. "Those guys are here." She yawned.

The boys exchanged troubled looks. Rock asked. "What's going on, Robinson?"

"All in good time." Robinson yawned once more. "It's been a long night."

Rock didn't react well. "I don't care if it has been a long night, if you think—"

She held up a hand. "Wait a moment. Someone will be joining us. Care for some coffee?" She lifted a lipstick stained mug to her lips, inhaled deeply then took a sip.

"No, thank you," said Tony. Rock shook his head.

"You sure? Made it only ten minutes ago."

Tony declined. He was nervous enough as it was.

A doughy skinned fellow in a yellow jacket and beige slacks came up the hall. He leaned against the doorframe. His green eyes were small and close together, like someone had pinched them up to his nose. He had a receding hairline which he covered by keeping his head closely shaved. He was of average height and a little more than average weight and Tony figured him to have hit the big 4-0. He nodded first at the boys then at Robinson.

"This is Joe Carvin. He's one of our detectives."

Joe Carvin nodded once again.

Tony, despite his uneasiness, managed to smile and say hi. Rock was mum.

Joe Carvin was obviously a man of few words. What was he doing here? Shouldn't he be out practicing mime somewhere? Like outside the Grand Palace?

Robinson pulled a yellow pad from her desk drawer, ripped off the first page which was covered with tiny rows of numbers and tossed it into her little black trash bin. She caught Tony looking at the numbers. "My brother and I are trying to figure whether we can afford a bigger house."

Tony nodded politely.

"You see, Kenny, that's my brother, his wife got killed last year in an auto accident and he's got three boys to raise and, seeing as I'm not married, I moved in to help out. Be a mother figure, you know."

Tony nodded once again. "I think that's very sweet of you."

Rock's eyes were rolling around like a couple of those little roulette marbles.

"Thank you, I—"

Carvin cleared his throat.

"Right, then." Robinson picked a pencil out from amongst the clutter of her desktop and began doodling at the top of a fresh page. "Tony Kozol and Rock Bottom, that right?"

"Yes." Tony folded his hands across his lap, feeling suddenly quite the schoolboy.

"And you're friends with Jim Stafford?"

Tony nodded. He caught a quick look that passed between Robinson and Joe.

"That's right," said Rock. "Jim, Tony and I are good friends. The best of friends. Is he really here? Can we see him?"

"In a minute." Robinson held up her hand to shut him up. "I have a few questions." She turned to Tony.

"Okay," Tony said slowly. He squirmed. Were there upside-down, four inch long spikes planted under his cushion? Did they use this chair and this technique to squeeze confessions out of suspected criminals? Had the Spanish Inquisition finally reached Branson, Missouri?

"How do you know Mr. Stafford?"

Tony answered quickly. "We met him yesterday." Kozol explained how they'd run into him at a buffet in town.

Robinson chuckled and made a note. "Best of friends, eh?"

Rock scowled.

"And you're detectives? What brings you to Branson? What are you working on?"

Tony shot up. "Detectives? Where on earth did you hear that?"

"We're musicians, Robinson," said Rock. "Haven't you ever heard of Nanci Dement?"

Carvin stepped in. "Have you ever heard of being locked up for thirty days?"

"Listen," said Tony. "It's no big deal. We're hear this week working for Nanci Dement. She's a folksinger who's performing for Kewpiecon. She was hired by the organizers and hired us for her backup. I play guitar. Rock plays bass."

"Kewpie what?" Carvin scratched his forehead.

Tony turned. "Kewpiecon. It's an event celebrating the life and works of Rose O'Neill."

Robinson was nodding. "I saw something in the

Branson News about it yesterday. Sounds interesting. This Rose O'Neill was a famous artist. She lived in that Bonniebrook house outside of town."

Carvin looked almost impressed.

"We haven't been there yet," said Tony.

"But we're doing a story on Kewpie dolls while we're here," added Rock. "We freelance."

Tony groaned. Lying to the police should only be done as a last resort.

Carvin left his post in the doorway and entered the office. He loomed over Tony. His arms were folded across his chest. "Can you tell us what Jim Stafford's relationship was to B.A.D. Spike?"

"Who?"

"B.A.D. Spike. You know, the rap star."

"I know who you mean, I just don't know what you mean. I mean, how would we know what Mr. Stafford's relationship with B.A.D. Spike was?"

Tony crossed and uncrossed his legs. "Rock and I were at the B.A.D. Spike Crib yesterday. That's the name of his theater over on Highway 76."

"I'm familiar with the place," said Robinson. "What were you guys doing there? Trying to get something on B.A.D.?"

"I thought you said you were here for the Kewpiecon?" put in Carvin. "Thought you said you were a couple of musicians?"

"We are." Tony sighed. "That's where the Kewpiecon trade show and concert are being held. They've rented out the hall at B.A.D.'s theater. We ought to be there now, *working.*"

"Did Mr. Stafford speak with B.A.D.?" asked Det. Carvin. "Did they have some sort of an argument?"

"What? Huh? Not that we noticed. We never even saw them together."

Robinson said, "How about you? Did you speak to B.A.D. at that time? Did he say anything about Mr. Stafford?"

Carvin wasn't waiting for answers. "What is your relationship to B.A.D., Mr. Kozol? Have you worked for him in the past? What about you, Mr. Bottom? And what are you, musicians or detectives?"

"That's it," said Rock. "I'm not saying anything more." He rose from his chair. "And you shouldn't say anymore either, Tony." The big guy glared at the two men. "Not until these jokers tell us what's going on. Not until we've seen Jim."

Tony hesitated a moment, then nodded.

Carvin scratched his wrist. "Fine by me."

Robinson stood. "Come on."

Tony rose to his feet unsteadily. Where were they taking them? What was going on? Was somebody really dead? Was he going to have to identify a body? He didn't like blood. He'd seen enough of it in his life.

"Are you coming?" Det. Joe Carvin was beckoning with his finger.

"Huh?"

"Is something wrong Mr. Kozol?" asked Robinson.

"Oh, no. Nothing." Ignoring Carvin's ugly look, Tony mechanically followed the two men down the hall. They turned right and followed another quiet corridor which came out near a fancy communications center occupied by two women who looked at him like he was a criminal.

Tony had the irrational urge to shout that he was only visiting, but squelched it. Robinson motioned for the boys to follow and they entered a small, cold passage with several tightly closed doors. Tony didn't need to ask what these doors were. Jail cells—most definitely jail cells.

They came to a stop. Were he and Rock about to be locked up? Had they committed some crime that they weren't aware of? Had Rock abused the all-you-can-eat buffet? Did they toss you in the slammer first, in Branson, and charge you with a crime later? Despite the chill, Tony felt a sweat rising up along the bridge of his nose and behind his ears.

Robinson spoke softly. "Take a look" She was peering through the tiny, reinforced window of the first cell.

Curious, Tony edged up to the window. He had to rise up on his toes to see. "Jim!"

Rock pushed him aside and peeked in. "I'll be danged."

Jim was lying on a narrow cot, an olive blanket tucked up to his chin. Incongruous Disney characters, Donald Duck, Mickey and Minnie Mouse, Goofy and the gang, were painted on the otherwise unremarkable pink concrete walls. This wasn't a scene he could ever have imagined. A big star like that. What was the world coming to?

At the sound of voices, Jim opened his eyes.

Tony looked from Robinson to Carvin and back again. "What's going on? You've got Jim Stafford in a cell."

Rock pulled on the doorhandle. It was locked.

"Let's go back to the office, gentlemen." Robinson started off.

"Tell us what's going on here. Why have you got Mr.

Stafford locked up? What could he possibly have done?" Tony was angry now. Stafford seemed like such a good guy. "This has got to be some kind of joke. You don't really mean to say you think he killed somebody?"

Robinson's face remained noncommittal. Carvin was smirking. "No joke," said the detective.

"This is nuts," said Rock. "You've got him cooped up in there like he's nothing but a—"

"Cold-blooded killer?" suggested Carvin.

Tony turned on the detective. "Exactly." This couldn't be real. It also couldn't have anything to do with them. Except that Jim had called them.

Why?

Chapter 8

Robinson shifted her weight from foot to foot. The keys hanging from the leather belt circling her slender waist jingled. "Jim Stafford was found at the scene of a murder last night."

"Whose?"

"B.A.D. Spike's," replied Carvin stonily.

Tony could tell the detective was studying him, trying to gauge his reaction. Did the detective suspect he was some sort of an accomplice? Kozol folded his arms across his chest. "That's impossible. Just plain impossible. Somebody around here is making a very big mistake."

"I'm afraid it's true, Mr. Kozol. I found Mr. Stafford there myself."

"You did?"

Robinson nodded. "Someone reported some suspicious character lurking around the parking lot outside

B.A.D.'s theater. I responded to the call. I reconnoitered and saw a light on inside through a crack in the rear door to B.A.D.'s apartment in back of the place. The door had been broken. I went in and found your friend kneeling over the body."

"No."

"He had blood on his hands. B.A.D.'s blood," said Robinson.

"But he couldn't have killed him."

"How would you know that, Kozol?" Carvin asked. There was a hardness to his voice that said he had his own theories and that Tony wouldn't like them.

"I'm certain." There was a lot that Tony didn't know about Jim Stafford. But he was no killer.

"Can we talk to him now?"

"He's been calling you all morning. Says you're detectives," Robinson said. "Sure would like to know why." She arched one fine-tuned eyebrow.

Neither Tony nor Rock answered.

Carvin nodded and Robinson drew a key from her pocket and unlocked the cell.

Jim swivelled his legs from the bunk to the floor with a groan. "Hi, Tony. Like my new digs?"

Tony looked at the Disney characters dancing along the back walls. "If you wanted to go to Disneyworld, Jim, wouldn't it have been easier to buy a ticket to Orlando?" Kozol turned to Officer Robinson. "Can we get out of here and talk someplace more pleasant?" He stifled a shudder. The tiny cell was cold and clammy. Maybe it was just his nerves. He'd seen enough of jail cells in his short life, too.

Robinson and Carvin conferred a moment and then escorted Jim and the boys back to the office. "You can talk here," said Carvin. "Paula and I need to have a word with the assistant chief."

They left and Tony whispered to Jim, "You think it's safe to talk here? You think they've got the place bugged?"

"I don't know," he said, rather loudly. "It don't matter. I didn't do anything."

"Quiet," cautioned Tony. "You want to get yourself in more trouble? You're only going to make the cops mad."

"Let them get mad," Rock said. "Tell us what happened." Rock wasn't keen on cops. The big guy wasn't keen on authority of any kind.

"I spent the night in a jail cell. Never been so miserable my entire life." Jim went on to explain how he'd gotten Rock's number off his business card and decided to give the boys a call.

"But what happened, Jim?"

Stafford paced. "Got to stretch my legs. Cooped up all night."

"You should have called your lawyer or your wife," said Rock.

"I did. We're trying to keep all this hush-hush. That's why I called you boys. You're outsiders. Lawyer's on his way out from New York though. On the train. He doesn't like to fly."

"All *what* hush-hush, Jim?" And what on earth did they have to do with it?

Stafford paced the carpet some more. The boys waited for the explanations to begin. Soon enough, the story came.

Jim told how he'd had an appointment with B.A.D. last night. "When I got there, the place was deserted and B.A.D. was dead. Murdered!" Jim wrung his hands. "Well, almost dead. He managed to say my name and then he died."

"That's terrible," said Tony.

"Horrible," agreed Rock.

"Tell me about it, men," Jim said. "And that police officer—"

"Robinson?"

"Yeah, Robinson. She finds me leaning over the body and, next thing you know, I'm in cuffs and accused of murder."

Rock asked, "Why would the police think you would want to murder B.A.D. Spike?"

"That's the part where it gets worse." Jim groaned and pulled his hair. "You see, B.A.D. and I had rigged up this here publicity stunt."

"Publicity stunt?" Tony said.

"Yeah. We pretended to really hate each other."

Rock frowned. "That's weird."

Jim ignored the comment. "Then, on B.A.D.'s opening night I was going to come out and B.A.D. and I were going to do a duet."

Tony shook his head. Show biz folk were sure strange. He'd been witness to their crazy behavior often since entering the biz and this was the craziest yet. "So you two were pretending to hate each other and now the police think you've killed him?"

"You got it."

"Didn't anyone else know about your little publicity stunt?"

Jim shook his head. "Only my wife. And B.A.D.'s manager."

"That guy you were arguing with at the buffet?"

Tony asked.

"That's right. That's what I was trying to tell you yesterday. It was all a setup. Make believe."

"Could have fooled me," said Rock.

"Did fool me," Tony said.

"I didn't murder anybody, boys." Jim helped himself to an open bag of sugarless oatmeal cookies on Robinson's desk.

"I know that, Jim," said Tony, "and you shouldn't be eating Officer Robinson's cookies."

"Hey, this girl pointed a gun at me. A big one! I could've gotten shot. Helping myself to an oatmeal cookie is the least this lady owes me."

"She did see you leaning over a dead body," Tony said in Robinson's defense. "Imagine. What was she supposed to think? She was only doing her job."

Rock's eyes narrowed. "You like her, don't you?"

"No, of course not," Tony quickly replied. "But that doesn't mean we shouldn't be civil."

"Civil?" Rock thrust his arms out. "Jim was in handcuffs!"

"Well, he's out of them now. Let's see about getting him out of jail next. It would help if everybody would stay calm down and act reasonable." Tony made a face at Jim. "And stop stealing cookies!" Jim pulled his hand away from the bag like he'd been bitten by a snake.

"Was it rough?" Rock asked.

"Huh?" Jim wiped the crumbs from his stubbled chin.

"Finding the body."

Jim dropped his head. "Oh, yeah. But like I said, B.A.D. wasn't quite dead when I found him."

Tony whistled.

"No, men." Jim placed his elbows on the desk and used his hands to hold up his drooping head. "He was standing there, in the kitchen," Jim said somberly. "He called my name. He was trying to talk—to tell me something. Something about dolls."

"Dolls?" Tony chewed his lip.

"Kewpie dolls?"

Jim shrugged. "Maybe. I guess." He shook his head as if to shake the memories from his mind. "You should have seen the look in his eyes, boys. B.A.D. knew he was dying."

Tony commiserated.

Jim looked towards the door. "You think they'll let me out of here?"

"They ought to. It all sounds pretty circumstantial to me. But I'm no lawyer." Even when he used to be, he wouldn't have wanted to pass judgement here.

Jim said. "There was a knife on the floor. A big, old kitchen knife. It had blood all over it."

"Jim," groaned Tony, remembering every TV movie he'd ever seen, "you didn't touch it, did you? Tell me you didn't touch it."

"I didn't touch it."

Tony let out a sigh of relief, then glanced at his watch. "Those police officers have been gone a long time. Maybe I'll go look for them. But you," he commanded, "stay put. Don't even think about leaving this room."

"Don't worry," Jim said. "I'm not going anywhere. They just might shoot first and ask questions later."

"Good. Think that way." Tony could well imagine Jim getting up and leaving. He'd be on the lam, an escaped criminal. There would be a manhunt. It would be in all the papers. "You still haven't told us why you've called us, Jim."

"I checked you out after meeting you. Found out you'd done some detective work. Solved some murders. You're reporters, too. At least, that's what Rock said."

"Yeah," Tony said slowly. While he had been involved in murder in the past, Tony considered his best skill to be that of extricating himself from sticky situations. He was not a detective, trained or otherwise. As for the reporter bit, that was all a might fanciful on Rock's part.

"So, investigate. Help me out of this jam."

"We're not that kind of reporters," answered Rock.

"No, we're more photojournalists," Tony said. "You know, Kewpie dolls, car shows."

"Two-headed calves," added Rock.

Jim's shoulders sagged. "Does that mean you won't help? How am I gonna explain this mess to my wife, my kids? My fans? Besides," pleaded Jim, "you're fellow musicians—help a brother out."

Kozol surrendered. The poor guy looked like a muddied puppy dog left out in the rain. And Tony couldn't help but think about Jim's angelic little daughter. She had appeared briefly in his show the night before. She'd done a little joke and a dance with her daddy. Jim's young son had performed as well, amazing the audience with his multi-instrumental solos. And Tony was a sucker for kids.

Tony tipped his head and pulled Rock aside. They pow-wowed. "Look at the poor guy, Rock. He's asking for our help. We can't just turn him away, can we?"

"Why not? What can we possibly do for him? We're

not criminal attorneys."

Tony thought for a moment. "I don't know. There must be something we can do. We could poke around—ask a few questions. Who knows? Maybe we can get to the bottom of things around here."

"And what about our job, Tony? And our story? You do remember that little thing called a job that we're here to do? Nanci likes me, but I don't know if I can keep her off our backs forever."

Tony grabbed Rock's wrist. "Don't you want to find out who killed B.A.D.? Think of the story we could get out of that?"

Rock's black eyes lit up. "You just might have something." He turned to Jim. "We'll make you a deal. You give us the story, us and only us, and we'll help you out. But if we find out you're guilty," he wagged a stocky finger, "you're on your own." Rock looked at Tony. "Okay, Tony?"

"Okay."

"Ditto," said Jim.

"Great," said Rock. "Now that we're all friends, have you got some local lawyer you can use, Jim?"

"That won't be necessary," said Det. Carvin, appearing in the open doorway.

"Whoa, don't do that, man," snapped Rock.

"What won't be necessary?" Tony demanded.

"That lawyer. Seems some hotshot lawyer from New York City has already called and chewed the chief's ear off." Carvin said *New York City* like it was a suburb of Sodom and Gomorrah. "Screaming about circumstantial evidence."

"Hey, you were listening in on our private conversation," complained Rock. "Isn't that against the law or something?"

Carvin was all smiles. "I won't tell if you won't. Now get out of here, you're free to go." He stepped past the boys and stopped in front of Jim. "The chief wanted me to apologize for any inconvenience, Mr. Stafford, sir. Something has come up, so he's unable to tell you personally."

"Sure," answered Jim, affably. "No problem." He headed for the exit. "Coming men?"

Carvin added, "You can sign for your things at the desk."

"That'll be fine."

"Chief Schaum did request that you stick around Branson—in case we have any more questions. You understand."

"Completely." Jim waved his hand. "No problem. Got a show to do every night. Can't disappoint my fans."

"No, sir," Carvin replied.

Rock made a face and Carvin held him back. "Funny," he said, pulling a toothpick from his shirt pocket and twirling it in his fingers like a mini-baton, "how when we pick some guy up at the scene of a crime, they tell us that it's just a big, old coincidence. Just like Stafford did."

"You think he's guilty, Carvin?"

Carvin shrugged.

"Your chief just set him free."

"Me and the chief don't always see eye to eye."

"We'll get to the bottom of this and when we do you'll see that Jim is innocent."

"Stick to making music. Keep out of police business, Mr. Bottom, before we lock you and your friend up."

"You're blocking the door."

The detective stepped aside.

Rock hurried past and down the hall. He caught up with Tony and Jim in the parking lot.

Jim inhaled deeply. "Ah, fresh air. Freedom." He closed his eyes and tilted his face towards the sun. "I missed you, sun. I missed you blue sky. I missed you trees—" He paused. Came back to earth. "Can I give you men a lift?"

Rock answered. "That's all right. We've got a car."

"You think it's okay to take your car, Jim?" wondered Tony. Was it evidence in a murder investigation?

"Why not? They gave me these back." Jim dangled the keys. "I tell you what," said Jim, "there's a little place downtown where we can get a cup of coffee. Let's meet up down there and discuss the case."

"Case?" The mere mention of the word made the whole situation sound way too serious and way too much responsibility. It would be far more sensible to let the police do their job and catch B.A.D.'s killer. "I don't know," began Tony, glancing at his watch, "we've still got a gig to do." He'd explained how they were working for Nanci Dement.

"Come on, Tony. Don't worry about Nanci. We've got plenty of time. What's the name of this place?" With the promise of a story that could get him a byline in maybe even the Miami Herald, Rock was changing his tune quickly.

"Branson Café," answered Jim. "Y'all follow me. It's up Highway 76, then right on Main Street. It's in the old downtown section of Branson."

Stafford climbed into a big cream-colored Lexus

with a personalized SPIDRS license plate and waited at
the edge of the road for the boys to catch up.

"You do know we're supposed to be working for
Nanci?" Tony took the keys from Rock and pulled in
behind Stafford.

"I know, I know. But you should have heard Carvin
back there. I'd like to hear what Jim's got to say for
himself."

"You think Jim's innocent?"

Rock shrugged. "I'm keeping an open mind. Either
way, this could make a great feature." He rubbed his
hands together. He could see his byline already.

Chapter 9

They found a parking space on Main Street and joined Stafford. Branson Café was jammed but somehow he'd ended up with a great booth right up front. An 8x10 black and white glossy of Jim hung on the wall above the table. That might have explained things. Behind the register was a wall's worth of Branson celebrity shots.

"I ordered us up some coffee and pie."

"Thanks, Jim," Tony said. He smiled in the direction of an elderly couple sitting shoulder to shoulder and whispering behind a plastic-laminated menu.

Rock asked, "What kind of pie?"

"Apple."

Rock looked ready to complain and Tony quickly kicked him across the shin under the cover of the table. Rock replied with an 'accidental' elbow to Tony's ribcage. "Gosh, this booth is cramped, isn't it, Tony?"

Tony slid over. The place smelled of bacon and eggs and strong coffee.

The pie and drinks arrived quickly. While Jim attacked his pie, Rock attacked him. "So, if you want our help, you're going to have to give us more to work with, Jim." He was leaning back, making with his best prosecutorial stare.

"What more can I say?" replied Jim, chewing up a mouthful of apple and swallowing. "I don't know any more than you men do."

"You said you had an appointment with Donald," Tony began.

"That's right. He was worried about his grand opening and wanted to jaw."

"At night?" Rock said skeptically.

"Why not? I had a little time after the show. I'm a night person. Got to be in this business. You know that."

Tony broke off a bit of pie crust and nibbled on it. It was rich and buttery and smelled like Heaven on a spring morning. The filling was heavy on the cinnamon, just the way he preferred it. He was going to gain five pounds on this trip. Maybe he'd dust off the in-line skates once he got back home. He might be able to burn some fat off courtesy of the hot Florida sun, if nothing else.

Rock leaned forward. "You said you were helping him out. Were you two good friends?"

"Not to begin with, no." Jim sighed. "You see, it was like this. When B.A.D., Donald, first came to town, he looked me up."

"When was this?" interrupted Tony.

Jim pushed his pie around on his plate some.

"About a year ago. He came to see me at my theater. He said he was thinking about doing something in Branson."

"But why did he come to see you, Jim, if the two of you didn't know each other previously?"

Jim shrugged. "Not surprising. I've been here a long time, Tony. I first came to Branson back in eighty-three. I'll never forget that day," he said fondly. "I had a gig at the Roy Clark Celebrity Theater. I'd never even heard of Branson myself before then."

Jim stopped and sipped his coffee. "For me it was just to be another stop on the road, you know? But you should have seen it, men. I tell you, I was amazed. The bright lights, the music, the live shows. There's lots of talented folks here in Branson."

Tony agreed. "Sounds like fate."

"Sounds like we're getting derailed," murmured Rock. "Someone want to get this discussion back on track?"

"Hear me out, Rock." Jim turned to Tony. "You said exciting? Heck, I thought I'd stumbled into some town in the Twilight Zone. I couldn't believe it. I kept coming back here to Branson, playing dates along the way and finally moved here permanent back in nineteen-ninety." He wiped his lips with a paper napkin. "It about scared me to death, too."

"Why was that?"

"You kidding? It meant giving up my career. I had to say no to any other future dates, cruises, TV shows, everything; and make the commitment to performing here. And hoping that folks would come see me."

"I'd say it's worked out all right." Rock pulled the fork out of the center of his pie and licked it clean.

"I've been lucky. But it's been a whole lot of work. You can't just open up a theater here in Branson and expect the people to come. Some stars think that's all there is to it and that's why they fail."

Stafford shook his head. "Nope. Takes a lot of work, I tell you. And that's why I understood where B.A.D. was coming from. He was desperate in a way. I mean, his career had stalled. His previous attempts at reinventing himself and staging comebacks had all failed. But show business was all the fella knew. B.A.D. was determined to make this theater thing work. And I figured the guy deserved whatever little bit of help I could give him."

"I don't know," said Rock, "rap music in Branson?"

"I know, sounds crazy. And I agree with you. I told B.A.D. it was a pretty risky venture. But he had ideas. Good ideas. And he was going to go more mainstream, more traditional."

"B.A.D. Spike" Mainstream? Wow, he sure had changed."

"But the public feuding?" Tony waved for the waitress and asked for more coffee. "Whose idea was that."

"That was a little bit I worked up," Jim said. "In public, I was arguing with B.A.D. and telling him to get out of town and all that stuff. But it was all play-acting. Free publicity. Folks ate it up, the papers, too. Like I said, opening night I was going to show up at B.A.D.'s theater dressed up in my cowboy outfit. You know, the one I wear in the Cow Patti number from my show. With the black hat and all."

The boys looked skeptical.

"B.A.D., he had himself a cowboy outfit, too, with a

white hat. I was planning on coming into the theater, packing my six-guns and calling him out. We were going to do some back and forth repartee and then break out into a Cow Patti duet, but updated—sort of rap style."

The boys looked at one another.

"Only in Branson." Rock was shaking his big head.

"And that's why you went to his theater last night," said Tony.

"That's right. At least, I guess it was. Donald wanted to talk. I assume that's what it was all about. I tell you, Donald and I were friends. That's what I was trying to explain to you fellows when I saw y'all up at the Kewpie doll show."

"He didn't give you any other clues as to what else might be going on?" asked Tony.

"Mentioned anybody that wanted him dead?" Rock added.

Jim was shaking his head. "Nope. Donald called me and begged me to come by and see him after my show last night. Said it was important. That's all I know. I knew he was worried about getting all the work finished up on time for his opening. All sorts of stuff going on with the contractors. Plus he said Merel had been by getting him all riled up."

"Merel?"

"Merel Pearce," said Jim.

"Merel Pearce the country star?" Tony said.

"That's right. He's Donald's landlord. The Crib is Merel's old theater. Donald and Merel didn't get along. But then nobody much gets along with Merel.

"Donald seemed particularly upset when he phoned yesterday afternoon and wanting me to come by then.

But I had a meeting and then my own show to do, I told him it would have to wait. Maybe if I'd gone by early he'd still be alive."

"Or maybe you'd both be dead," Rock said matter-of-factly. Jim and Tony looked shocked. "What? It's possible."

"So that's the reason you left your theater so fast last night, Jim," Tony said, "because you were meeting Donald?"

"That's right. How'd you know?"

"We wanted to go backstage and thank you for our tickets. But we were told you'd left already."

"That's where I was, at Donald's."

Tony was rubbing his chin. He hadn't had time to shave and itched badly. "What time did you get there?"

"Some time between ten-thirty and eleven. Probably closer to eleven. That's what I told the police."

"Why so late?" Tony inquired. "B.A.D.'s Crib is just up the street from your own theater."

"I had to stop at the Walmart first."

"Walmart?" Rock repeated.

"Promised my son I'd pick him up a new DVD for his DVD player. He likes something to watch back-stage. So I stopped at Walmart, then drove on up to the Crib."

"That seems an awfully odd time to be stopping at Walmart," Rock said. "Especially right before B.A.D. is going to get himself murdered."

"Why? Place is quieter then. Nobody bothers me and they've got just about everything. I do it all the time. Besides," he added, "I didn't know what was going to happen. I didn't know B.A.D. was going to get himself killed."

Tony said, "Think, did you see anyone else around Donald's theater, Jim?"

"Nope. Not a soul."

"Then who was it that saw you and reported you to the police?" Rock wanted to know.

"I don't have a clue. The police told me it was some anonymous tip."

"Somebody simply called up the police to complain that you were hanging around outside the theater?" There was a current of skepticism running through his words like low voltage electricity.

"Well—" Jim squirmed in his seat.

"Well what?" demanded Rock.

"You see, actually, men, they reported seeing me running off with that Kewpie doll." He dropped his eyes.

"Okay," said Rock, shredding his napkin, "we're back to you and that Kewpie doll." Rock picked up his pie with two fingers and stuffed the remaining half of it into his gaping mouth, chewing with exaggerated, angry movements of his wide jaw. The muscles on each side bunched up like knots of steel.

The waitress was wiping down the table next to theirs. Tony whispered, "That was the Kewpie doll I saw in the box on the desk in the police station, wasn't it?" He'd noticed it on their way out.

Jim nodded. "I'm afraid so."

"But what was an expensive thing like that doing in the parking lot?"

He shrugged. "Beats me. I knew from going to the trade show that that there doll had to be valuable. Nobody would throw a thing like that away. I was going to take it to the police station in the morning. I never had the chance."

"Weird," remarked Tony.

"Yeah. Now the police think I stole that dang Kewpie and killed B.A.D."

"I remember your daughter looking at that exact Kewpie doll yesterday afternoon," said Tony.

Rock said, "I'll bet that's the Kewpie doll that B.A.D. was trying to tell you about before he died."

Jim nodded. "Looks bad, doesn't it?"

Tony agreed.

"But still," said Rock, "Jim Stafford steal a Kewpie doll? I mean, he's loaded."

"Rock!"

"What? You are, aren't you?"

"I get by," Jim replied, all modesty.

"Besides," continued Rock, "how much can a Kewpie doll be worth?"

"According to the police, that particular doll is worth about eight grand, maybe more."

Tony whistled.

"Maybe somebody was stealing the Kewpie and B.A.D. caught him?" suggested Rock.

"Let's say that's true," Tony began, playing devil's advocate. "So how did B.A.D. end up in the back of the theater and the doll in the side parking lot?"

Rock had several answers, none of them much good. "Okay, then let's say the killer breaks in, steals the doll. B.A.D. chases him and gets knifed somehow. The the killer runs out with the doll. Maybe he hears a noise, too, and gets frightened. The killer drops the doll and runs."

Jim snapped his fingers. "I'll bet you're right!"

Rock grinned triumphantly.

Tony picked up the thread. "Did you see or hear anything suspicious?"

"Nothing but that doll in the lot."

Tony's phone rang. He checked the number. "It's Nanci again."

Rock said, "Don't answer."

"I won't." Tony laid the ringing phone on the table. "Jim, didn't anybody else know about this publicity stunt you and B.A.D. had cooked up?"

"Just me, him, his manager and Annie, my wife. I mean, we didn't want everybody to know. That would spoil all the fun."

"Yeah, fun," Rock said drily. "Like tossing wet cowpatties into an audience every night."

"Ouch." Jim tapped his chest, directly over his heart. "Now that hurts, son."

"Sorry," Rock mumbled.

"We'll have to talk to Butch," said Tony. "Where can we find him?"

"I don't know." Jim called to the waitress. "Is there a charge for this, honey?"

"It's on the house, Jim."

Jim thanked the woman and laid a twenty next to his plate. He rose. "So what's the plan, men?"

Tony picked up his phone and dusted off the pie crumbs. "Plan?"

"Yeah, we had a pact, remember? We've got to nail this killer."

"Better keep your voice down, Jim," Tony whispered. "People are looking at us kind of funny."

"Oh, big deal." Jim waved. "Hi, everybody. You all know me, Jim Stafford. Don't forget to come see the show. Eight o'clock, every night. Matinee on Wednesday"

Startled faces smiled uneasily. Some nodded.

Tony headed for the door.

Jim caught up with him on the sidewalk. "Come on, Tony. Help a fella out."

"Jim, I'd like to help you, really I would. But I'm not a real detective."

"That's not what I hear on the grapevine. I hear you've helped out lots of fellow entertainers."

"Not really. You see I—"

Tony desperately wanted to explain to Stafford that he really would be of no use to him, but just then two youths on heavily stickered skateboards, wearing baggy, over-sized shorts and torn, dirty T-shirts, whizzed up to them. "Hey, Stafford, you don't like spiders and snakes," yelled the first one, sporting the backward Raiders ballcap, "but is it true you got a thing for Kewpie dolls?"

His friend laughed. They kicked off and the skateboards clattered down the sidewalk. The sidewalk ended and the kids shot across the street to the accompanying blare of angry drivers' car horns.

"What was that all about?" Tony asked.

"Uh-oh."

Tony looked at Jim whose eyes were on a newspaper vending machine leaning up against the wall outside the cafe. It was some local paper called *The Branson Bugle*. The big headline read: *A B.A.D. Ending for Rapster*. That was bad enough. A second headline read: *Kewpie Kaper for Komic?*

Tony bent down and began to read, "Local celebrity, Jim Stafford, was found at The Crib, scene of Donald Milquist's, aka B.A.D. Spike's, murder late last night.

Police sources say Stafford had a priceless Kewpie doll in his possession. He—"

Stafford groaned, fished around in his pocket for a couple of quarters and dropped them in the slot. He pulled out all the remaining papers, tossed them into the trunk of his car and sped off.

Chapter 10

Butch kicked the door.

It slammed against the doorjamb then bounced back in his face. He pushed it away. "This stinks. This really stinks. I'm broke!

"I always told B.A.D. he ought to have himself some sort of life insurance policy. What am I supposed to do now?"

Cyndi rubbed her red eyes. She'd been up half the night crying and the other half worrying. "Can't you think about anything or anyone but yourself, Butch? Poor B.A.D.'s lying in the morgue dead. Doesn't that mean something to you?"

Butch snarled. "It means the end of the road. No more gravy train." He paced up to the girl. "Not for me and not for you, honey doll."

"I don't care about any of that," Cyndi retorted. She was decked out in something more conservative this day, a close-cropped white peasant blouse that leaned towards the sheer side and a pair of low-rider, spandex-enhanced jeans with fringed cuffs.

Butch laughed callously. "Sure you do, honey. We all do."

"That's not true. I loved Donald." She stepped away from B.A.D.'s overbearing manager and paced the office. She'd never been able to stand being too close to him. She thought he smelled like a New York subway station. His personality stank as well. She often wondered what B.A.D. saw in the unlikable man and why he kept the oaf around. So they were cousins, big deal.

The office was quiet. Outside, the stage was deserted. The employees had been questioned by the police as they trickled in that morning and were then sent home. Some had already heard the news of B.A.D.'s death before coming in, others were caught by surprise. A few broke down.

Cyndi and Butch weren't allowed back in Donald's apartment yet either. The Branson police still had the area taped off.

She'd had to spend the night at the Radisson up the road. They hadn't even let her pack a suitcase. An officer let her pick out a change of clothes and only with the chief's permission was she allowed to take that much with her.

Cyndi twisted the blinds open and looked out the window across the deserted parking lot. She couldn't stop crying.

Butch didn't seem to care. "I've already had a call from that fool, Pearce. Man says he wants us out of here as soon as the police are through."

Cyndi turned. "What?"

"You heard me."

"But he can't do that. We—I mean, Donald, has a lease."

"Man says he's already got his lawyers tearing into that lease like they's gobbling up a meaty old bone and going for the marrow."

"But this is our theater."

"How you going to pay for it? You have any idea how much the bills have been adding up to?"

Cyndi shook her head. B.A.D. didn't go into too many financial details with her.

"Well, I do. And with B.A.D. dead, we're dead." Butch spat into the steel trash can beside the desk. It rang out like a shot from a BB gun.

"No, Merel Pearce wants us out of here and we're out of here. Just as well." He spat again. "We've got no show anyway."

"I hate that man."

Butch was tickled. "Line forms to the right."

Then Cyndi's eyes grew wide. "What about a tribute show, Butch? We could do a B.A.D. Spike tribute show. It could be wonderful."

Butch looked at her like she was some sort of trigonometric equation that he'd been asked to figure out. And the only numbers he cared about had dollar signs in front of them and lots of pretty little zeroes after them. "That's stupid."

"No, it isn't. We could celebrate the life and times of B.A.D., pay tribute to his music and his career in show business. There could be songs and big dance numbers. The works."

"You're looney, girl. Guess love does that to a

woman."

"No, I'm not. We can do this, Butch. B.A.D. would want us to."

Butch's face grew hard. "Honey doll, I don't care two bits what B.A.D. would want us to do. He's dead. Time to pick yourself up and move on. Just like I'm going to do. Find yourself another sugar daddy."

"All you care about is money. Isn't that right, Butch?"

"Finally you understand me."

"Think about the money we can make doing a B.A.D. Spike tribute show then, Butch, if money is all that matters. Let's make some money. We'll be partners, fifty-fifty."

Butch was shaking his head. "You still going on about that? It isn't going to happen. We haven't got the money and nobody is going to give it to us. And fifty percent of nothing is still nothing."

"We can try, Butch. We can try to raise the money."

"By the time you do that, if you do it, Pearce will have had us tossed out of this theater on our ears and he'll have struck up a deal with someone else for this place."

Cyndi chewed her lip. "It's not fair."

"Geez, Cyndi, not fair? Where'd you grow up, Sesame Street?"

Cyndi crossed from behind the big desk and gently took hold of the pleat of Butch's crisp, white dress shirt. Despite his obviously dipping himself in eau de cologne, he stank. It was a repugnant mix of that NY subway and Calvin Klein. "Don't underestimate me, Butch."

Butch laughed nervously, shifted his feet to adjust

his bulk. "Why?"

She tugged. "Because that would be a mistake. A big mistake."

Butch pulled himself free. "Don't mess with the clothes." He sauntered cockily to the door.

Cyndi's hard, flat eyes glared at Butch's retreating backside.

Chapter 11

Rock stepped from the car and planted his feet on the hot, gooey blacktop.

Tony checked to make sure he had his notebook and grabbed his guitar. "What do you suppose those police cars are doing up there?" Two squad cars sat next to the entrance. There was no sign of the officers who'd driven them.

"Searching for clues, I guess." Rock said. Despite the size of the crowd, the mood was noticeably subdued. The boys slipped their gear under the rear of the stage. "No sign of Nanci," said the big guy. "That's good."

"Unless she's out looking for our replacements." Tony fiddled with his pen.

"Maybe Jim will give us jobs."

Tony refused to even entertain that dream. "I'd like to go from table to table and talk to everyone about their collectibles, what they are, what they represent. Find out whether the pieces are considered rare or not. That sort of thing. I'll leave it up to you what shots to get. The papers will want some photos of some of the more ordinary Kewpie, plus some of the more rare and valuable ones, I expect. Make sense to you?"

"What do you suppose those two are up to?"

"Huh?" Tony followed the line of Rock's finger.

"What do you think is going on over there?"

"I don't know," Tony replied.

"That's that guy from the hotel. The same guy that was driving that pickup with that stupid *Booze or Gas* sign on the back of his boat."

"What?"

"The guy the cops are talking to. The one with the red hair and the beard. He's even wearing that threadbare herringbone jacket. Doesn't he ever take that thing off? I'll bet he sleeps in it. I'll bet he showers in it."

This from a guy whose only variation on the theme of black was his pair of black and white, image-of-prison evoking, p.j.'s. "Do you think we can get started now, Rock?" asked Tony. "Before Nanci shows up and expects us to do something crazy—like play some music?"

"No, on second thought I'd say he doesn't bathe with it on. Too dirty. That jacket's probably never seen the inside of a washing machine, let alone a proper Laundromat."

Tony shook his head, rolled his eyes and headed for the nearest dealer's table. "I'll be over here—*working.*"

"I'm right behind you, Tony." Rock instead made a beeline for the redheaded man's tables across the room. He had three tables laid out in a U-shape configuration near the edge of the center wall. He was standing behind the middle table and the two police officers were speaking with him.

One of the officers glanced in Rock's direction as he approached. Rock didn't recognize either one of them from the station. He dropped his gaze and pretended to be staring at a sheet of labels with Kewpie doll pictures on them. They were pea can labels. Man, those Kewpie images were everywhere, thought Rock.

He took out his cheesy little digital camera and focused in for a closeup.

"I didn't have any insurance," bemoaned the fellow. "In a business like ours, it is extravagantly expensive and hard to procure."

The man had a strong accent which Rock guessed to be Scottish.

He was wringing his hands. "I drove all the way to Missouri to make a few dollars, be near my friends who share this passion for Rose O'Neill. I ask you, gentlemen, who, who would do such a terrible thing?"

Rock froze. Was he talking about the murder? Was it spoiling his Kewpiecon? Talk about heartless.

"I don't know, Mr. Daniels," said the officer nearest Rock, "but we'll do all we can to recover the rest of your collectibles."

The rest of his collectibles?

"Consider yourself lucky that you're going to get that one Kewpie doll back so quick."

"Yeah," said the first officer. "Eight grand. Man, no way I can buy my daughter one of these things. You know," his voice dropped, "just between us, I hear Jim Stafford had it."

"I heard that, too," said the second officer. "Nice fella. I met him last year when he did that charity for those cancer kids at the hospital. A real regular guy."

"The woman watching my table for me yesterday told me Mr. Stafford's daughter was looking at the figurine for quite some time," said the dealer.

"Pretty weird," said the first officer. "Jim Stafford. Now there's a guy who can afford to buy his kid a Kewpie doll if he wants to."

The redheaded man smiled. "I do have some very nice, very reasonable reproductions." He reached to the side table, said "I'll be right with you, sir," to Rock, and brought over a plastic Kewpie doll for the officer's inspection.

He took it. "Yeah, not bad." He held it up to his friend. "What do you think, Mike?"

"Cute."

"How much?"

"Thirty-five dollars only. In fact, for an officer of the law, whom I admire greatly, twenty dollars, tax included."

The policeman pulled a twenty out of his wallet. "Thanks. Stef's gonna love this. And when you've got that list of the stolen merchandise completed, just give headquarters a call. Ask for me by name, Hank Pankovits. I'll come pick it up myself."

"Thank you, Officer Pankovits." Mr. Daniels bowed. "And you as well, Officer Midkiff. It will take a little effort for me to complete my inventory, I only hope I have not lost too much."

Rock waited until the officers left then scooted in close.

"Duncan Daniels at your service, laddie. Can I help

you with something in particular?"

"I couldn't help overhearing," said Rock. "What happened? Did you have something stolen?"

Mr. Daniels nodded. "Didn't you hear, laddie? This place has been buzzing all morning. It's like listening to a swarm of flies lingering over a dead heifer in the glen."

Rock felt the man's eyes, green as gherkins, giving him the once over, probably estimating how much money he could squeeze out of him. Good luck, thought Rock, whose pockets were virtually empty. An inch long, wide deep red scar ran under the man's right eye, twitching to a beat all its own.

"No," said Rock, all innocence, "what happened?" He leaned forward like a good co-conspirator should. He liked playing detective almost as much as he liked playing the bass.

"Someone broke into the trade hall last night. They killed B.A.D. Spike and robbed the place. Personally, I've lost a number of my best dolls and figures, and some china."

"That's terrible!"

"Yes. But don't worry, laddie. I hear they've caught the murderer."

"They have?"

He nodded. "Caught him at the scene of the crime. Standing over the body. I heard he's some sort of celebrity."

"I see," said Rock glumly. Word was spreading quick. "Mr. Daniels, did anyone else have anything stolen?"

"Call me Duncan. I believe in first names." Daniels looked about the room. "A piece or two here and there.

But Elf," he shook his head, "he lost the most."

"Elf?" Did this guy also believe in elves? If so, he'd been hanging around all these fairy-like creatures way too long.

"Rick Elf, the ROSE vice president. He had his Kewpie Mountain on special display in the other room. Brought it all the way from Colorado."

"And someone stole it?"

"Yes," said Mr. Daniels. "Smashed the case with an ashtray and snatched it, he did."

"Wow, I'll bet he's upset. Probably kind of expensive, huh?" A little bait and reel him in. This guy was *so* easy.

Daniels leaned back and laughed. "Expensive? Try one hundred thousand dollars expensive, laddie."

"One hundred—" Rock stammered.

Daniels was nodding, his hands resting over his paunch. "Maybe more."

"For a Kewpie doll? You're pulling my legs, Duncan."

"No, laddie. A Kewpie mountain and I kid you not."

Rock's camera hung limp in his hand. "What is so special about this Kewpie Mountain? Do you have one? Can I see it?"

Duncan's eyes sparkled. "Ah, if only. If only I had one. You ask what is so special about the Kewpie Mountain. What is not special about the Kewpie Mountain?"

He pressed his hands down on the tabletop, eyed a prospective customer, who quickly moved on, and spoke. "The Kewpie Mountain contains seventeen action Kewpie figurines arranged on a small mountain. A lone tree trunk on the left curves back toward the center at its highest point." He twisted and bent his wrist to demonstrate.

"The charming little figures are arranged in various poses. In the center, on top, there is a small combo of musicians playing drums, bass and violin. Another baby Kewpie swings from the tree. There is too much for me to describe adequately. And the piece is entirely bisque, of course."

"Of course," nodded Rock. "What's bisque, again? I mean, I thought it was a soup."

"The word bisque comes from biscuit. The term is generally used in ceramics to indicate porcelain which has undergone a first firing."

"I see. But what I don't see is what makes this Kewpie Mountain worth a hundred thousand of somebody's hard-earned dollars."

Duncan shrugged. "Elf's was a very fine piece. Beautiful. Not a single flaw," he said with obvious appreciation. "And rare, laddie. Why, there are only two Kewpie Mountains known to exist in the entire world."

A youngish Japanese couple in matching black cargo shorts and button-down black shirts approached and began poring through Duncan's prints. Boxes of prints were stuffed alphabetically in two brown cardboard boxes to Rock's left.

"Who has the other Kewpie Mountain?"

"It is in a private collection owned by a woman in New Jersey, I believe. I can't be sure. I believe her name is Eudora Pandolfo."

Daniels turned to his customers. "Very fine prints, don't you agree? Very reasonably priced. Fifteen dollars each, but in honor of our Japanese allies, whom I greatly admire, two for twenty dollars." Duncan showed his teeth. "Tax included."

Rock grinned and moved away. Turning about, he spotted Tony scribbling away in his notebook. Rock ran to Tony and twisted his shoulder. "Wait till you hear what I found out, Tony."

"Where have you been?" Kozol held up his note-book and waved it in Rock's face. "I've got pages and pages of notes here and no photographs to go with them."

"I was talking to Duncan."

"Duncan?"

"Duncan Daniels, that guy over there."

"The one from the hotel?" Tony turned and studied the man. "The one with the tacky sign on his boat?" he said incredulously. "Why on earth would you want to talk to a clod like that?"

"Turns out he's not such a clod, Tony." Rock pulled Tony to the side of the room, away from the milling crowd. "You saw the police talking to him when we got here."

"Yeah, I was hoping they were going to arrest him for crude behavior, not to mention bad taste in bumper stickers."

"You've got a point there," admitted Rock. "But listen, Tony. I was talking to Duncan. I thought he might know something and he did."

"Like what?" Tony looked skeptical.

"Duncan had some things stolen from his booth, including that Kewpie doll that Stafford says he found in the parking lot."

Tony whistled. "Really? What did he say? Does he know anything that might help Jim?"

Rock was shaking his head. "No, at least I don't think so." His shark-like grip clamped down on Tony's forearm. "But listen to this."

Tony's eyes were scanning his notes.

Rock shook his arm. "Are you listening?"

"Yes, I'm listening." Tony pulled himself loose. "Go ahead already."

"There's a Kewpie Mountain missing," announced Rock grandly.

Tony's eyebrows shot upwards. "A Kewpie Mountain, eh? Well, I sure do hope the Branson police put out an All Points Bulletin quick. I mean, someone might drive off with that mountain and how, oh how, will anyone find the dastardly criminals, what with them driving off with, what? A mountain sticking out of the back of their truck?"

Rock glared. "Are you done?"

Tony was smiling. "I guess so. Now can we get on with this? This whole story thing was your idea, remember?"

"Kewpie Mountains are some kind of ceramic bric-a-brac. Only two are known to exist in the whole world."

"That's wonderful," said Tony, obviously not meaning it. "Now can you take some pictures?"

Rock said slowly, "Duncan says this one's worth over a hundred thousand dollars."

"You can start with getting a shot of—" Tony's jaw dropped. "Did you say one hundred thousand dollars?"

"Yep." Rock looked triumphant. "One hundred thousand pretty little Georgie Washingtons."

That was some serious money. "Your new friend, Duncan, must be pretty upset." Tony hadn't seen that much money since. . .Hell, he'd never seen that much money!

Rock was shaking his head again. "It didn't belong to him."

"But you said he had some things stolen."

"He did. So did some of the others here. The Kewpie Mountain belonged to Rick Elf."

"Rick Elf? His name sounds familiar." Tony flipped through the pages of his little notebook. "Here. Rick Elf, a vice president of the Rose O'Neill Society of Enthusiasts."

"That's the one. The suddenly poorer Rick Elf of the R.O.S.E."

"Interesting," Tony said. "I suggest we have a talk with this Rick Elf."

"You see? I suggest you listen to me more often, Tony. I am an expert at prying information from people. I make a great detective."

"Fine, Mr. Detective, any idea where we find this Elf fellow?"

Rock was smiling. "Follow me, my man."

Grudgingly, Tony did.

Rock led the way to the second room where they bumped into Virginia Plat, ROSE president, in the entryway. "Good morning, Virginia."

"What?"

"Good morning, Miss Plat," Tony said. "Are you all right?" Poor Miss Plat looked even mousier than usual. The circles under her eyes presaged incipient black holes. "You poor thing," Tony said, laying a gentle hand on the other woman's shoulder. "It's all these thefts, isn't it?"

"And the murder, I'll bet," added Rock.

"Thefts? Murder?" Miss Plat ran a nervous hand through her hair. If she'd had whiskers she'd have rubbed them off by now.

"Yes," Rock said with what Tony felt were over-the-top dramatic tones, "the dolls, the figures," he whispered, "the Kewpie Mountain."

"Oh, my, yes. The thefts. It's a nasty business. And it's all my fault." Ms. Plat wrung her hands.

"All your fault? What do you mean, Ms. Plat?" Tony held up his notepad, pen at the ready.

"It's nothing. . .probably." She squinted. "Aren't you the musicians?"

Tony nodded. "What's nothing?"

"I don't know. . .Can I trust you, gentlemen?"

They nodded.

Miss Plat swallowed hard and said, "You see, I saw—"

A voice in the crowd called Miss Plat's name. She looked up.

"You saw what?" asked Tony.

"Later." Miss Plat scurried away. Like a mouse. A frightened mouse.

"When?" called Tony.

Miss Plat turned. She seemed confused by the question. Then she replied, "Tonight, after the banquet." And then she was gone.

Tony watched her go.

"What a kook," Rock said.

"You do know, my dearest friend, that there are those who would say you are a kook, Rock?"

Rock shifted his not inconsequential weight. "Sure, I know. But that's because the folks saying it are the real kooks. I happen to think I'm pretty normal." He stuck out his jaw. "Now let's go find this leprechaun guy."

"He's not a leprechaun, he's an elf," said Tony. "I mean his name is not Leprechaun. It's Elf. Rick Elf."

"Leprechaun, Elf. They're all little green guys in tights, aren't they? Streaking through the forests, chasing rainbows and hoarding gold and stuff like that?"

Tony followed Rock's quick steps. "Please, do not share this theory of yours with Mr. Elf, Rock."

"What kind of a good life is that, anyway?" yammered Rock. "Imagine. Running around all day in nice fitting clothes, counting your gold. Maybe granting a wish or two to some poor slob. Man, sign me up. I could live a life like that."

Tony had a feeling Rock already did lead such a life. If not precisely, then very close indeed.

Chapter 12

Merel stomped across the hardwood floor.

"Where's my lighter?" He rummaged around on his desk and came up empty. "Dang wife's been cleaning up again, no doubt. Drivin' me crazy the way Dolly goes around fussing and cleaning up all the time."

"Yes, Mr. Pearce." Johnny Jones, Merel's chief assistant, gofer and doormat, shifted uneasily. He was a small man with a knobby pink nose and cold black eyes. His boss was angry and that meant his own life was going to be all the more uncomfortable.

Johnny was sixty-two years old, the same age as his boss, Merel Pearce. And he'd been with Merel for thirty-one of those years. Half his life. And it seemed like half of that half Merel had been teed off about one thing or another. It was Johnny's job to listen to Merel's rambling rants and raves and do what he could, and/or what he was told by his boss, to make things better.

"I've told her I don't know how many times she don't need to clean up the office. Got a service for that. Got a service for everything." Merel found a pack of matches in his drawer, twisted one off and lit up his cigar.

Pearce pulled on his cigar a while, one hand behind his back. He gazed out the window to the hills. He liked this new theater much better than the old place. In town, all he saw were signs and cars. Out here a man could see God's country.

He'd also gained a bigger theater and a way bigger parking lot. That meant he gained more money in the bank. For Merel Pearce, there wasn't much that could beat that.

Much as he hated to, Merel had to admit Tom E. Landry had had the right idea building out this way, away from the crowds. It had been a bit of a risk at the time. Some folks thought that a theater off the beaten track would fail. But Tom had succeeded and so when the time came that Merel felt he had outgrown his theater in town, he decided to follow Tom's lead.

Of course, Merel had made sure that his architect built the new Merel Pearce Mongrel Theater a bit bigger and even a smidgen taller than Tom's place. That had gotten under Tom's craw, he was sure. And that had made the extra expense all the more worthwhile. Merel had always been running second to Tom, on the sales charts and in the airplay stats over the years.

Merel was determined to be Number One in Branson. Top dog and top draw.

"Where's that idiot lawyer of mine, Slootsky?"

demanded Merel, stamping out his cigar against the marble windowsill. "Why ain't he here yet?"

"He went up to Forsythe, Mr. Pearce."

"Oh, that's just great. What do I bother to pay him a retainer for? Just so's he can irritate the bejeezus out of me? Get him on the phone."

"I tried, sir. There was no answer."

"He probably shut his phone off."

"Maybe there's trouble with the signal?"

Merel glared at Johnny.

Johnny realized he'd crossed an imaginary line. He fidgeted. "Anything I can do, boss?"

"You can take a shotgun out to the old theater and run off those squatters."

Johnny swallowed. "I was by the place earlier, Mr. Pearce. The police still have the place sealed off. Excepting for the Kewpie show. I don't think there's much I can do about those folks."

Merel looked down on Johnny from across the room. "No," he said heavily, "I don't suppose there is anything *you* can do."

Johnny lowered his eyes. He felt like a whipped dog. But then, he was accustomed to the feeling.

Shel Slootsky burst through the office door. He had short, unruly black hair and always decked himself out in a wrinkly black suit and tie. With the little moustache he was sporting of late, he looked a little like Oliver Hardy. He certainly had the weight down pat.

Slootsky tossed his black leather briefcase over onto the sofa. "Afternoon, Merel. Bad news. I'm afraid there's not a whole lot we can do about that rap bunch over at the old theater, at least not straight away. The contract you signed with B.A.D. is pretty ironclad. I warned you. I told you that you were giving too much away in the deal." Slootsky ran an unsteady hand through his greasy head.

Merel scowled. "Don't you ever knock? Didn't your mama teach you any manners?"

Slootsky looked nervously from Johnny to Merel. "Sorry," he mumbled. He flopped down into a chair across from Merel's desk. "I pored over every word of the contract. I even had a little chat with old Judge Simons—you know he likes you, Merel—but he said there was nothing we or him could do."

"Nothing?" Merel's hands wrapped around the stub of his cigar and ripped it to shreds which sprayed across his desk. "I thought with that fool B.A.D. dead my troubles would be over."

Slootsky shrugged. "Not until they default on their payments over there." He grinned. "But hell, that shouldn't take long. They've got no star. No show."

Merel said nothing.

"I mean," said Slootsky, tugging at his tie, "they're bound to run out of money soon. What I don't get is why they haven't capitulated. That Butch Domino fella wouldn't even listen to me when I tried to talk to them. And I did like you told me, offered to let them out without any penalty at all. Even though it is your legal right."

Slootsky had a copy of the contract in his hand. He slapped it. "It's right here. Says you've got the right to be paid six months rent if they default. I mean, you've been generous with them, Merel."

"Very generous," said Johnny.

Merel fumed. "More than generous." He crossed

from behind his desk and grabbed the contract from his lawyer's hand. "It's Butch Domino and that girl. They're up to something."

"What girl?" asked the lawyer.

Merel replied, "Parker."

"Parker, Parker. Cyndi Parker?" Slootsky said.

Merel nodded.

"She's nobody. B.A.D.'s girlfriend is all. She doesn't pose any sort of problem."

An evil grin crossed Merel's face. "He doesn't know much about women, does he, Johnny?"

Johnny chuckled. It was part of his job description. Laugh at boss's jokes. Laugh when boss laughs. Commiserate when boss laments.

"What's that supposed to mean?"

Merel turned to Slootsky. "It means you can go."

Startled, Slootsky rose and skedaddled out the door.

"Something's got to be done, Johnny," Merel said softly. "I want everybody out of that theater."

"Yes, sir."

"And that includes the police and the Kewpie dolls, the reporters and the lousy Dallas Cowboys if they show up and anybody else within ten feet of the place!"

Johnny nodded. "Yes, boss."

Merel nodded for Johnny to leave. He twisted the contract up tightly in his hands, wringing it like he was relieving a chicken of her need for air. He threw the twisted papers across the room. "I'm surrounded by incompetence."

His jaw wriggled back and forth as he assessed his options and his chances. "One thing is certain," he muttered, "you want something done right, you do it yourself."

Chapter 13

"Hi. Rick Elf?"

Tony knew it was a dumb question even as it came out of his mouth. The name tag on the string draped around Elf's neck made the answer apparent to anyone who could read. But he figured everybody was entitled to a minimum of one dumb question per day. And as they say: Use it or lose it.

Elf nodded and set down his coffee mug. He wore thick black-framed eyeglasses which he pulled off his nose and stuck in the pocket of a yellow and white striped shirt with a button down collar.

Without the glasses, he was a fairly handsome guy with classic middle American features. He did have a slight paunch, but that was pretty classic American as well. Besides, Tony could sympathize with that dilemma himself.

Elf had a pleasant face but he looked tired, like

he'd had a rough night. Probably had.

"I'm Tony Kozol and this is Rock Bottom. We're here doing a story on Kewpiecon."

"I know who you are." He made a sour face. "You're those musicians."

So much for pleasant faces and first perceptions. "Great, then you wouldn't mind answering a few questions?" said Tony, ignoring the slight. He'd developed a reasonably thick skin over such prejudicial attitudes and issues. "You are the vice president of the Rose O'Neill Society of Enthusiasts, is that right?"

Elf rubbed his jaw. "Now is not a good time, buddy."

As always, Rock decided to forego tact and go straight to blunt. "It's because of the Kewpie Mountain, isn't it? It must hurt to lose something so valuable?"

"You guys should know." Elf was looking directly into Rock's eyes. "Musicians don't make much, do they?"

"Was it insured?" Tony asked.

"Yes. But only when it was kept in my home. I've got a secure cabinet in my office, you see. I brought it out here because the club members asked me to. My insurance agent tells me the policy is void under these conditions. No security. No alarm." He hung his head. "No insurance."

"Ouch," said Tony.

"Yeah, ouch," he replied, sourly. Elf was still staring at Rock. "My partners aren't exactly all excited about the situation either."

"Partners?" Tony pulled out his notebook. There could be something in this.

"You think I can afford a thing like the Kewpie Mountain on my own?" He didn't wait for Tony's answer. "I'm a bookkeeper at a lumber supply house. No," Elf shook his head, "a group of us formed a small partnership and bought the Kewpie Mountain as an investment."

"Seems like an unusual investment. I mean, why not real estate or bonds or something?"

"It's none of your business," he said, sticking his hands in his pockets. "But I'll tell you. It's because I know Kewpies. And I know the art market. I'm a part-time investment adviser. Collectibles are good invest-ments. I calculated we could see a twenty-percent return on the Kewpie Mountain inside of a year."

Tony whistled. "Can't be too many people to sell a thing like that to."

Elf shrugged. "I know a few interested parties." His eyes were like tiny time bombs about to go off.

Rock spoke up. "What did you mean when you said we should know? What exactly are you trying to im-ply?" He puffed out his robust chest in a display of machismo.

Elf came around his display table and planted himself between Tony and Rock. "Your friend took it. I want it back."

"What?" glowered Rock.

"Don't look at me like that, buddy. The police are acting all coy, but I heard all about it."

Rock fumed.

"Stafford broke in here last night, killed the poor guy that owns this place and stole the Kewpie Moun-tain and who knows what all else?"

"You're crazy!"

"Mr. Elf," Tony began, "believe me, Jim Stafford had nothing to do with the burglary."

"Or B.A.D.'s murder," Rock added.

"I want my Kewpie Mountain back, buddy." Elf's voice was hard and threatening. "And it better be in one piece."

"You aren't going to be in one piece in a minute, you four-eyed, fairy collecting—" Rock's arm shot out and caught Elf behind the ear.

Elf howled and reached for Rock's arm. He twisted. Rock hurled a punch that Elf dodged, barely.

Tony threw himself between them. "Knock it off!"

"Out of the way, Tony," hollered Rock. "I'm gonna kill this creep!"

Elf put a hand up to his ear. It was turning as purple as an eggplant and looked like it was going to puff up nicely.

"What's going on here?"

Three heads turned.

Oh, no. Tony inwardly groaned. It was Officer Robinson. Rock, who had been struggling against Tony's grip, suddenly let his arm go limp as a ribbon.

"It's about time you got here, officer. You ought to lock up this big dumb animal. He assaulted me." Elf dusted himself off. A look of superiority hung to his face.

Rock felt like knocking it loose. He ground his fist into his palm. "I'm gonna knock you up alongside your—"

Tony shushed the big guy. "It's all just a big misunderstanding, Officer Robinson."

"Misunderstanding?" Elf thrust an accusing finger towards Rock's chest. "This man's a raving lunatic!"

"Calm down, Mr. Elf. I know. I heard him." Robinson studied Rock a moment. "I'm sure he didn't mean it. Just the man's way of letting off steam. And by the look of him, I'd say he's got a pretty good head up."

Tony was grateful that Rock was for once doing the right thing—keeping his big mouth shut.

Robinson folded her arms across her chest. "You men better come with me."

Tony gave Rock one of his 'what have you done to us now?' looks.

Officer Robinson led them to the corner of the room near the restrooms. She opened a white, unmarked door leading into a small, brightly lit alcove. "You gentlemen created quite a little scene back there. Do you really think it's wise for you to be here?"

"We're supposed to be here. We've got a job to do," Rock said. "Is there a law against that?"

"No." Robinson was smiling.

"Good."

"Rock's right," Tony began. "I'm sorry about the ruckus back there, but we really didn't start it. Mr. Elf started in on Rock—"

"He accused Jim of killing B.A.D. and stealing his stupid Kewpie Mountain."

Robinson was nodding. "The man's got a right to be upset. He's suffered a big loss. Maybe you should stay away from him for the time being."

"That suits me just fine," declared Rock. "In fact, I'm leaving right now." He laid his hand on the door handle.

"Wait," said Robinson.

"What?" said Rock. "Decide to throw us in cuffs?"

Robinson laughed. "Elf's out there. I wanted to say

that you might want to leave through the other door here on this side." He pointed to the door opposite the one they'd come in. "This door leads down a corridor running along the seating area of the main theater. There's an exit at the top."

"Oh." Rock frowned and opened the door. "You coming, Tony?"

Tony nodded.

"I'd like a word with you, Mr. Kozol." Robinson laid a finely turned hand on his arm. "If you don't mind?"

"Huh? No, I-I guess not." Tony looked at Rock. Why did he suddenly feel trapped?

"Fine. Give me a call when you're done, Tony. But don't blame me if she sticks you in cuffs, locks you up, or pulls a gun on you, like she did Jim. And if you need bail, just remember, my credit cards are maxed out already."

The door swung shut and Rock was gone.

Robinson was still chuckling. "Your friend's a little high strung."

"Rock really is a sweet, kind-hearted boy."

"He hides it well."

Tony laughed. "So," said Tony, stuffing his notebook into his back pocket, "what did you want to see me about, Officer Robinson?"

"Call me Paula." She nodded towards the door. "Come on. There's something I want to show you."

"Okay." He told her to call him Tony.

"Did you know, Tony," Robinson began, as she trod, "that until Walt Disney came along with Mickey Mouse that the Kewpie was the most famous, widely merchandised figure in the history of the world? Images of the Kewpie appeared on magazine covers, in books, on food packaging, all sorts of things. And there were the figurines, of course. Rose O'Neill was wildly successful.

"In fact, at her peak, O'Neill was the highest paid female illustrator ever. She died broke though. Funny, isn't it, in a sad sort of way?"

Tony stopped dead in his tracks. "To tell you the truth, I didn't know any of that stuff."

Robinson turned. "I thought you were doing a story on Kewpies?"

Tony flushed. "I am. We are. I've just been so busy what with Jim getting arrested and all. I haven't had time to do much research. Consider me impressed that you are so knowledgeable." Tony was beginning to wonder if this moonlighting as a writer was a big mistake. Even this cop knew his subject better than he did.

"Don't be," Robinson said slyly, "I got it all out of a book." She nodded towards the Kewpiecon room. "In there."

"Cute."

"I thought so." Robinson led him up onto the stage. The curtains were drawn. Even with the klieg lights on, the corners were dark. She stopped. A man and two women were conversing at the opposite end of stage. "Go on inside. I'll be right with you." She motioned to the door on Tony's right.

Tony ducked under the police tape and headed into what it soon became apparent was B.A.D.'s former living quarters. This was where Jim had found the body. He slowed. Did he really want to go in here? And what did Officer Robinson, Paula, want to show him?

Kozol heard noises up ahead and it gave him

confidence. It was the silence—the silence of the dead—that disquieted him.

A small closet was half-open and Tony nudged it open further. A white cowboy outfit hung inside on a lopsided hanger. So at least that part of Jim Stafford's story checked out. B.A.D. and Stafford must have been planning some kind of cowboy number. Why else would a rapper have a gaudy, rhinestone outfit like that?

A hand shot out in front of him and a uniformed officer stopped him. "Excuse me, sir. But this area is off-limits."

"Sorry, miss, I mean, officer. You see, Paula, I mean, Officer Robinson," Tony couldn't stop stammering, "told me to come inside. I thought she meant here, so I—"

"It's okay, Elizabeth."

"Hi, Paula. This Nervous Nelly with you?" Elizabeth was a squat, dark-haired lady—all muscle by the look of her—with Asian features.

"Yep."

"Okay." Elizabeth stepped aside.

Tony took notice of a locksmith working on the backdoor. "Changing the locks already?" On hearing himself mentioned, the locksmith looked their way and nodded.

"According to B.A.D.'s assistant, one Cyndi Parker, the lock got broken yesterday by B.A.D. himself."

"He was throwing out Merel," Officer Elizabeth said with obvious relish.

"Merel?" asked Tony.

"Merel Pearce," replied Robinson.

"The country singer, again?"

"You know him?"

"Sure. Country's not really my thing. I'm more of a sixties Beatles fan, but I've heard of him. Worked for a country act myself once in fact. And I've been hearing his name bandied around. Why was B.A.D. tossing him out?"

"You see, Merel owns this place. It's his old theater. He performed here for years."

"So I heard." Jim had said the same thing. "I take it B.A.D. and Merel weren't best friends?"

"Not hardly," said Elizabeth. "You should hear Ms. Parker. Girl's got a poisonous mouth and most of her venom is aimed at Merel. He's a tough old turkey."

"Tough enough to kill B.A.D.?" wondered Tony.

Robinson shrugged. "It was Jim Stafford I found lingering over the corpse."

"Find his prints on the knife?"

"Wiped clean."

"Why would he stick around? I mean, if Jim had killed B.A.D. Spike—and I said if—and he'd cleaned the knife, why was he still here?"

Robinson was mute.

"Doesn't make sense, does it?"

"Murder rarely does. People do some goofy things."

"Like Jim Stafford with a stolen Kewpie doll."

"Exactly. And he had means, motive and opportunity," Robinson said, ticking the words off on her fingers.

"You don't really believe he killed B.A.D.?"

"That's not for me to say."

"You know, Jim explained that he and B.A.D. were really good friends. All that feuding in public business was only a publicity stunt."

Robinson was nodding. "I heard that. It's the same story he told the chief. Butch Domino says different. He says he has no idea what Jim Stafford is talking about."

"What?" Tony found this hard to believe. "Butch must be lying."

"Why would he lie?"

Tony didn't know and said so.

"Face it, Tony, it's not a question of what you or I believe. It's a question of what a jury is going to believe—what a smart lawyer gets them to believe."

"That's an awfully jaded outlook, Paula. True as it probably is." Tony looked around the smallish apartment. It was in complete disarray. Was this the way B.A.D. lived or had the police turned the place upside down? "Why did you bring me here?"

"A couple of reasons." She grabbed Tony's hand and pulled him across the floor. "You know what this is?" She was stooped down in front of the kitchen counter looking up at the underside of the granite top.

Tony had to get down on his knees to see. He squinted. "Is that a—"

Robinson clamped a warm hand over his mouth. She whispered in his ear, "That's right, a bug."

Tony cupped his hands and whispered, "What's it doing there? Who planted it?" Truth be told he was a little curious about the bug business; and a little aroused with this intimate ear whispering business.

Tony straightened and helped Paula to her feet. She led him to the far side of the kitchen. "Those are a couple of good questions that we'd like to have a couple of equally good answers to."

Robinson motioned for Tony to follow. She lifted the

phone on the desk against the opposite wall. "There's one in here, too," she mouthed almost silently.

"Well, Jim certainly didn't plant them there," Tony said, though he had no proof one way or the other. They were back in the far corner of the kitchen again, out of range of any unknown listeners.

"Maybe. But he might have. They appear to have been there a while. Lots of dust near the edges."

"Maybe B.A.D. planted them himself? Keeping tabs on his employees."

"That's a possibility."

"Are there any others, bugs, I mean?"

"We're still searching. There's an awful lot of space to cover in a theater this size. In the meantime, we're letting them stay. The chief thinks they may prove to be useful. We're keeping our knowledge of their existence under wraps."

"Why tell me then?"

"I figured I could trust you. Keep what I've told you to yourself, however. In exchange, if you or your partner turn up any info, fill me in." She winked. "I'd like to make detective myself someday.

"Deal." Why did everybody think he and Rock were detectives? Maybe he should have talked to Jim about paying them. No, he couldn't do that. Tony couldn't think of anything else to say to Paula and he did have a job to do. His cell phone had rung twice in the last hour. How much longer could he and Rock avoid Nanci? "Thanks for the tour. I'd better be going."

Robinson stepped in his path. "I wanted to tell you that it's been a pleasure meeting you, Tony."

Tony's ears fired up.

"I was wondering if we might have dinner sometime?" She was looking coyly at the ground.

"Lock's ready," announced the locksmith. "You want the key?"

Robinson held out her hand and the locksmith dropped the key in her palm.

"Who do I make the bill out to?"

Robinson thought a moment, then smiled. "Why not send it to Merel? After all, his name's on the deed to this place."

The locksmith cocked his head. "Think I'll just do that. My middle daughter was up for a job as an usher in his new theater last month and she didn't get it. Think I'll send him a real fine bill." He tipped his head and exited through the newly repaired door.

Robinson cleared her throat. "What do you think?"

Tony considered. "I think Merel Pearce might have killed B.A.D., could have killed B.A.D."

"I meant about what I just said."

Tony smiled. "Are you asking me out, Paula?"

"Are you gonna make this difficult for me?" Robinson stepped close. "Am I going to have to do like your friend, Rock, said? Am I going to have to bring out the handcuffs?"

Chapter 14

"She what?" Rock hit the brakes. "That woman's got some nerve."

"I don't know. I mean, Paula is kinda cute."

"Now she's Paula," groaned Rock. "You told her no."

"I didn't tell her anything. I didn't know what to say. It was out of the blue. I froze. I'm not used to women asking me out."

"Well, I am," boasted Rock. "But she's a police officer. She pointed a gun at Jim. And we're supposed to be on Jim's side. Not to mention—" Rock shut up. He knew better than to mention Tony's troubled past. A gentle honk came from the blue station wagon behind them. Rock waved them off. The driver honked a second time. This time longer.

"I think you'd better drive, Rock."

Rock took his foot off the brake. They quickly caught up with the snarl of traffic ahead. "Fine."

"Can we talk about our gig now, please? Our *paying* gig. Nanci keeps calling. She wants to see us and we can't afford to blow her off. We need the money."

"That suits me fine. I need some fresh coin." The big guy cracked open his window as they hit I-65. Fresh air was always preferable to conditioned air. "You leave Nanci to me."

They were on their way out to Bonniebrook, Rose O'Neill's former home, now a historical landmark, located several miles north of Branson.

The little car fought its way valiantly up one steep hill after another. Clouds had turned the sky dark. Would it rain? Minutes later they spotted the turnoff and followed a small twisting road to Bonniebrook.

Rock pulled into the parking lot and joined up with the small herd of cars already present. They gathered up their gear, locked up the car and bought tickets to the Rose O'Neill house inside a combination museum/store and named the Maggie Fisher Center.

"Let's make this quick," said Tony, anxious to get back to town and assuage their boss.

They took a peek in the museum then headed down to the house. Tony rang the bell and they waited for the guide inside to answer as per the instructions printed on a small sign at the entrance.

Rock pressed his face against a dirty pane of glass looking into the primitive kitchen. "I wouldn't want to have to cook in there."

"You don't cook."

Rock pointed across the way. "What do you suppose that is?" Behind them, directly across from the front door, up the side of the hill stood a tiny, ancient looking ruin of a building, a vertically aligned, rectangularly-shaped monolith. There was no door.

"I don't know." Tony approached the edge of the walkway and tried to see through the dark opening. "Outhouse?"

"Made out of cement?" Rock stepped up over the stone wall and peered inside. The ground was damp. There were no windows.

The front door popped open, followed by the sound of a sharp cough. A gray-headed woman, her hair done up in a tight little bun, was staring at Rock. No, make that glaring. She swirled towards them in an ankle length denim skirt with a billowy white blouse and black sneakers. Lacy pink socks curled up over her ankle bones. Her cheeks puffed out like a howler monkey getting ready to let loose.

Rock scrambled down the hill.

Tony approached the docent. "Hi." He held out their tickets. "We're here to tour the home."

The guide pursed her wrinkled lips together generating the appearance of having had all the fluid precipitously sucked out of her body, from head to toes, through her lips by an invisible, yet powerful vacuum hose.

"Come this way," she said sternly. "The hidey-hole is off limits." The plastic Scootles-shaped name tag pinned to her shirt read *Sue*.

"Please, do not touch anything," she said with a voice like an automaton. "Do not sit on the furniture. And do not stray from the tour. If you need to leave, depart only by the main door. The others are to remain locked at all times." The guide looked at everyone to make sure they'd understood.

A half dozen more visitors had arrived. Some faces

the boys recognized from Kewpiecon. Tony and Rock blended into the rear of the crowd and far away from Sue's eye and grasp.

Tony made notes fast and furiously. The house was nothing like he'd been expecting. While it might have been large for its time, it was small and low-ceilinged by today's standards. Still, it must have been a quiet, inspiring place to spend one's years.

Tony was surprised to learn from Sue that the original structure had burnt to the ground back in 1947. The house they were touring was an elaborate and detailed reproduction of Bonniebrook. There were spectacular views in every direction, another extravagance for its time. For according to the guide, homes in those days were taxed based on the number of windows they had and Bonniebrook had plenty.

Looking across the grounds through one of the windows now, Tony tried vainly to see the cemetery that the docent was describing but it wasn't visible through the dense trees. They'd have to go search it out when the tour was over. Rose O'Neill was buried out there in the family plot along with her mother, brother, James, and sister, Callista.

Tony had a certain fondness for cemeteries, though why he couldn't say. Maybe it was just knowing that when his time was done, he'd be lying in a soft piece of ground somewhere with plush green grass and plenty of fresh flowers.

He sort of liked that.

There in the garden stood two of O'Neill's most famous works, the statues of the reclining *Faunesse* and *Embrace of the Tree*, the latter a ten foot tall piece of rock with a nude, woman-shaped rock being embraced from behind by an equally nude hulk of a man.

Tony called out. "Rock, you have got to get some pictures of that." There was no response. "Rock?" Tony frowned. There was no sign of Rock. He slipped away from the group and found Rock pawing over a vase in the living room. "Rock!" Tony slapped Rock's hand.

The Chinese vase fell to the rug with a thud and rolled under an antique sofa.

"Rock!" gasped Tony.

"Are you crazy, Tony? Look what you made me do." Rock checked to see if the coast was clear then bent over to scoop up the vase. He turned it round and round in his big hand.

"Is it broken?"

Rock returned it to the table from which he'd borrowed it. "No. Lucky for you."

"Lucky for me? You heard the lady. You're not supposed to touch anything."

"You're not supposed to go around causing people to drop things either. Which do you think old Sue is going to care about most?"

"Let's just catch up with the group."

"Hey, look."

Tony looked out the window. A small, dry creek ran along the back end of the house. There were some wooden benches between the trees. "That's Rick Elf and Virginia Plat."

"I know. That's why I said, 'Hey, look.' What do you suppose they're doing out here?"

"Why do you have such a suspicious nature? They're here for the same reason we are—to see Bonniebrook. I've recognized several faces from Kewpiecon here."

"I suppose." Rock didn't seem satisfied with the explanation. Perhaps it was simply too ordinary for him. "Look, he's taken her hand."

"Oh?" Tony leaned against the window ledge. Sure enough, Rick and Virginia were holding hands.

Rock took a picture. "Interesting. Who'd have thought those two were a couple?"

"Let's go say hi."

"What about the tour?"

Tony shrugged and headed for the front door. "Sue will have to carry on without us."

"Oooh, you wild man, you."

They left the house and crossed the garden. Rock wanted to stop and get some pictures of the statues but Tony hurried him along.

"What's the big deal? Why are you in such a hurry to talk to Rick Elf and Virginia Plat?"

"I need some info for our piece. Besides, I'd like to hear what Virginia thinks about these Kewpie thefts. She's big on all this Rose O'Neill Kewpie stuff. Maybe she knows someone whom she thinks might have taken them. Could help Jim. And she seemed really worried about something. I wonder what it is?"

"Maybe the mousey Ms. Plat swiped the Kewpies herself. Makes a nice little nest egg. Or maybe she's going to make it the centerpiece of some private Kewpie shrine in her bedroom."

"Right," said Tony. Rock and another of his wild theories. Still, one never knew.

"I'd like to get my hands on that Kewpie Mountain myself." Rock gripped his camera to keep it from bouncing off his chest. "I could use a quick hundred grand. When I think of the things I could do with money like that. . ."

Tony headed down the path. The wooden benches were empty. But it was the last place they'd seen Ms. Plat and Rick Elf. "Yeah, that would be just great. You with the Kewpie Mountain. With your luck, the police would catch you standing over it and then you'd be arrested for grand theft mountain."

Rock frowned. "You always have to look for the bad in everything, don't you, Tony?" He crossed his arms. "Your friends aren't here." There was an odd but invigorating odor in the air. A rare scent of Mother Nature, he suspected.

"I know that." Tony squinted through the trees. "Where do you suppose they went?"

Rock knelt and put an ear to the ground. "Me hear horses. Two." The big guy rose and pointed. "They go that-a-way."

Tony stomped off in the opposite direction. Sometimes Rock just wasn't funny. Wasn't funny at all.

Chapter 15

"It was very sweet of you to agree to see me, Mr. Pearce."

Cyndi Parker had decked herself out in her sexiest white dress, the one with the big scoop taken out in the front. It was snug in all the right places. And she'd 'forgotten' to wear a bra.

Cyndi leaned over the entertainer's desk, unleashing vistas she figured the old man hadn't seen in years.

She was right. Merel ogled her but retained his outward composure. "You've got five minutes, little lady."

She sat on the desk and crossed her legs, revealing a fine pair of long, shapely legs. "That's all I need."

Merel leaned back in his chair and crossed his hands over his stomach. He'd already sucked in his gut but had been forced to cease the effort after several minutes of straining that had his stomach tied up in thick knots.

"I won't try to con you," Cyndi began, already working her con, "I'd like to find," she put her palms on his desk and pressed closer, "some arrangement where the I.C.G.C. could hold on to the theater."

Merel broke into a grin. "The danged I.C.G.C.!" He banged his fist on the table.

"That's what got me into this mess in the first place. Inner City Gospel Corporation," he spat derisively. "Your boss and his manager really hoodwinked me with that one. I thought I was leasing the old theater out to some religious organization, not some washed up, bad mouthing rapper."

Cyndi laid her hand over his. "B.A.D. hadn't named his company that to trick you, Mr. Pearce."

He eyed her hand. "Call me Merel."

She batted her eyelashes. "Merel. He only came up with that name so that folks wouldn't know it was him that was interested in renting a theater here in Branson. He didn't want people taking advantage of him. Charging more because of his name.

"You can understand that, can't you, Merel?" She stroked his hand. "I'm sure a famous star like you gets people trying to take advantage of your wealth and fame all the time."

Merel pulled his hand away and reached for a fat cigar. "Oh, yeah. But it never works." He glanced meaningfully at his gold watch, then looked Cyndi in the eye. "And you got one minute."

"Look," said Cyndi, "I have an idea for a B.A.D. Spike tribute show. I just know that it will make money. I've already made some calls. I realize it seems perverted, but B.A.D.'s death has really renewed everybody's interest in him, from the press to his fans. We can pack the place. We'll cut you in for a percentage of the door."

Merel stood. He passed around the big mahogany desk and put a rough, calloused hand on the girl's bare thigh. "You'd do just about anything to keep that theater, wouldn't you?" He leaned closer.

"Yes, I would." She dared him to look her in the eye—to see the infinite possibilities open to him.

He stepped back. "All the more reason I get a kick out of telling you no." He rubbed his watch. "Your time is up. The maid will see you out." Merel opened the study door.

Cyndi hopped down from his desk. She pushed down her dress. "You'll be sorry. Do you believe in karma, Merel?"

He looked at her blankly.

"I believe people get what they deserve."

"And I believe that people get what they can take." He nodded for her to leave.

The door in the back of the study opened. The smell of fine tobacco wafted into the room. "Helping yourself to my cigars?"

The big man in the suit grinned. "Didn't think you'd mind, bro.' "

Merel returned to his desk and opened the bottom left hand drawer. He withdrew a thick envelope. He extended his hand and the heavyset man took the envelop greedily. "Twenty-thousand dollars."

The man set his cigar down in an empty glass and opened the envelop to verify its contents. He appeared satisfied. He should be.

"Now, you do like I told you. I want you to strongly encourage B.A.D.'s people to leave town. Leave town quickly." He pointed his thumb at Butch. "Get that Cyndi Parker out of my theater. Get them all out of there. Kill all this B.A.D. tribute garbage. I want you all long gone. And I don't care how.

"I don't never want to see or hear from any of you again. And don't even think about taking my money and reneging. Merel Pearce has a long memory and a long reach."

Merel stepped up to the fellow and ran a hand along the edge of the man's lapel. "Twenty-thousand dollars is a lot of money. I will get my money's worth. Is that clear, Butch?"

Butch nodded and tucked the envelope of cash into his suit coat. "Nice doing business with you, Mr. Pearce. If there's anything else I can do—"

Merel gave him a shove. "Yeah, you can get your sorry behind out of my house." He closed the study door and looked out the big bay windows overlooking the private golf course. His property extended for about a hundred yards along the fourteenth hole.

His daughter, his only daughter, Sherry, was out at the tee now with that no-good boyfriend of hers. The kid had his slimy mitts on her hips, like he was helping her with her swing.

The entertainer clenched his fists. He'd like to take a swing at that piece of scum with a three-iron, right upside the head.

Merel went to the bar and poured himself a tumbler of JD. Sherry always could pick the bad apple on the tree. This one, Aaron Amsterdam, was as bad as any yet. Merel had been forced to give him a job as a gofer.

The kid wasn't good for anything else.

Aaron was going to have to go, but not just yet.

There was one more thing to take care of. Pearce rang for Johnny on the in-house phone. Johnny was in the billiards room. "Domino is leaving, Johnny. You keep an eye on him."

Johnny laid down his cue stick and headed quietly to the garage.

Chapter 16

"I do hope you will keep everything I tell you in confidence." Ms. Plat nervously peeled a strip of bark off the side of the nearest tree. She had no idea what kind of a tree it was. She wish she knew more about such things as trees and bushes and plants in general. But she was not a tree person. Truth be told, she was not an outdoor person at all.

'Of course, Virginia," said Rick. "But I must admit, I don't understand all the secrecy. Why did you want to meet me? And why did you want to do it way out here?"

The two ROSE officers stood in a small, wooded glen a little ways from the house. Bonniebrook was not visible from where they stood.

"I saw some of our ROSE members back at Bonniebrook. I didn't want them to see us talking."

Elf looked puzzled. "Okay." He found himself a seat

on a flattish rock. "So, what's this all about?"

Ms. Plat sighed. "Oh, I don't know. Maybe I should just say nothing."

"That's exactly what you've said so far," Rick said, a smile on his face, "nothing."

"I'm sorry. I-I simply don't want to make false accusations. And I don't want to get anyone in trouble."

Rick rose and placed his hand on Virginia's shoulder. "What is it, Virginia?"

She looked him in the eye. "It's about the Kewpies."

"What do you mean?"

"About the thefts, that is."

He spun her around. "You know who stole the Kewpies? My Kewpie Mountain?"

She pulled herself away from him. "I-I'm not sure."

"Sorry." Rick held out his hands. "I'd give anything to get that Kewpie Mountain back. I was responsible for the thing. I have no idea how I am going to explain its loss to my partners, let alone pay them back." He shook his head. "I don't have that kind of money."

"Have you told them?"

"No. I haven't. The police asked me for the names of my partners. Maybe they gave them the news. Heck, my wife doesn't even know about this yet. She's gonna kill me when I tell her.

"She's been home taking care of our baby, Rhonda, since she was born." He was shaking his head. "This will mean Rhonda will have to go to daycare. My wife will have to go back to work."

He pleaded with Ms. Plat. "If you know who took the Kewpie Mountain, you've got to tell me."

Virginia tugged at her hair. "But I don't know, not

really. I only have a suspicion. And it probably isn't a fair one at all. After all, he had Kewpies stolen, too."

"He?"

She wrung her hands. "Maybe I shouldn't say anymore. Maybe I shouldn't have said anything at all. It would be so embarrassing for me and for—this person—if they should get arrested and be innocent."

"Did you hear that?" Rick froze.

"No. What?"

He scratched his head. "Thought I heard a sneeze. Now, Virginia, listen to me. We don't have to involve the police. We're Kewpie people, you and I. We can handle this. Tell me, who is it that you suspect?"

She let out a long, slow breath. "It's Mr. Daniels."

"Duncan Daniels?"

"That's right."

"But he had thousands of dollars worth of Kewpies stolen himself. What makes you suspect him?"

Ms. Plat shrugged. "I don't really. It's simply that—well, you see, Mr. Daniels approached me that evening at the hotel. He said he'd left his wallet behind at his booth. I had a dinner to go to. I didn't have time to go back for his wallet myself. He assured me it would be all right. So—and I know I shouldn't have, I wasn't supposed to—"

"Shouldn't have what, Virginia? Wasn't supposed to what?"

"I gave Mr. Daniels the key to the building. So he could get his wallet." She wrung her hands. "And now all those things are missing and some poor man's been killed. . ."

Elf straightened. "I see." This time he'd definitely heard a sneeze, two of them, in fact. Virginia must have heard them, too, because she was looking in the same direction.

Virginia said, "What do you suppose—"

Elf motioned for her to be silent. He swung around, wondering where the sound had come from. "Is somebody out there?"

They turned at the sound of footsteps heading their way. A man in dungarees and a flannel shirt waved to them. A two days' growth of beard clung to his face like coal dust and a frayed, olive green hunter's cap hung loosely on his skull. "What are you two doing out here? You folks lost?"

"No," said Rick, "only enjoying the grounds."

"I'm Clyde, the caretaker around here. Bonniebrook's a big place. In case you are lost, the house is back that way." He pointed towards the sun and the west. "Besides, it's always best to keep to the trails. We don't like seeing any visitors getting hurt."

Rick looked dubious. "Hurt?"

"Oh, yeah," explained Clyde. "There's all kinds of things out here in the woods can get you. Spiders, snakes. You might trip over a rock and sprain your ankle. Bust your leg."

"Thanks, we'll keep a lookout," said Rick. "Besides, I suppose we should be getting back. Right, Virginia?"

She nodded.

"That's fine," said the caretaker. "You go on up that hill, between them rocks. You'll find a trail takes you right to the parking lot after a quarter mile or so. Or take the branch to the left and you'll end up by the house."

"I don't like this," said Rock. He gripped and

regripped the steering wheel. His palms were sweaty. "How are we going to get in? We could get arrested for breaking and entering."

Merel Pearce's Mongrel Theater was one of the most imposing theaters in Branson. It was even larger and more grandiose than Tom E. Landry's place up the street. A huge bronze-colored statue of a mongrel dog sat on the lawn in the middle of the long, circular drive leading to the main entrance. The statue had to be twenty-five feet long and about as tall. The dog was a symbol of Merel's success. The song, *Mongrel*, had been Merel's biggest. Double platinum.

"What are you talking about, Rock? You've seen all those folks going in. The doors are unlocked."

"But those people work here. They're probably getting ready for tonight's show."

"So?" Tony was shaking his head. "All we have to do is walk up there like we own the place. March right in like we know what we're doing and where we're going. No one will dare stop us. We just have to look like we belong."

"I don't know if I can."

Tony jumped out of the car. "I'm going. You can sit out here and sweat, if you want."

Kozol marched over the neatly manicured lawn, ignoring the sidewalk, leaving deep footprints, making a beeline for the doors.

Rock slipped the car key into his pocket and hurried up the sloping sidewalk after him.

With what Paula had said about Merel Pearce, Tony really wanted to talk to him but when they had called the theater and asked to speak with him, they'd been put off. Politely but firmly.

Tony was inside by the time Rock reached the doors. Tony was talking to a young woman in a Confederate gray uniform. He had his python-like arm around the girl's shoulder as if they were best friends. "Hi, Rock. Glad you could make it. Come on, I'll take you back."

"Huh? What's going on? I—"

"Don't worry. I've made all the arrangements for your visit. You run along now, Tracy." The young girl nodded and loped off. Tony grabbed Rock's arm and dragged him along the carpeted hall.

"What was that all about?" Rock whispered.

"I told her I was with Merel's management company and I'd set up an interview for a reporter from Country News Tonight."

"Country News Tonight? Is there even such a show?"

"How would I know?" Tony pushed his way through a set of heavy double doors and turned right. "Come on, Rock. Merel's dressing room is this way."

They passed several workers, some wore Confederate uniforms similar to the one the girl, Tracy, had on. Others, Tony soon discovered, were wearing Union blue uniforms. Tony couldn't help wondering if the two sides got along or if there was the occasional fray.

At the top of a short flight of stairs, Tony paused. He ran his fingers over Merel Pearce's nameplate. "Here it is."

"It says *Do Not Disturb*."

"Oh, please. Who are we disturbing?" Tony twisted the handle, opened the door and shoved Rock on in.

Rock stumbled over his feet. "Watch it, Tony. I could have—" Rock looked up. "Sorry." He backed into the doorway, bumping straight into Tony. "I thought this was Merel Pearce's dressing room." The big guy looked at Tony for help.

Tony pushed him back inside the room.

There was a woman sitting at the small desk beside a window. Behind the desk was a bar. Beyond the bar, a big-screen television was built into the wall. An acoustic guitar was leaning against the wall under the window. The instrument had Merel's name on the fretboard in pearl inlay.

The woman quickly shut the desk drawer. She had a cassette tape in her hand. The lady had to be in her sixties. She had a nineteen-sixties style Loretta Lynn hairdo, at any rate. She wore a lovely Laura Ashley print dress, though. Tony immediately liked her for it. Reminded him of the style of dress his own mother used to favor.

The woman dropped the tape in her open purse and stood. She couldn't have been over five foot and that was in her heels. "It is. I'm Dolly. Dolly Pearce. I'm Merel's wife." She held out a soft white hand. Tony came back into the room and shook it.

"I'm Tony Kozol and this is Rock Bottom." Rock nodded. "We're journalists. Doing a story on Branson. You know, entertainers, Kewpie dolls."

"How nice." Smile lines appeared at the corners of her sparkly blue eyes. "Are you gentlemen here to interview my husband for your article?"

"That's right," Rock said boldly. "I'm surprised he isn't here. He should be expecting us. We're with Country News Tonight."

"Expecting who?" The heavy pounding of cowboy boots preceded Merel's entrance. "Dolly, what are you doing here?"

"Just straightening things up for you, dear."

He shook his head. "Cleaning up again. I keep telling you, we got us a service for that. You don't have to work."

She smiled wanly. "I know. I only like to keep busy."

"Well, you don't need to make no fuss over me, Dolly." Pearce pulled off his cowboy hat and hung it on a hook beside the door.

"I'll leave you to your interview, dear." Dolly went to the door. "Lovely meeting you gentlemen."

They returned the compliment. A fellow in a Union uniform, complete with cap, came bustling past into the room. He had a thick black moustache that looked about as real as the dime store Groucho Marx version. He was carrying a towel and a tray with a couple of bottles of spring water balanced on it. His eyes were a mischievous blue.

Rock studied him. "Hey, that's Jim—"

Tony's elbow shot out, catching Rock between the ribs. "Yes, that is one jim-dandy ashtray you've got there." Kozol reached over Pearce's table and plucked a completely ordinary looking, ash-filled, glass tray and held it up to the light. "Swarovski?"

"What?" Rock was looking at Tony like he'd lost his mind.

Merel was watching Tony and Rock each like they'd both lost their minds and a couple of other folks' minds to boot. He snatched the ashtray from Tony's hands, sending a small cloud of ash into the room. "Will you all get the heck on out of here?"

He looked down. The worker was on his knees,

trying to wipe the ash off the floor. Not a good idea. The floor was carpeted, white no less, and the towel he was using was damp. Not a good combination. Not a good combination at all. "Go, son!"

The mustachioed Union man let out a quick 'yes, sir' and fled, keeping his eyes to the ground.

Pearce went for his drink at the bar, then fell into his chair at the desk. "You two still here?"

"I'm Tony Kozol." Tony extended his hand. "And this is Rock Bottom."

"I know who you are."

"We're here doing a story on Kewpies and thought it would be really special for your fans if we could do a story on Merel Pearce, as well."

Pearce tipped back his drink. His Adam's apple bobbed up and down like it was tied to the end of a fishing line. He set down his glass. The look on his face was hard. Dead hard. He could have given Medusa a run for her money. "Don't try to hornswoggle me, little man. I know who y'all are and I know why y'all are here."

"You do?" Tony felt his palms getting all sweaty. He looked at Rock for support but none was forthcoming. Rock looked like a prairie dog caught in the path of a rampaging herd of bison. Sometimes the big guy was no help at all.

"You're here because you found out that I own the theater where Donald Milquist, alias B.A.D. Spike, met his maker." He half-rose from his chair. "And you're friends of Stafford's. You've also got a reputation for nosing around in business that's no concern of yours, Kozol.

"And," he added triumphantly, "you're musicians

working for Nanci Dement."

Tony had to admit, the guy was good. Maybe he should be the detective. Tony asked, "What do you know about B.A.D.'s murder, Mr. Pearce?"

"I know who done him in."

"You do?"

"Yep."

Rock said it first. "Who?"

"Stafford."

"Jim Stafford?" both men asked at once.

"Yep."

Tony wiped some ash from his jeans. "You really believe that Jim Stafford murdered B.A.D., Mr. Pearce?"

Pearce lit up a fat cigar and began pacing. "Why not? It's common knowledge around town that the two of them have been feuding for months. Stafford wanted B.A.D. out of town." He waved his cigar. "I can't say as I blame him. B.A.D. wasn't right for this town."

"Why is that?" Rock said, coming to the dead man's defense.

"Not the right image. We're good, simple, country folk."

"You know, Mr. Pearce, according to Jim, that whole feud thing was all a publicity stunt."

He shrugged. "Maybe. So what? He was arrested for stealing those dang Kewpies. That means he was at the scene. No, if you ask me, Stafford is your killer."

"Besides, they didn't exactly arrest him. They only had him in for questioning," Rock clarified. "They let him go."

"Close enough," Pearce muttered. "Besides, I hear he spent the night in a jail cell."

Tony said, "Why would Jim kill B.A.D.?"

"Who knows? Maybe they had a falling out. Or maybe over that Kewpie stuff. I hear tell some of that junk is mighty expensive."

"Jim doesn't seem to be exactly hurting for money," countered Rock.

Pearce shrugged this off as well. "Maybe Stafford's one of them there kleptomaniacs. He sees all this Kewpie stuff and decided he had to have it. Donald caught him in the act and gets himself killed."

"I don't know," said Tony, "it doesn't sound like the kind of thing Jim would do."

"Now what do you know about that, Kozol?" Pearce kicked at the dirty spot on his rug and looked him in the eye. "You ain't from here. You don't know Stafford like I do. Did you know that he likes to ride the little mechanical horsie outside Dick's 5&10 up on Main Street?"

The boys were shaking their heads.

"Well, he does. And it's a kiddie ride, for crying out loud. He done broke the motor on it three times." Pearce held up three arthritic fingers. "Burnt the motor right out. The man's too heavy. The thing's got an eighty pound weight limit on it. It's a kiddie ride, for crying out loud."

"You said that," put in Rock.

"They finally had to put a sign up saying *Children Only, Please.*"

Tony had seen the sign. "Still that's hardly a reason or an explanation for his murdering a man."

"Let me tell you boys something else." Pearce had worked himself into a lather so bad he actually had to wipe the spittle off his chin with the back of his sleeve.

And by the look of the sleeve, it was a bad habit. "That Jim's a trouble maker. Where there's trouble, there's Jim. You see this theater?"

Rock replied, "Kind of noticed it on our way in."

"Well, I got me more than thirty cacti out there."

The boys nodded, wondering where this story was going.

"Those cactus cost me plenty, I can tell you. You know what Stafford does?"

Tony bit. "What?"

"He tells folks, in the middle of his shows, he goes and tells the folks in his audience to take my cacti. Tells them just like that. Says, 'folks, you've seen that lovely theater Merel Pearce has got himself, the Mongrel Theater, well, Merel says he wants you all to come by after tonight's show and take yourself home a nice cactus for a souvenir. Help yourself,' he tells them."

"Oh, come on," said Rock, "we heard him say that during his show. It's only a joke."

"Sure," added Tony, "he says so himself. He says he's only joshing."

Pearce turned purple. Something about Jim Stafford obviously didn't agree with his constitution. "Folks do it anyway! They come up here, dig 'em right out of the ground and haul them off!"

"You're kidding?" Rock looked more amused than upset. Tony found himself hiding a snicker with the back of his hand.

Pearce's head was bobbing up and down like there was a trout on the other end of an invisible line. "Dig 'em up and haul 'em off. I lose better than a couple dozen cacti a year. One night alone, some fool made off with nine of them. Those danged cactus ain't what you'd call ingenious to Missouri."

"Indigenous," corrected Tony.

He didn't take well to being corrected. "Whatever. I got to have them hauled up all the way from Arizona. Cost me thousands of dollars. I can't tell you what that does to the profit margins." He told them anyway. "Shoots it all to hell."

Pearce was perfectly apoplectic now. He quenched his nerves with a bourbon. He was pacing.

"I take it you and Jim Stafford aren't exactly friends?" Rock quipped.

"You take it right. And if he didn't kill that dang rapper it's only because that girl of B.A.D.'s, Cyndi, beat him to it."

"Cyndi?" Tony had heard that name before. Had Paula said anything about Cyndi?

"Cyndi Parker." Merel spat the name out like it was some kind of Third World disease. "That girl's trouble. She's B.A.D.'s assistant, girlfriend, whatever."

"Why do you think she might have killed B.A.D.?" Rock asked.

"Old B.A.D., he might have felt like he was the boss, but trust me, that girl of his, she was running things. Still trying to. A world class gold digger, if you ask me. But she ain't got a chance. Nope."

Merel slammed down his glass. "That little lady isn't going to do any more gold diggin' out here in the Ozarks at any rate."

Tony remembered now Paula mentioning that Cyndi Parker worked for Donald. "I still don't see how you not liking this Cyndi Parker gives her a motive for murder."

"Yeah," quipped Rock—he had picked up a Merel

Pearce 'Greatest Hits' CD off one of his built-in glass shelves, which was literally packed tight with records, CDs and tapes, and stuffed it down his shirt without asking—"because if you not liking a person was a good reason to accuse them of murder, I expect half the folks in Branson would be suspects."

"Make that three-quarters." Merel held out his hand and Rock reluctantly gave him back his recording.

"Cheapskate," muttered Rock.

"Crook," retorted Merel.

"Do you know where we can find this Cyndi Parker?" Tony interjected between the two bickering children.

"What do I look like, Columbo?"

"You do share a nasty habit for cigars," Rock said.

He scowled at them. "Get out."

Tony and Rock headed for the door.

"Go gnaw on Stafford's leg for a while. Maybe you can beat a confession out of him. That character is nothing but trouble. If they don't lock him up for murder, they ought to lock him up for his own good."

Merel shook his fist. "For everybody's own good!"

Chapter 17

"Pssst. Pssst."

The boys turned. They were standing in the hall leading to the stage, a couple doors down from Merel's dressing room. People were running in every direction. No doubt getting ready for the show.

A man in a Union uniform was wiping a wall with a towel. He turned his head slightly in the boys' direction as he moved the rag uselessly about. "Hey, men."

"Jim!" shouted Rock. "I knew it was you!"

"Shhh!" cried Tony.

Jim turned around. His moustache was falling off on one side. Tony adjusted it for him. "What are you doing here, Jim?"

"I'm looking for clues."

"Clues? Are you crazy?" quipped Rock. "In that getup? What if Merel catches on?"

Jim looked affronted. He tugged at the uniform. "What? This is a great disguise. It's an official Mongrel Theater uniform."

"Where did you get it?" whispered Tony.

"I rented it from one of the kids that works here."

"What if he tells somebody?" wondered Tony. "What if he tells Merel?"

"Nah, kid wouldn't do that." Jim seemed sure of it. Tony wasn't.

"Still," said Rock, "it seems to me you're taking a big chance being here."

A stagehand stood across the boards eying them. Tony motioned for them both to follow. They went down a small stairs and huddled in front of one of the exits, where the light was low and they were far less visible to prying eyes.

"I'm not taking any more chance than you men. You're here, aren't you? Why shouldn't I be?"

"Because, Jim—"

"Oh, give it up, Tony. Jim's got a point," Rock said. "Besides, he's here, we're here. Not much we can do about it now. What's the sense in arguing the point?"

Tony was forced to agree. "But what made you decide to come here in the first place? And in that costume?"

"I got to thinking about what we talked about. You know, about Merel. I got to thinking that maybe that old cuss was behind all this. And I couldn't exactly call him up and ask him. 'Say, Merel, did you kill B.A.D. Spike?' And I couldn't exactly walk on in."

Jim's voice dropped. "I have a confession to make, men."

"What's that?" asked Rock.

"Merel and I aren't exactly the best of friends."

Rock snorted.

"We know," said Tony, remembering Merel's diatribe against Jim.

"So I got this disguise. Worked pretty good, too, if I do say so myself," Jim said proudly. "Ole Merel never even recognized me back there."

Tony nodded, but had the feeling that Jim was more Maxwell Smart than James Bond. And what if Pearce had recognized Jim and only kept mum about it because it suited some private agenda of his own? There was a lot going on below the surface around here, though what it was and who was connected to it, Tony had no idea.

"Did you find anything out, Jim? Is Merel the killer?"

"Saw a Kewpiecon schedule on his desk."

"That doesn't mean anything," said Rock.

"No, I suppose not. I haven't had time to find much else out about old Merel. There is something else going on that strikes me as funny. You see, I—"

A brawny young fellow in a highly decorated Union officer's uniform was heading their way, flashlight in hand. He was frowning and had the look of someone about to toss out some gatecrashers.

"Why don't we continue this outside?" Jim suggested. He hurriedly pushed open the exit door.

Tony and Rock shouldered past each other in their haste to get out.

Jim was about to hustle on out of there himself when the young man in uniform laid a firm grip on his upper arm.

"You the new guy that's taking over for Quince?"

"Uh," Jim looked helplessly from the man to the boys. "Yeah, that's me."

"I'm Craig Whitlaw, the crew chief around here. I need another hand unloading a truck around back. What's your name?"

"Um. You can call me Clyde."

"Well, let's get a movin', Clyde. Trucks don't unload themselves. And it's fifteen minutes till show time. Mr. Pearce don't want any chance of noise or distractions when the show's in progress, so we gotta get it done quick."

"But, Jim," blurted Rock, "what about—"

Tony was shaking his head and giving Rock the evil eye.

Craig paused. He was beating his flashlight up and down in the palm of his hand. Slap. Slap. Slap. "Who's Jim?"

Behind Craig's back, Jim/Clyde shrugged his shoulders.

Tony cleared his throat. "That's me."

"You're Jim?" The flashlight maintained a steady four-four beat against his fleshy palm.

"That's right, Mom named me after James Dean because I look so much like him."

"Huh? That don't make any sense. You don't look nothin' like James Dean."

Rock quipped, "Sure he does. You just have to squint a little. And look sort of sideways." Rock twisted his head.

Whitlaw was now rubbing the flashlight against the side of his skull. It made the hair on that side stick out like a scared cat's.

Jim tapped the crew chief on the shoulder. "Say,

we'd better get to unloading that truck, Craig."

Craig nodded. "Right," he said slowly.

"Thank you for all your assistance, *Clyde*." Tony waved.

Craig stepped forward and grabbed the door with his free hand. The exit door closed in their faces.

Walking back to the car, Rock said, "You know, Mr. James Dean, if it's fifteen minutes until Merel's show time. . ."

"Yes?" Tony was fishing around in his pockets for the car key. Rock had it.

"Then isn't it also fifteen minutes until Jim's show time?"

Tony stopped. He looked back towards the Mongrel Theater. Jim was in there somewhere, decked out in a Union army soldier's uniform, unloading a truck under the watchful eye of the dour and beefy Craig Whitlaw.

Miles away some two thousand people, give or take, would be making their way to their seats at the Jim Stafford Theater, expecting a show. "Uh-oh." Tony stared unblinkingly at Rock. "You know what's worse?"

Rock was shaking his big head side to side.

"It's also just about fifteen minutes until Nanci's show time." His features tightened. "Our show time."

"We'll never make it," groaned Kozol. "Nanci's going to kill us. Kill us and then fire us."

"Maybe," said Rock. "You leave Nanci to me. Let's see if we can help Jim out."

"Just how do you propose we do that?"

"Drive around the building. I'll think of something."

"Oh, that's a great plan." Tony stuck the key in the ignition and backed up. Slowly, he cruised around the huge complex, while struggling to raise a halfway decent plan of his own.

"There!" pointed Rock. A sapphire blue *Boadi Springs Company* truck was parked at the loading dock. "Stop."

Tony complied. "Now what?"

"Here comes Jim."

Tony nodded. Jim was hobbling awkwardly down the metal ramp from the truck to the loading dock, two cases of shrinkwrapped bottled water in his unsteady arms. Craig Whitlaw was leaning against the wall, marking up a clipboard.

"Quick," cried Rock, "let's go!"

"Go where?"

"There. Step on it, Tony!"

Tony sighed and stepped on the gas. The little car whizzed towards the loading dock.

Some poor soul in a Coupe De Ville, an old woman in a bonnet, no less, was forced to slam on her brakes or become part of a T-bone sandwich as they shot through a four-way intersection.

"Sorry," hollered Tony as he pressed on.

Rock leaned across and pressed on the horn. "Roll down your window, Tony."

Tony hit the switch.

"Hey," shouted Rock, "Clyde, get in!" Rock waved and honked the horn once again.

Jim/Clyde teetered on the ramp, the water balanced precariously in his arms. A look of recognition crossed his face. He glanced at Craig and made up his mind. Jim dropped the water and ran. He didn't hesitate to leap the four feet from the dock to the pavement and he hit the ground running.

Rock had the side door open and Jim jumped in

back.

"Hi-ya, men." Jim was grinning. "Dang this is fun." Sweat cascaded down his forehead. He'd lost his hat. Stafford looked like he'd just returned from the Battle of Antietam.

Craig was yelling and waving his clipboard, but his words and brawny figure disappeared as Tony gunned the engine and hightailed it out of there.

Chapter 18

"What's all the commotion?" Merel strutted out onto the loading dock and planted his arms on his hips. "You know I don't like all this activity when I'm fixing to go on stage."

Craig lowered his head. "Sorry, Mr. Pearce. But the water truck was late and the snack bar was low on supplies. I thought it would be okay. I thought we could get it unloaded quick like."

"Well, you're going to need more than one kid out here if you want to get done on time. We get a good markup on that water. See that it gets unloaded. Get some more help out here."

"Yes, Mr. Pearce, sir. I had another hand. You won't believe this, but he just jumped off the dock and ran off in that car!" He pointed to the little car as it sped out onto the main road regardless of oncoming traffic.

Merel stepped to the edge of the dock. "He did?"

The cowboy had removed his hat and was scratching his head.

"That's right, Mr. Pearce. Just up and jumped right off. Dropped those cases of water right there. Rode off with two strange men. Don't worry, sir. I'll see he never works here again."

Two cases of water lay crumpled on the dock. Pearce kicked them with the toe of his boot. One bottle had broken and warm water leaked out of its side. "Two men, you say?"

"That's right."

"A tall, buzz-headed, burly guy and a shorter one with wavy brown hair?"

"That's right, Mr. Pearce. One of them said his name was Jim."

Pearce's eyes bloated up on his face like a threatened bullfrog's chest. "Jim?"

Craig nodded. "Do you know them fellas, sir?"

Merel smiled liked he'd just swallowed the canary. "You know, son, I think I do." He slapped his knees and laughed. Jim Stafford. "Listen to me, now, Craig, if you see that worker around here again, you just let him work."

"But, sir—"

"Don't *but* me, boy, just do like I say."

Craig was confused but not too confused to nod.

"Let him be, but come tell me about it. If I ain't around, you tell Johnny."

"Yes, sir, Mr. Pearce."

"Daddy."

Merel turned. One foot went over the edge of the loading dock. Craig caught him by the shirt and pulled him back. Merel slapped the kid away. "Get this dang truck unloaded and be quick about it." He turned to his daughter. "Sherry, honey, what are you doing here?"

Sherry Pearce, eighteen years of trouble, dressed provocatively in a pair of low rise short-shorts and a sleeveless white blouse that she'd tied off below her woman-sized breasts, was stamping her sandaled foot. Her lip was twisted into a snarl reminiscent of her father's trademark image. "You know what I'm doing here, Daddy."

He gave her a look of heavenly innocence.

"I'm talking about the way you're treating Aaron."

Merel laid his hands on his daughter's bare shoulders. "Honey, I've got a show to do. I don't have time for this now." He patted her on the head. She had her mother's thick brown hair. "We'll talk about this later."

Sherry twisted her head from underneath. "We'll talk about this now, Daddy."

Out of the corner of one eye, Merel saw Craig looking at them. He reddened and pulled his daughter inside. "Listen," he whispered, "don't go talking to me like that in front of the help. It ain't proper. And do you have to go around dressed that way? It ain't proper neither."

"There's nothing wrong with the way I dress, Daddy." It was clear from her voice that he'd admonished his daughter for her dressing habits a thousand times in the past.

"You're half-naked and your bellybutton's all sticking out. You look like one of those California tarts in one of those trashy MTV videos you're always watching. I've warned you, baby. That stuff's rubbing off on you in a bad way."

"It is not, Daddy. This outfit is stylish. Aaron likes it."

"I'll bet he does," grumbled Pearce.

"And don't change the subject."

In the background, there came a wave of applause. Merel knew that would be Owen Plunkett, the comedian, out warming up the audience. That meant he had five minutes to deal with his daughter. Good thing he already had his stage clothes on. "Fine. What's the subject?"

He continued before she could tell him. "I know, Aaron. Like you said. Well, let me tell you, the bum isn't good enough for you. That's all there is to it."

"You aren't being fair. You aren't giving him a chance. And you keep giving him all these lowly little jobs to do around here."

"It's all he's good for."

"Well, me and Aaron talked and we think you should give him a bigger job. A more important job. And what's he doing for you that's so important he had to break our date last night?"

"What did Aaron say?"

"He said it was a secret, that he couldn't tell me. Said *you* would be mad."

Merel nodded. "Good. Maybe the boy's smarter than he looks, after all."

"Good? I think you're only trying to keep us apart."

"Of course I'm trying to keep you two apart. You deserve the best, honey."

"Daddy," warned Sherry, "don't start that again. I'm in love with Aaron."

He groaned. "How many times does that make now, Sherry?" Merel answered for her. "Six in two years.

That's how many. That's how many times you've fallen in love with one loser or another in the past two years. If you're going to keep falling in love so easy, can't you at least make it with a higher class of fella?"

"There's nothing wrong with who I pick to fall in love with. Besides, Aaron is—"

"—Different. Yeah, I know." He'd heard it all before.

One of Merel's assistants called out the two minute warning and ran on past.

Sherry was sobbing. He'd gone too far. It was time for a hug. "Sherry, honey, you're right." He planted a big, sloppy kiss on her warm, gardenia scented cheek. "I promise, I've got big plans for Aaron." He wiped away her tears with his thumb. "And I'm fixing to give Aaron his due. Trust me?"

Sherry nodded.

"Great. Is my tie straight?" He waggled the bolo back and forth.

"Looks fine, Daddy."

Pearce flashed his teeth. "Showtime."

Merel loped to the side of the stage, held his breath as his name was announced. One hand rubbed Johnny's head. It was part of the ritual. He counted three beats then swaggered out through the curtains and onto the big stage.

"Break a leg, Merel," hollered Johnny, just like he'd been doing every show for the last thirty-one years. Merel insisted on it. Said it brought him luck. Johnny was his lucky charm. It was half the reason Merel kept Johnny around and on the payroll at all. Don't mess with success.

Right on cue, an assistant thrust an acoustic guitar into Merel's hands as he came around the front curtain to the thunder of fifty-six hundred hands clapping; and that wasn't counting the shills.

Chapter 19

Tony bounced out onto the highway and only then eased up on the gas. He looked at the clock on the dash. "Eight o'clock," he pronounced as if he were proclaiming the onset of doom.

"Eight o'clock?" gasped Jim. "Uh-oh." In Branson, if you were a performer, this could spell doom.

The capital D kind.

Jim ran his fingers through his sweat-soaked hair. "Hot in here, ain't it?" He unbuttoned the brass buttons of his blazer. "Hot in this outfit. I'm late for my own show."

"We know," said Rock. "So are we. But don't worry, Jim. Tony will get you there, even if he has to run every red light on Highway 76."

Tony looked dubious. "I'm not breaking any laws. We'll get there in time." Tony was ever the voice of reason.

"What are you talking about? Jim's already late. Come on, Tony, step on it, will you?" Rock was never the voice of reason.

Jim leaned up between the seats. "I would appreciate it mightily if you sped up just a little, Tony. Why, I've only missed two shows out of more than three thousand in the past ten years."

"Do you two even see all the cars on this road? Or am I the only one?" Highway 76 was as clogged as his great-grandmother's arteries.

"You could go up the middle lane," suggested Rock.

"That's the turn lane. It's for turning only. The signs say so."

"Oh, please."

"Tony does have a point, Rock," said Jim. "I guess I'll have to miss my own show." He leaned back and shook his head woefully. "It'll be the first time in years. Folks sure will be disappointed. Come from hundreds of miles away, some of them do. Theater manager told me there was going to be some orphans coming in to see the show tonight. . ."

Jim looked especially forlorn sitting back there in the cramped little seat, all sweaty, his goofy-looking moustache drooping and half-off. Every time he talked, it flapped in the breeze like a kitten's tail. "My kids will be wondering what's happened to me. . ."

What else could he do? Tony gritted his teeth and guided the little car into the center lane. "I hate this," he grumbled.

"Tell us what you were going to tell us before, Jim."

"Huh? You men got any water? I'm awfully thirsty."

"No, sorry," replied Rock, though he checked the floor just in case. "Back at Merel's theater you started to tell us about something you thought was kind of funny. At least, that's what you called it."

"Oh, yeah." Jim scratched his head. "You got a minute?"

Tony actually turned around and stared at Stafford this time.

"Right. I guess you do. It's like this—"

"Tony, look out!"

Tony turned around. A red Ferrari was hurtling straight at them. "What's that nut doing driving in the center lane!"

"He's trying to make a turn!" shouted Rock. "Get out of his way!"

Tony looked around. There were thick rows of cars on either side. "There's nowhere to go!" He jammed his foot down on the brake pedal. So did the driver of the Ferrari.

Tony held his little remaining breath, waiting for the screams of agony and screeches of twisting metal. The smell of burning rubber turned his stomach, but instead of a head-on collision it was more of a head-on nudge.

Tony slowly let out his breath.

"Holy cow, Tony, that was close. You ought to be more careful." Rock was adjusting his seatbelt and stuck his head out the window, checking out the Ferrari. "Nice car. Here comes the driver. Hope he isn't too angry with you— driving in the middle of the road like that."

Tony, a deep growl emanating in his throat, held down the sudden urge he had to strangle Rock right then and there.

A bearded, curly haired fellow got out, walked

slowly to the front of their car. He was rubbing his chin. He laid his hands on the side of Rock's door. "You fellows okay?"

Tony nodded. "Sorry."

The stranger looked at Jim in the back and rubbed his jaw some more.

Jim was holding up his moustache.

"Do I know you?" asked the man.

Jim cleared his throat and waved. "How y'all doin'?"

Rock and Tony were surprised that Jim had suddenly developed a thick Tennessee twang.

A police cruiser arrived, lights blazing. He slowly exited his car, inspected the damage to the front of the vehicles then approached Tony's side of the car. "Everyone all right here? No one's hurt?"

"Everything is wonderful, officer. Not a scratch. Can you believe it?" The bearded fellow was actually smiling and didn't seem upset at all.

Tony was relieved.

The officer stepped away with the bearded man and they talked for several minutes. All the while, the bearded fellow kept glancing at his watch.

A moment later, he was in his car. The police officer stopped oncoming traffic and the man pulled up beside Tony and rolled down his window. "Have a good night, fellows."

"Hey," snarled Rock. "What about your license number and getting an accident report?"

The stranger smiled, all white perfect teeth. His eyes were twinkling like he'd swallowed a couple of Christmas tree lights. "There's no real damage. Your car is unharmed. Mine suffered only a tiny ding. I suggested that we let it go. This fine Branson police officer says he will take care of everything."

"But—" Tony didn't like the sound of that.

The bearded gentleman waved. "I love this country."

"Dang that Chernov," muttered Jim, letting his moustache fall. "Guy gets away with murder."

Rock's eyebrows rose. "Murder?"

"Forget it, Rock, we've already got enough suspects as it is." He looked at Jim via the rearview mirror. "You know him, Jim?"

"Hey, wait. I thought I recognized that guy." Rock thumped the dashboard. "That was Chekov Chernov, the Russian comedian, wasn't it?"

Jim nodded.

"Rats." Rock snapped his fingers. "And I didn't even get his autograph."

The officer was approaching their car. "Listen, here. You really ought to be—" He leaned over and stuck his head in the window so far that Tony had to move over to keep from getting butted. "Mr. Stafford, sir. I didn't realize you were here."

"Evening, officer." Jim nodded.

"Shouldn't you be on your way to your show? It's after eight."

There was a sound of awe and wonder in his voice that irked Rock. It wasn't fair.

The officer opened the side door. "I'd be honored to give you a ride, Mr. Stafford."

"In the squad car?" Jim was already halfway out.

"Sure."

"Can I work the lights?"

The officer grinned. "Heck, Mr. Stafford, you can drive if you want to."

Tony and Rock watched helplessly as Jim and the

officer sped off.

"Well, I like that," huffed Rock. "What about us?"

"We never did find out what Jim wanted to tell us. And we're still stuck in traffic."

"I'm hungry," complained the big guy.

"Not that I care, but you're about to get your wish. Because if we hurry we can still make the Kewpiecon banquet and Nanci's show."

"Great. I hope there's a bar. I could use a beer right about now."

"What you could use is a bass and me a guitar. Let's hope that Nanci's brought them and that the show is running late. And don't forget your little camera. We'll get some shots at the banquet after the performance. There are supposed to be some special Kewpie displays set up from what I hear. We can also talk to Virginia Plat."

"What do you want to talk to her about?"

"She wanted to talk to us, remember?"

Rock nodded. "Maybe she thinks you'd make good ROSE executive material."

Tony enjoyed a moment of silence before Rock started up again.

"And what about the way that cop just left us there? I mean, he holds up traffic for Chekov and then gives Jim a ride in his cruiser. Us he leaves stranded."

Tony maintained a diplomatic silence. After all, he knew full well that any reply was senseless.

"You ought to talk to your girlfriend, Paula, about it."

"She's not my girlfriend, Rock."

"Could've fooled me."

Det. Carvin was chewing on his fingernails and interviewing some robust-looking fellow in a hardhat. Chief Mark Schaum had his hands wrapped around a cup of coffee, listening in. It seemed like just about everybody on the force was there. Robinson half-expected to find the Branson PD secretarial and support staff lurking around the corner.

B.A.D. Spike's Crib was packed like it was opening night, at least backstage. All the lights were up bright, making the space intolerably warm. The smell of cigarettes fought with the scent of coffee for control of her nostrils.

Robinson worked her way toward the bottom of the stage near the back wall. An entire section of it had been half-demolished. Concrete dust and bits of rubble coated the floor. Bright spotlights blasted beams of light into the crevices as if they were intent on burning holes clear through the cement.

Robinson shouldered her way past a cohort and chewed her lip. "Is that what I think it is?" she asked no one in particular.

"If you think it's the prehistoric remains of a hundred million years dead archaeopteryx," answered the nearest officer, "you think wrong."

He paused and offered Robinson a peppermint-scented stick of gum which she declined. "Now, if you think it's recent human remains, you think right."

Chapter 20

Robinson watched as a couple of technicians carefully brushed away concrete dust. The body was a jumble of spare parts surrounded by decayed clothing and bits of hair. Not a pretty sight. Especially right after that enchilada she'd had for dinner.

She stepped back and Chief Schaum called her over.

"I'd like you to hear this, Paula."

"Sure, chief."

Carvin nodded towards the hardhat. "This here is Andrew Jergen, the general contractor that B.A.D. hired to do a remodel of the stage."

"But B.A.D.'s dead and this place was supposed to be off limits." Robinson looked around at the milling construction workers. "What are all your people doing here in the first place?"

Carvin answered for Jergen. "Says he was hired to

work round-the-clock."

"And that's just what we're doing," Jergen said belligerently. He was a wide, pasty skinned fellow with one strand of hair that stuck out the side of his hardhat. His irises were as gray as nailheads. "Just because the man that hired me is gone, I shouldn't finish the job?" He pressed a dirty and calloused hand against his chest. "I gave my word."

"If you ask me," Carvin said, jaded as any detective, "the only reason you're out here is because you're hoping to get paid."

"What's wrong with that? I have already invested my own money in this project. Scheduled it in the books. Put off other jobs. Mr. B.A.D. was supposed to give me a check on Monday." Jergen looked bothered. "Someone needs to pay me. I work, I get paid."

"Not now you don't work," Carvin said. "Not with that body over there. As for getting paid, my guess is you'll be needing a lawyer for that."

If Jergen looked bothered before, he looked perfectly livid now.

"Why are you tearing up the stage to begin with, Mr. Jergen?" asked Robinson. "It looks fine to me. At least, it did before now."

"Mr. B.A.D. he tells me to do this. He says he wants it bigger." The man's arms stretched out. "And he tells me, orders me to finish before next month's opening. I tell him that's okay. I know this theater. A few years ago, I did some work for Mr. Pearce. I know it like the back of my hand. So, it's no problem. But my men must work overtime. This costs me much."

Robinson asked, "How did you get in?"

"Mr. B.A.D., he gave me a key."

"To that door?" Robinson pointed to the newly refitted backdoor.

The contractor was nodding.

"Forget it, Robinson," said Carvin. "We've already been through this. The lock uses the same key as it did before."

"Are you sure?"

Chief Schaum replied, "I called the locksmith myself. He rekeyed it to work with the old key." The chief swirled up the dregs of his coffee then drank them down. "No one told him not to."

"And you conveniently didn't notice the police tape, Jergen?" Carvin asked.

Jergen shrugged. "I had a contract. We came to work. I did not think this would interfere with your policing. After all, Mr. B.A.D., he is already dead. What harm could we do?" He stared Carvin down. "And we did find the bones."

Jergen turned to the chief. "And when we did, we telephoned the police immediately."

Chief Schaum sipped slowly, making sucking noises. "A couple of Mr. Jergen's employees were breaking up the concrete back here with sledgehammers and noticed the remains," he explained for Robinson's benefit. "Poor fellas. Scared the dickens out of them."

"They go crazy," added the contractor, throwing his arms about. "I thought they'd seen a ghost or were drinking on the job or something."

"That's them over there," Carvin said, gesturing to two young men sitting on metal folding chairs off in the corner.

They looked shell-shocked. Finding a dead body,

even an old one could do that to a person. Robinson tilted back out of the way of Jergen's windmilling arms. What was it with this guy and his arms? Early stage Parkinson's or a desire to fly like Daedalus? "Any idea whose body it is?"

"None," replied Chief Schaum. "They say it's a man, though there was no ID found on the body. No wallet, nothing. It's going to take some time to figure out who he was unless something more turns up at the dig."

"Not to mention, what he was doing there," Robinson added.

Carvin said, "You don't accidently end up swimming in concrete."

Robinson nodded. If you asked her, this theater was cursed. She kept this opinion to herself. You didn't last long on the force believing in curses. At the very best you'd end up in the Records Room right up until your retirement party. It was tough enough being a woman in this job without spouting off out of the ordinary beliefs.

She was all for keeping her mouth shut. No way she was working Records. Being stuck on the night shift all month had been bad enough. This was not her idea of the way to spend a Saturday night. She could be home right now at her brother's house, watching football, her brother's favorite sport. Instead, she was feeling like it was the end of the fourth quarter and her head was the game ball.

Robinson's thoughts ran to Tony Kozol. She wondered where he was now and what he was up to. Tony had given her his cell number. When she could safely duck out of here and out from under Chief Schaum's eye, she'd give him a call. Maybe they could meet for coffee somewhere. Was she being too pushy?

Paula rubbed her eyes with the fleshy part of her palms as Chief Schaum dished out orders.

Chapter 21

"Any sign of her?" Tony's guitar case bounced off Rock's bass case. They'd picked up their instruments on the way over.

Rock asked, "Any sign of who?"

"Virginia Plat."

Rock shrugged. "I haven't even looked for her yet." The big guy inhaled through his nostrils. "Can't we get something to eat first? I'm famished."

"Fine. Let's look around for our table." Tony scooted between tables and chairs, not easy loaded down with their instruments. The round tables, big enough to accommodate eight, were clustered close together.

He figured they'd be seated next to Nanci, but was told she had come and gone after performing two songs solo on her twelve-string. He groaned. They were in trouble deep.

The banquet hall was a smallish, inconspicuous,

single storied building across the parking lot from a mid-century Presbyterian church located on the other side of the White River. They'd driven past the unmarked building twice before stopping to check it out.

There were blacked-out plate glass windows on either side of the solid front door. The place was almost dark. Inside, dusty chandeliers hung from the ceiling like old memories.

"Is this a party or a wake?" Rock quipped.

"Shh." Tony brushed against someone's shoulder and excused himself.

"Hello there, boys."

"Hi. Sorry." Tony recognized the old man from Kewpiecon. He'd been sitting next to Tony at the first meeting. Pretty hard not to recognize the guy, even if he couldn't remember his name. He had a flowing white beard and walked with a limp for which he carried an intricately carved wooden walking stick with a dragon's head handle. The staff was multicolored, brown, blue, red and green. Tony had never seen anything quite like it.

"There's no need to apologize. Looking for a place to sit?"

Tony nodded.

"We're starved," added Rock.

"We've got two seats right here. Join us. Sit between Mother and Evie."

Tony scanned the table. He recognized the man's mother. She'd been with him at the meeting. And that was Evie from the hotel sitting a couple chairs away. She had given them their conference materials.

Tony nodded to the woman. Before he could say yes, Rock plopped himself down next to the old man's mom. "Thanks. I'm sorry, but I've forgotten your name." He'd introduced himself at the meeting, he was sure, but he hadn't made so much as a mental note of it.

He held out a large, crooked hand. "Dewey Rood. My mother's name is Cleo."

For a large man, he had a small, whispery voice. It was like straining to hear a distant creek in a dense forest.

"Sit yourself down now, Tony, and we'll get the server on over. The banquet's first rate this year. We've got four kinds of meat."

Tony said hello and resigned himself to sitting next to Evie. White table cloths spread across the tables and halfway to the floor. The centerpieces were little wicker baskets of flowers with plastic Kewpies and goodies. They shoved their instruments under the table as best they could.

"Good evening, dear," said Evie. "Are you enjoying Kewpiecon?"

"Very much," Tony answered, diplomatic if not wholly honest. B.A.D. Spike's murder and Jim's arrest had sort of put a damper on things. He pulled on his napkin. "Has anyone seen Nanci?" Maybe she was still around somewhere.

"No, she seemed upset. Left directly after her performance. Weren't you boys supposed to be playing with her?"

Tony groaned.

Rock slapped him on the back. "Buck up, Tony. You leave Nanci to me."

"This is my roommate, Becky," said Evie.

Tony waved hi. This might as well be his last

supper.

The server arrived.

"What will it be, Tony?" asked Dewey. "Beef, chicken, ham or pork?"

"Actually," Tony said, "none of the above. I'm a vegan. So's Rock." Though Rock was new to the club.

"You're from Vegas?" said Cleo. "Why didn't you say so? We're from Las Vegas, too."

"No, Mother." Dewey was shaking his head. "They're vegans. Vegetarians. Don't eat meat."

Tony's face turned beet red. A nice vegetarian color. Au natural.

"How nice," said Evie. "I always said vegetarian was the way to go." A fist-sized slab of baked ham slathered in honey went from the tip of her fork to the depths of her gaping mouth. "Yes," she said, chewing and talking, "that's the way to go. I envy you, Tony."

The waitress smiled. "You're the two veggie plates. Don't worry. Got them in the kitchen. Wondered who they belonged to. Be right back."

To busy himself, Tony fingered a small replica of a Kewpie coloring book. Someone had gone to an awful lot of trouble creating these centerpieces.

"Lovely, aren't they?" remarked Becky, a silver-haired woman with a pasty complexion and a button nose. Her teeth were unnaturally white. "No two centerpieces are alike."

"They're raffling them off after the banquet," added Evie. "If you're interested, you can still buy tickets."

"Thanks," said Tony, "maybe I will." He was only being polite at first, but the more he thought about it, the more he realized his Aunt Louise might like a little souvenir and one of these Kewpiecon centerpieces would be about perfect. "How much are the tickets?"

Evie grinned like a carnival huckster. "Dollar a chance. And you can pay me. Becky's got the tickets right here."

Becky deftly pulled a spool of yellow tickets from her purse. "How many you want, Tony?"

Tony handed over a ten dollar bill and Becky tore off ten tickets.

"Thanks."

"Good luck, Tony."

"Ah, dinner." Rock cleared his silverware out of the way and grabbed his plate from the server before it even had a chance to touch down. "Ouch, hot!"

As Rock dug into his veggie plate special, carrots, broccoli, cauliflower and white sauce on a bed of fettuccine, Tony asked about Virginia Plat.

Dewey frowned. "I don't know." Using his cane, he half-lifted himself from his chair. "Virginia must be here someplace. She'd never miss this. Besides, she's got a presentation to make." He scanned the room. "And now that you mention it, Tony, she was supposed to introduce Susie. Instead, Secretary Farland did it."

"Maybe she's in the ladies room," Evie suggested. "Want me to go see?"

"Oh, no," said Tony. "Don't go to any trouble." Ms. Plat would just love it if Tony sent Evie into the ladies room looking for her. Tony already had a feeling that Ms. Plat didn't like him. How much less would Ms. Plat like him if she was responsible for someone interrupting her trip to the toilet? "It wasn't important. I was only wondering where she was. I wanted to interview her for our story."

"Story?" said Dewey. "I thought you were musicians?"

"We're writing up a little story on Kewpie dolls, too," put in Rock.

Evie smiled and patted the big guy's hand. "Kewpies are addictive, aren't they?"

Rock grinned.

The scent of steaming vegetables slowly wormed its way into Tony's consciousness and his stomach started doing somersaults. He satisfied its entreaties by twirling up a mouthful of noodles and carrot. The buttery noodles all but melted in his mouth. Before long, eating was all he was thinking about.

Incoming ROSE president, Susie Garcia, a youthful, raven-haired woman, with an offbeat beauty and laugh was wrapping up her obligatory speech and thanking everyone for their votes and their confidence in her upcoming tenure.

"Most of all, I'd like to thank my husband, Shelby, for indulging my passion for all things Kewpie and for taking care of the kids while I come to Branson every year for the past nine, without complaining. At least, not much."

Some folks laughed.

Susie cleared her throat. "And now I'd like to introduce Rick Elf, whom you all know. Rick has some interesting news to report on our ongoing efforts to construct a virtual Rose O'Neill museum."

Rick Elf rose from a table near the podium to a smattering of applause.

"I see Mr. Elf is here." Tony turned his chair and craned his neck for a better look. "He was out at Bonniebrook with Virginia Plat earlier."

Becky giggled.

"What's so funny?" asked Rock.

"When Susie comes," Evie replied, "Rick is always here."

Becky snickered. "You mean *there*." Becky and Evie giggled some more and Becky gripped Evie's hand. "Oh, yes. Rick wouldn't miss Kewpiecon for anything, would he?"

This time Evie snorted like a pig. Rock frowned. He hated inside jokes. "What's that supposed to mean?"

Becky looked at Evie who shook her head. Becky shrugged. "Oh, it's nothing."

Elf pushed a pair of reading glasses up his nose and began reading from a sheaf of papers he'd brought with him to the podium.

"It's terrible about the thefts, isn't it?" whispered Tony. "I hear Mr. Elf lost some very expensive collectibles."

"I'll say," said Dewey. "A fella could retire on the sale of that Kewpie Mountain alone."

"So could a bass player," quipped Rock, wistfully. The big guy had polished off his plate and was motioning for someone to pass the bread rolls.

As for Becky, there was something going on there and Rock vowed to get the woman alone and get to the bottom of it. The woman had more than one secret and Rock believed in sharing. "Jim did not steal anything and he didn't kill anybody."

Dewey's mom broke the silence. "Most of us Kewpie folks don't believe for one minute that Jim Stafford could commit such horrible crimes, child."

"You don't?" said Rock.

Tony asked, "Who do you suspect, Mrs. Rood?"

Cleo was quick to reply. "I'm not sure. Truth is, I

don't have any idea at all. Except that it had to be someone who knows Kewpies."

"And Kewpie values," added Dewey. "Let's face it, there's a lot of stuff on display down at the theater." He nodded as he sliced then buttered up his third roll and turned it into a meat sandwich. Dewey had picked the pork. "Someone with intimate knowledge of Kewpie prices went after the best stuff. Someone like Jim, an amateur, would have grabbed whatever was at hand."

"Meat's tough." Cleo Rood struggled with a plateful of beef.

Her son ran a finger along the edge of her steak knife. "Blade's no good, Mother." He unsheathed a six-inch blade from a leather pouch attached to his belt. "Use this."

Evie picked up on what Dewey had said earlier about Kewpies. "And some of the items for sale at the show aren't worth much at all."

"They're just reproductions of originals, like ours," explained Cleo, deftly dicing the beef into small cubes with her son's knife. "We make molds of Miss O'Neill's statues and create miniature reproductions."

"And kitchen magnets," added her son.

"That's right," Cleo said, "kitchen magnets. Dewey carves them himself. He's great with a knife." She patted her son on the leg.

Dewey beamed.

"So," said Tony, "it was an insider."

"The question is: who?" Rock propped his wide chin on his elbows and looked from one tablemate to the next.

"Miss Plat?" suggested Tony.

Dewey laugh. "I can't imagine. She's a harmless

little woman."

"If you say so." Tony took a look around the room. "Where could she be? Has anyone seen her lately?"

"We haven't seen her since we left Bonniebrook," answered Evie. "Have we, Becky?"

"No, that's right. Last place we saw her was Bonniebrook. Same as you. Saw her car in the parking lot. The blue Dodge. It was closing time and hers and ours were just about the only cars left."

"We saw her in the garden," replied Tony. "She was with Mr. Elf."

"Maybe he knows where she is," Cleo said.

"Let's ask him later," Tony said.

"Mother and I haven't seen her at all. Have we, Mother?"

She shook her head.

On the third bite, Dewey's sandwich disappeared down his gullet. He cleared his throat of debris, bent low to the table and looked directly at Tony.

Rick was droning on and on about the difficulties and costs of a dedicated server versus leasing space, so Tony was glad to continue the conversation.

"I hesitate to say this, but Duncan Daniels—" He paused.

"What about him?" whispered Tony.

"I could be wrong, but I've heard he has troubles."

Tony's brow wrinkled up like a crinkle fry. "Troubles? What sort of troubles?"

"Money troubles."

"A hundred thousand dollars solves a lot of money troubles," Tony whistled.

"It would solve mine," joked Cleo.

"But Duncan had a number of collectibles stolen as

well, including the Kewpie that Jim Stafford said he found," Rock said. "Duncan told me."

Dewey's big shoulders jerked up and down. "I'm only repeating gossip that I've heard around. I'm not saying the stories are true."

Tony leaned back in his chair. "You think maybe Duncan stole the Kewpie Mountain and added a few of his own pieces into the lot to throw the police off the trail?"

Dewey grinned.

Tony was tapping on the table with his dessert spoon. Rick Elf threw him a dirty look and he stopped. "Mr. Daniels did go back for his wallet. Ms. Plat told me that. He said he'd left it at his table and she let him have her key so he could get it back."

Evie and Becky were looking perplexed. Evie spoke up. "Wasn't Duncan at dinner with us last night, Becky?"

"I believe so." She was scratching her head. "But he wasn't at our table. A bunch of us were out at the Red Lobster. I'm pretty sure he was there though, Tony."

Rock drained his ice tea, wishing it was Jamaican rum. "What time was this?"

"Pretty late, wasn't it, Evie?" Becky said.

"After the window display contest and we didn't get out of the hotel till after nine-thirty."

"Could have been ten even," figured Becky.

"Could have been," repeated Evie.

"And Duncan couldn't have been in two places at the same time," Rock said morosely. "Oh." He suddenly realized he may have cleared yet another suspect, leaving the Branson police an unobstructed path to Stafford. Could Jim be guilty, after all?

Rick wrapped up his speech to twice the applause he'd gotten on starting. But then, it was getting late and this crowd wasn't much interested in the internet.

Another speaker was heading to the podium. "Let's get out of here, Tony." Rock pushed back his chair, snatched up his bass, and headed for the door.

Tony caught up to the big guy outside. "That was rude, Rock. You didn't even say goodnight to anyone. What's the rush?"

"I've got this feeling in my gut."

"You always eat too much."

"It's not that." Rock stared up at the gray sky. "I'm just wondering if we're wrong."

"Wrong about what?"

"Face it, Tony. Jim Stafford could be guilty of murder." And he did not like backing the wrong side.

Chapter 22

"Come on, Rock. You don't really believe that."

Rock looked uncertain. "I don't know, Tony." He scratched his head. "What if Jim really hated B.A.D.? What if he wanted him out of town? Dead?" The big guy looked his friend in the eye. "Face it, Tony. What do we really know about Jim Stafford? He could be a cold-blooded killer." Rock paused. "And he's got us helping him. We've been conned before. Remember?"

Tony remembered all too well. Friends weren't always what they appeared to be. "There's only one way to know for sure."

"Yeah?"

I think it's time we got a little more proactive."

"What do you have in mind?"

"We're going to Bonniebrook."

"Now? In the middle of the night? It won't even be open. Why go all the way out there? And what about

Nanci?"

"I'll let you take care of Nanci. We're going to Bonniebrook because Miss Plat implied that she has some answers. Answers to some very important questions. Maybe she can clear Jim. And that's the last place she was seen."

"Okay, Tony." Rock jumped in the car. "But I don't know what good it's going to do."

They drove the now familiar route up Highway 65 and found the drive to Bonniebrook blocked by a set of low metal gates—not much more than a pair of namby-pamby poles with wheels on the ends. Rock pushed them open.

The tires hissed along the road. Invisible crickets chirped in the dark. "Man, this is spooky. Reminds me of the swamps back home." The parking lot was tenebrous. The moon kept playing hide and seek behind a patchy sky of dark angry clouds. There was only one other car on the lot.

Tony trained the headlights on the other vehicle. They got out and approached on foot. It was a late model, four door Dodge. It was in bad need of a car-wash. Bugs and dirt stuck to the body and windows like nature's glue.

Tony pressed his face against the glass. There was a Scootles air freshener dangling from the rear view mirror.

Rock tried the doors. "Locked tight. You think it's Virginia's car?"

Tony slowly walked around the car. "Definitely. I recognize that scarf of hers on the front seat. Plus, this car has got Iowa plates."

"So?"

"Don't you remember? Miss Plat is with the Iowa chapter of ROSE."

Rock looked with trepidation at the dark buildings and forbidden-looking woods. "Where do you suppose she is?"

"Maybe her car broke down and she got a ride into town with someone else. Like Rick."

"Then why wasn't she at the banquet?"

"Good question." Tony walked to the edge of the parking lot. There was a low railing along the side looking down into the woods. "Miss Plat! Miss Plat, are you out there!"

"No one's home, Tony. Looks like this is a dead end. Let's go back to the hotel." The wind kicked up and sent a shiver along his arms. "Should have brought a jacket."

"Not yet. Let's have a look down by the house and garden first."

"What for?" Going down into that dark nether world was the last thing that Rock wanted to do. He had a palpable fear of the netherworld. The darkness represented fire and brimstone to him.

"To have a look around. Come on, Rock. We're here anyway. Maybe Miss Plat is lying out there helpless somewhere. Maybe she fell and broke a leg or something."

Rock wasn't convinced.

"Besides, it's kind of peaceful. Imagine how nice the garden must be on a night like this. It'll be just the way it was when Rose O'Neill lived here. A peaceful, idyllic retreat."

"My idea of a peaceful retreat is a day at a five-star spa, with some ample-chested young woman with a foreign sounding name, like Giselle, giving me a back rub."

Nevertheless, Rock reluctantly followed Tony down the path. The museum and gift shop were locked up tight. Bonniebrook was dark and the door secure.

They called out Virginia Plat's name as they searched the grounds. There was no reply. None human anyway.

Going around to the garden, O'Neill's giant statues stood out like monstrous dark angels to Rock. But none of it seemed to disturb Tony. He was making notes in his pad. Rock couldn't begin to imagine what for.

Rock rubbed his arms. "Can we go now?"

Tony considered. "Want to go check the cemetery?"

"You're out of your mind. I'm not going down there in the dark. Cemeteries give me the creeps, even in the daylight. Too many loose souls looking for new homes. Like hermit crabs."

"Oh, please."

Rock grabbed Tony's arm. "Come on, Tony, let's get out of here. It looks and smells like rain coming up. Besides, you left the headlights on. What if the car battery runs down? We'll be stuck out here miles from anywhere."

Tony closed his notebook. "You're right. Let's get back to Branson."

With an audible sigh of relief, Rock headed up the now familiar path around the garden and up the side of the house leading to the parking lot. For a big guy, he was sure skittish sometimes.

"Wait."

Rock turned. "Now what?"

"I thought I saw something."

Rock said, "Are you kidding? I can barely see you, let alone anything else." The boys stood on the path, sandwiched between the house and the stand of trees near the front door. "What could you have possibly seen?"

"I don't know. I guess it was nothing."

"Fine, can we go now? Headlights, remember?"

Tony took a step. "I thought I saw a glint of something shiny—"

"The window of the house, maybe? Come on, Tony."

"No, over there. Across from the house."

Rock came back down the trail and grabbed Tony by the arm. He'd haul Tony up himself if he had to. Sometimes a person simply had to take control.

"There's nothing out there," Rock said, "now let's go. I am not spending the night out here with the bears and the wolves and the boogeymen just because you saw an empty soda can or a burger wrapper."

A gust of wind blew through and the clouds parted long enough for the light of the moon to capture the boys like a spotlight.

"There it is!" Tony whispered.

Rock followed Tony's pointed finger. "What? I don't see any—" He scowled. "Oh. I see it now. That's coming from the hidey-hole."

"The what?"

"You remember. The guide told us that was the hidey-hole. The reinforced concrete box where folks flee in a tornado."

"Right. What could be shiny in there?" The clouds had buried the moon once more and the hidey-hole all but disappeared in the depth of the trees.

"It's damp in there. You're probably seeing the light of the moon reflecting off the water when it hits just right."

"I suppose that must be it." Tony laughed. "This place is starting to get to me, too."

"Spooky, ain't it?"

Tony nodded. "Let's get out of here."

"Now you're talking, buddy." Rock started back up the walkway. "You know, Tony, I appreciate what you're trying to do and all, but don't you think we should go link up with Nanci and beg forgiveness?" Rock figured that would get them out of here. Oddly, Tony made no reply. "Tony?"

Rock turned. "Tony, where are you?" The big guy didn't like this. Didn't like this one bit. He was beginning to regret every slasher movie he'd ever seen. Had Tony met his maker?

Rock took a couple of steps back toward the empty house. "Tony?" His fear-driven thoughts considered silent body snatchers lurking in the woods. He'd heard about such evil spirits growing up. What had happened to Tony? Had the evil spirits claimed him? Was he about to be next?

"I'm in here."

With a start, Rock turned toward the sound of rustling trees. "Where?"

"I want to take a quick look at the hidey-hole." Tony's voice sounded distant and muffled.

"Well, tell a guy, would you?" Rock climbed over the low wall and followed the sound of his friend's voice. "Don't disappear like that."

"Sorry. Watch out. It's slick up here."

"I know." Rock bumped into Tony at the entrance

J.R. Ripley

of the hidey-hole. It was dark enough to be the entrance to Hell. "Satisfied?"

Tony gripped the rough edge of the doorway and stepped into the hidey-hole. It was damp and rank. His foot hit something soft. Tony slowly bent his knees, all the while testing the air with his hands. "Get out of the doorway, Rock."

"What?"

"Get away from the door."

Rock stepped back. "Fine, but why?" Tony was awfully snappy all of a sudden.

"Because I feel something down here and you're blocking the light." Tony's hands fumbled in the blackness. He drew his fingers over something soft and cold. It felt like fabric. Kozol's eyes were adjusting to the dark now and the moon was once again creeping into view.

Tony screamed but not before Rock did. "It's Virginia!" Rock yanked his cheesy camera from his pocket, adjusted for flash and began shooting.

"What in heaven's name are you doing?" Tony was getting woozy. Miss Plat lay spread out on the wet ground, her face frozen in a grimace of fear and death. She didn't look so mousy now. "Ugh." The shiny glint had apparently come from Miss Plat's silver wristwatch, hanging needlessly now on her bent and twisted arm.

Rock was shaking. "I don't know. It's a reflex, I guess."

"Well, come inside and do it again." Tony's teeth were chattering. There was a large red circle on Miss Plat's chest and Tony didn't think it was part of the original design.

"What for?"

"My phone slipped out of my pocket in here some-where and I need to find it so I can call Paula."

Rock did as he was told, but he didn't like it. *See A Dead Body* was not on his 'To Do' list and he'd already seen too many.

Tony scooped up his phone, exited the hidey-hole and called Robinson. "Hello, Paula?"

"Speaking."

"This is Tony Kozol."

"Oh, Tony. I'd been meaning to call you. But this isn't exactly a good time."

"I know. There's been another murder!"

"What?"

"Yes, I'm standing right next to the body. It's Miss Plat." Tony was breathing hard. He explained how they were out at Bonniebrook and had stumbled on Virginia Plat's body. "You'd better get out here."

"Stay put," she ordered. "And don't touch anything. Better yet, go back to your vehicle and wait for me there."

"Okay, Paula." Tony dropped his phone and looked at the big guy. Rock's white face presented a stark contrast to his dark clothing. The only thing whiter was Virginia Plat's own blood-drained face.

Chapter 23

The cops arrived.

In twenty minutes they had transformed the place into a scene reminiscent of a late night Miami model shoot. Lots of lights, cameras, action. Virginia Plat played the part of the model. She played it well, though she only had the one pose in her repertoire.

Tony and Rock huddled under the roof of the Rose O'Neill house. A light rain was falling. Robinson, covered in a raincoat, approached. She held a wet flashlight in one hand. In the distance, Det. Carvin and the rest of the crime unit were monitoring the removal of Virginia Plat's body.

Robinson slapped her flashlight against her leg and turned off the beam. Water fell from her hat and she wiped a cold drop from her nose. "I'll take over here, Noelle."

The uniformed officer, who had been silently

standing watch beside the boys throughout their ordeal, nodded and moved off.

Robinson said, "Looks like our victim was stabbed several times."

Tony shuddered. "What a place to die. Someone must have lured her there and then—" There was no need to complete the sentence.

Robinson was shaking her head. "Not enough blood."

"What do you mean?" asked Rock.

"It means Miss Plat was killed elsewhere and her body dumped in that shed."

"Hidey-hole," corrected Rock.

"Huh?"

Tony explained. "Do you think the same person that stabbed B.A.D. stabbed Miss Plat, Paula?"

Robinson was looking at Rock. "Could be." The sound of a fading siren echoed through the trees as Miss Plat's corpse was taken away. They followed Robinson back to town and police headquarters. Det. Carvin was there, looking exhausted. Even his paunch looked paunchier than usual. It was nearly midnight.

"You mind telling me what you were doing out at Bonniebrook?"

"We were looking for Miss Plat." And they'd found her. Tony shivered.

Det. Carvin sat at the head of the table, notebook in hand. "Bonniebrook's closed at night. Why there?"

Tony explained his reasoning.

"You men are messing in an official murder investigation. I ought to lock you both up."

"Go ahead," quipped Rock. "I could use a good night's rest. And how about breakfast in bed? I'll have the yogurt and fruit salad. Coffee, no cream, no sugar."

Carvin told Rock to keep quiet. He made a phone call and declared himself finished with them. He told them they were free to go. Carvin and Robinson rose.

"Wait just a minute," Tony began, "what about sharing with us now? We've told you everything we know. You owe us."

Carvin laughed. "You're funny. I like that." His features stiffened. "Now go home. Get some sleep."

"But that's not fair. Tony's right," put in Rock, giving Carvin his most unpleasant look. The kind that said: There's a fist coming your way. "At least tell us what happened to Virginia."

"I'm afraid that's police business, Mr. Bottom." Det. Carvin pushed open the conference room door and held it open. "Now, if you don't mind?"

Rock held his ground. "I do mind."

"Come on, Rock," Tony said loudly. "If the police don't want to cooperate with us, maybe we won't cooperate with them anymore. Maybe we'll keep all our information to ourselves."

Carvin stuck out his hand, effectively blocking Tony's way. "What information?"

"We know certain things," Tony said boldly, if not completely honestly.

"Yeah," affirmed Rock, "we're in the middle of this thing. People talk to us. And we're reporters, we know how to investigate. From the inside."

"Listen, you creeps, if you're holding anything back—" Det. Carvin let his threat hang there in the air unfinished.

"Holding anything back?" Tony repeated innocently. "Why, we're just doing like you said, detective." He pulled on Carvin's sleeve and delicately moved his arm from his path.

"Yep," Rock said, "going home to get some beauty sleep. A boy needs to look good, doesn't he, Tony?"

"Absolutely."

Robinson laughed.

Carvin surrendered. "I'm going home." He was looking at Robinson like it was all her fault. "These two are your problem, Paula."

After Carvin had disappeared, Robinson refilled Tony's mug and poured Rock and herself some coffee. "We don't know much more than you about Virginia Plat. Preliminarily, it looks like she was stabbed several times in the chest and stomach. Once in the back. She was killed somewhere yet to be determined and her body dragged into that hidey-hole."

"Her car?" Rock asked. "Maybe the killer murdered her in the car and then dumped her out there where she'd be less visible."

"The car was clean. No signs of violence there." Robinson wrapped her hands around her paper cup for warmth. "No, my guess is that she was killed some-where on the property. Bonniebrook's a pretty big place, as you well know. Even if Miss Plat had been killed earlier in the day, there's a good chance no one would have heard it happening."

"Maybe even while we were there," stated Tony.

"What time was that?"

Tony told her.

She shook her pretty head. "According to the ME, it's more likely that Miss Plat hadn't been dead more than two or three hours before you discovered her. The question is: What was she doing out there that time of night? The place was closed up."

"We saw her out there this afternoon, talking to Rick Elf."

"Rick Elf?"

"He's a ROSE vice president."

"Right. The guy with the Kewpie Mountain. Maybe we'll have a talk with him."

"He could have killed her," said Tony, "though I couldn't imagine why."

"No," said Rock, "he couldn't have done it."

"Why not?" Robinson poured a second sweetener into her cup. She reached for a spoon, then held it suspended over her cup a moment before setting it back down.

"Because we saw Rick at the Kewpiecon banquet this evening."

"Are you sure?" Robinson squinted and blew on her coffee.

Tony nodded. "Rock's right. Mr. Elf even gave a speech."

Robinson frowned. "I'll mention it to the chief, anyway. Mr. Elf may have seen or heard something while he was out at Bonniebrook. You never know."

Tony said, "I still don't get why anyone would kill poor, defenseless Miss Plat. I've never met a less likely victim."

Robinson grinned. "Looks can be deceiving, Tony."

Rock bit. "What's that mean?"

"We searched Miss Plat's room just a short while ago."

"And?"

"And found a number of Kewpie collectibles."

Rock shrugged this information off. "That's nothing.

You should see these rooms out at the Ramada. These folks fill their rooms with all sorts of Kewpies and Scootles and Ho-Hos. They're fanatics about the stuff."

Robinson was still grinning like she knew a secret and the rest of the world was in the dark. "These dolls and collectibles were special."

"Yes?" said Tony. "What was so special about these?"

Robinson had the pleasure of dropping another bomb and watching Rock and Tony's faces. "They appear to be the missing property from the Kewpiecon trade show."

"They what?" cried Tony.

"Have you checked with Duncan?" Rock said. "A lot of the stolen stuff was his. Has he confirmed this?"

"We haven't been able to find him this evening," replied Robinson. "We'll catch up to him tomorrow at the show."

Rock rubbed his weary eyes. "In spite of everything that's happened, I know one person who's going to be happy."

"Who's that?" Tony wondered aloud.

"Rick Elf, of course. Now that he's got his Kewpie Mountain back he'll be breathing a big sigh of relief."

"Not just yet he won't," said Robinson.

Rock set down his coffee, untouched. What he needed was sleep, not caffeine. "What do you mean?"

"We didn't find the Kewpie Mountain."

Tony tilted his head. "You mean, it wasn't in Miss Plat's room?"

"Nope."

"Maybe Virginia killed B.A.D., too," suggested Tony. "He might have caught her in the act."

Robinson rose. "That's all well and good. An interesting theory. But there's no evidence. Yet."

"I think Tony's right. Virginia might have let herself into the theater where, who knows, maybe B.A.D. hears her burgling the place and she kills him—"

"You're forgetting that B.A.D. was killed in his apartment behind the theater, not on the trade show floor."

"She might have dragged him there," Rock suggested, realizing the impossibility of mousy little Virginia dragging anybody several hundreds of feet across the floor, up the stairs and into B.A.D.'s apartment.

"Maybe they went back to his apartment for some reason. Maybe he was going to call the police from there. He turned his back and Virginia panicked and grabbed the nearest thing she could find—the knife—and stabbed him in the back."

Robinson admitted it was possible, if unlikely. "And with Virginia Plat herself dead, we may never know."

"We've got to discover who killed Miss Plat," said Tony, resolutely.

"Two stabbings. A real knife freak," remarked Rock.

"Seems to me, both killings could be the work of the same person," replied Robinson.

Tony nodded. "Somebody good with a knife."

Rock's breath caught in his throat. "I know somebody who's good with a knife."

Tony and Paula looked at him. Tony spoke, "You do?"

Rock nodded. "So do you."

Tony looked puzzled. "I can't think of anybody who—"

"Dewey Rood."

"Who?" asked Robinson.

"Dewey Rood."

"Rock, you don't mean that nice old man from dinner tonight?"

Rock was nodding vigorously. "Don't you remember his mom telling everyone how good he is with a knife?"

Tony searched his memory. "I guess I do." There had been some discussion at the table. What was it that Mr. Rood had said he did?

Rock explained for Robinson's benefit. "Dewey Rood makes carvings of Kewpie dolls, statues, and the like. Turns them into kitchen magnets and all sorts of things that he and his mother sell at shows like the Kewpiecon."

"Cleo, that's Dewey's mother, did say how great he was with the knife. I remember now," Tony found it hard to believe that harmless looking old man and his even more harmless looking and older mother could be involved in multiple murders but he wasn't naive enough to completely discount the idea either.

"Well, well," said Robinson. "Wait till Carvin and Chief Schaum hear about this. Do you think this Dewey character had time to kill Virginia Plat and still make it to the banquet?"

"Don't ask us, Miss Policeman. That's for you to figure out."

Robinson engaged Rock in a staring contest. "Miss Policeman will look into it."

Chapter 24

"I feel kind of bad throwing Mr. Rood to the police," Tony said the following morning as the boys headed out towards the Radisson.

"Don't," replied Rock. "All's fair in love and war and homicide investigations, especially if it gets Jim off the hook. Besides, old Dewey just might be guilty. He's got those squinty eyes and those weak lips. The killer type, if you ask me."

Tony nodded. Rock could be right—for once. He was looking forward to having a little chat with Cyndi Parker, B.A.D. Spike's now ex-assistant.

"Shall we check at the desk and have her called?" Rock was already heading through the automatic doors to the counter on the right.

"No," said Tony, grabbing Rock's arm and stopping him. "What if she doesn't want to talk to us?"

Rock shrugged. "Why wouldn't she?"

"Why would she? We're looking for suspects in her boss's murder. I wouldn't talk to us, if I was her. No, the element of surprise is what we need."

"What do you suggest then? Did you see the size of this place?" The Radisson was at least nine or ten stories tall and looked about a thousand feet long. "We can't exactly go knocking on every door. There are hundreds of them."

Tony looked around. "I've got an idea. Come on." Kozol found a house phone in an alcove near some offices, took a breath and picked it up. Tony called the front desk.

"Reception, Eric speaking."

"Hi, Eric, this is Larry, from room service." He struggled with his lame attempt at a deep-fried southern accent. "I've got an order for a Cyndi Parker. But there's some sort of mixup, I thought she was in six-thirty-nine, but when I got there it was the wrong darn room. I could call my boss, but I've only been here a couple of days and I don't want to get in any trouble. I'm kind of on probation and I was hoping maybe you could help me out. I'd be very appreciative."

"What was your name again?"

"Larry, Larry Fine." Tony shot Rock a nasty look and gave him a jab to stop his snickering. "Just moved to town. Lucky to find this job, I can tell you. Got a wife and a baby daughter."

"Just a sec—" Eric came back on the line and rattled off a number.

"What's that? Nine-oh-four? Got it. Thanks, Eric. I really owe you." Tony hung up.

"Sweet," said Rock, approvingly. "Such trusting naiveté. Only in Branson."

"Thanks," said Tony. "You think so? It was nothing." He pulled Rock across the lobby to the elevators on the opposite side. "Now let's just hope we can catch Miss Parker in her room."

Looking out over Branson through the glass-walled elevator, Rock said, "I still don't see why we're spending time talking to Cyndi Parker. If you ask me, there are more interesting suspects to interrogate."

"We've been all through this, Rock. Miss Parker could very well have been the last person to see Donald alive, besides the killer, that is. Who knows what she might have seen or heard? She may even be the killer."

"I'm sure the police have interviewed her thoroughly."

Tony smiled as the elevator opened on the ninth floor. "Suddenly you're a fan of the Branson Police Department, I see. That's a one-hundred and eighty degree switch in attitudes."

Rock scowled. He pushed the maid's cart out of his path and strode forward. The door to nine-oh-four was wide open and the maid was slowly, and not very well, from Tony's perspective, straightening the sheets. It was a poor job at best, with the ends of the sheets all clumped up in the corners, and the stout maid looked rather poorly herself.

Across the spacious room, Cyndi Parker sat half-buried in a plush chair in the far corner near the window, a telephone to her ear. The curtains were open, revealing an unencumbered view of the Grand Palace, Branson's largest theater. With four thousand seats, the Grand Palace was an imposing Southern plantation-style white mansion with a red roof. Towering white columns flanked the entrance.

The maid glanced in their direction then lowered her eyes quickly. There was something about those eyes that made Tony hesitate but he forgot all about them when Cyndi leveled her own peepers on him. She was the kind of woman that could bring a grown man to his knees.

Cyndi dropped the phone and shouted, "What are you doing here?"

Tony answered. "We came to talk to you about Donald's murder."

"Ha!" cried Cyndi, turning in her chair, recovering her phone from the floor and slowly replacing the receiver. "You aren't the police. You're those nosy musicians I been hearing about."

The woman was dressed to thrill in a pair of tight blue pedal pushers and an even tighter white spandex shirt. Tony wondered how the girl kept from suffocating. Miss Parker's feet balanced on stiletto heels that looked capable of punching holes in the thick carpet and maybe even the floor.

Rock winked at the maid, who quickly turned her head. "We're investigating B.A.D. Spike's murder."

"Everybody's a detective." Cyndi folded her legs and arms. She sat rigid in the chair, keeping her eye on the boys. "What do you want from me?"

The maid had shifted to the other side of the bed and was watching the action out of the corner of her eye. Tony looked sideways at the maid and the maid began fluffing the pillows to no avail. They laid there looking limp and lifeless as before.

"You were the last person to see Donald alive, besides the killer."

"Maybe. But, like I told the police, I was out when Donald was killed."

Rock couldn't help mouthing off. "Probably stabbed him on your way out."

"You! You there!" Cyndi was pointing to the maid.

The maid lifted her eyes and cleared her throat. "Me?"

"Yes, you," Cyndi said, arrogantly. "You see anybody else around here working? What's your name?"

The woman nervously cleared her throat. "Patty, ma'am."

"Patty, you think you can do up the bed so's it looks better than it did before you started?"

The maid reddened. "Yes, ma'am." The voice was squeaky and crackling.

Tony didn't recognize the voice, but by now he recognized those eyes. It was Jim. He'd gone all out this time, blonde wig, maid's uniform, black stockings and all. And was that a touch of mascara and lip gloss he was wearing? What on earth was he up to?

The maid fiddled with the covers a bit, turned her back to the group and began wiping the deep sink at the wetbar near the bed with her cleaning cloth.

Cyndi Parker shot a look of exasperation at the maid whom she obviously took for useless. "I'm gonna tell you what I know. I know that Donald was alive when I left the theater."

"Why did you leave that night?" Tony inquired. "After all, it was kind of late—for Branson, at any rate."

"Because Donald asked me to. Said he had some meeting, some business and he didn't want me around."

"Do you have any idea who might have killed him?"

"I told you, mister, I was out when Donald was murdered. I don't know what happened. If you don't believe me, ask the police, why don't you?"

Rock wiggled his fingers in the maid's direction. The big guy looked goofier than ever, having purchased a souvenir black Kewpiecon T-shirt with a picture of a coy looking Kewpie on the front with the expression—I ♥ Kewpies—along the top.

"Besides, Jim Stafford was the one found standing over his body. He was the one arrested." Parker was grinning. "Not me. Now, if you don't mind—" She waved towards the still open door.

"Come on, Rock."

"Okay," Rock reluctantly agreed. "But," he said, wagging a finger at Cyndi, "we believe Jim is innocent."

"Maybe."

"Is there anyone else you think might have had a reason to see Donald dead, Miss Parker?" Tony asked.

Cyndi shrugged. "A strong man makes enemies." She paused, deep in thought. "Still, not too many would have taken the step of killing him. I mean, Donald was a good man. Gonna miss him. If it wasn't Stafford," Parker said, "then I'd bet on Pearce."

"Merel Pearce?" Tony asked.

"Yeah. He's one ornery son-of-a-gun. I wouldn't put it past him."

"But what did he have to gain?"

"He'll get his theater back, won't he?"

"He wanted the theater back?" Rock said.

"That's right. He wasn't happy with what B.A.D.'s plans for the place were. You see, he thought the club was going to belong to some church and hold religious services."

"Where on earth did Mr. Pearce get that idea?"

Cyndi smiled. "The name of Donald's company is the Inner City Gospel Corporation."

"Cute," said Tony.

"Cute is right," agreed Cyndi. "So when Merel found out this black rapper dude from the city was coming in to do his show and going around tearing up the stage and remodeling big-time, he flipped out. Merel didn't want any part of it. That old cowboy didn't like what B.A.D. was doing to his town or his theater. Tried to get the theater back."

"And Donald wasn't giving it up?" Rock said.

"Not a chance." Cyndi shook her head. "And now he's dead and Merel wins."

There was a pregnant silence as Tony and Rock considered this information.

Cyndi Parker had stepped in front of the mirror and was shifting around some of her assets. "Sounds like a happy ending for somebody." She turned sideways, ran her hands along her thighs and seemed content with her profile.

Tony nodded then thanked Cyndi Parker for her time.

The maid was slowly straightening the closet, actually she—Jim—was more pushing things around senselessly. Empty hangers flitted from side to side across the metal pole. Tony tried to get Jim's attention but he acted like he was oblivious to them.

"There is one other person that I can think of who might have wanted Donald dead."

Tony and Rock stopped in their tracks. Tony turned. "Who is that?"

"Butch Domino."

Rock looked surprised. "Donald's manager?"

Cyndi nodded.

"But why would Donald's manager want his own client dead?"

"Yes, isn't that a bit counterproductive?" Tony added.

"You might think so, but Butch has a temper of his own. And Donald owed him money. Not to mention, Butch is from New York City and he didn't much appreciate moving out to Branson, Missouri. He didn't think much of B.A.D. Spike's Crib either. Butch always said being stuck in Branson was like being stuck in neutral and he couldn't wait to get out."

"Why did Donald owe Butch money?" Rock asked. "I mean, Butch worked for Donald, not vice versa."

"Going into business here cost all Donald had and more. He strong-armed Butch into loaning him about a quarter of a million. Butch didn't put up the cash very willingly. It was about all the money he had left.

"But Donald promised him it would pay off. He even promised to make him a partner eventually. I think the longer we stayed here the less Butch was coming to believe that."

Tony decided to take a chance. Dangle some bait. "Did you know that B.A.D. Spike's Crib was bugged?" asked Tony.

"Bugged? What do you mean?" Her brows formed a deep V over her nose.

"The police found several miniature listening devices in the apartment. Last I heard, they were looking for more."

Miss Parker scrunched up her face. "Who'd do a thing like that?"

Instead of answering, Tony asked another question. "Do you think Donald might have done it? Keeping tabs on his employees?"

Miss Parker scoffed at the idea. "No, that sounds more like the kind of no-good Butch himself would be up to. Maybe spying on Donald." A light went off in her head. "And me. Why, that son of a—"

"Where can we find him?" Tony asked.

Miss Parker's brain made a sharp right turn, but both the boys could tell this was only a temporary detour. "Butch has himself a room out at the Ramada."

"The Ramada?" This got Rock's attention. "The Kewpiecon rooms are at the Ramada."

Cyndi shrugged as if this meant nothing to her. "I don't know if he's there still. I tried to telephone him this morning. There was no answer."

Chapter 25

"What do you think?" Tony pressed the lobby button. They had the elevator to themselves.

"You sure got her attention with that bit about Donald's theater being bugged."

"You think Miss Parker really didn't know about it?"

"I don't think Cyndi Parker's a good enough actress. No, I think she was genuinely surprised."

"You think Butch Domino could be involved in all this somehow?"

"Why not? I'll bet Butch wouldn't have minded getting his hands on that Kewpie Mountain and selling it for one hundred thousand dollars," replied Rock. "That would go a long ways towards getting back what B.A.D. owed him."

Tony nodded. The elevator doors opened and they headed for the car. "He certainly had access, what with the trade show going on in B.A.D.'s theater."

"Yep." Rock took the wheel before Tony could intercede.

The Ramada wasn't far from the Radisson. Still, Tony braced himself for a rough ride.

Rock wormed his way into the flow of cars. "Means, motive and opportunity, isn't that what they say?"

"Okay," Tony stifled a yawn. This was turning out to be an exhausting week. He shook himself, struggling to keep his focus. And this trip wasn't even over yet. "Let's say Butch Domino is the killer. He's killed two people." He rattled them off on his fingers. "Donald Milquist, aka B.A.D. Spike, and Virginia Plat."

"Gives me the creeps," said Rock. "Remember the first time we saw him? At that restaurant where we met Jim? What a jerk." Rock was nodding and playing with the radio.

Tony twisted nervously in his seat. Neither of Rock's eyes seemed to be on the road, increasing his fear factor ten-fold. "He's stolen the Kewpie Mountain and the other collectibles. All together, let's say they are worth one hundred to one-hundred and fifty thousand dollars."

Rock whistled. "Sounds good to me." Rock parked, managing not to run over any possums, pedestrians or parking bumpers. The boys went to the inn's office. They had fished out their Kewpiecon badges to gain some respectability with the staff.

"Hi," Tony smiled broadly. "We're looking for Mr. Domino's room. He told us to come by this morning."

"He's got some Ho-Ho's for sale that I'm simply dying to see." Rock poured it on thick. He was a veritable honey pot when he wanted to be. And with that goofy shirt on, he fit right in with the rest of the Kewpie enthusiasts.

The smiling clerk, with puffed out platinum hair and fine, porcelain skin, shook her head. Her sharp blue eyes twinkled. "You Kewpie folks sure do love your dolls. And those windows y'all do up," as she spoke, her fingers checked the registry, "I sure get a kick out of those. Took my granddaughter over to see them yesterday, you know. Amazing." She looked up. "That's room three-forty-four, across the way."

"Thank you," Tony said.

"You men have a good day."

Rock waved and pulled open the door. "You, too."

The curtains to Butch's room were drawn. Rock put up his hand to knock. Tony wrapped his hand around Rock's and pulled it back. "Wait," he whispered. "Stop and think. If Butch is a killer, he may be armed."

They moved back away from the door.

"Good point. What do you suggest, Tony? I'm not exactly packing heat, are you?"

"Not unless you count my mentholating cream and I left that in my toiletry kit. Any suggestions?"

"I suggest I wring his neck, punch his lights out."

Tony knocked. They'd just have to take their chances.

Butch, in a wrinkled brown suit stepped briskly out, filling the entire gap neatly as a door-sized plug. He took one look at the boys. A flash of recognition appeared on his face and he slammed the door shut once again.

Rock lunged at the door. He grabbed the handle and pulled. It was locked. He banged. He kicked.

A maid across the parking lot was giving them funny looks.

"Hold it, Rock." Tony nodded towards the maid and Rock stopped assaulting Butch's door.

Rock was breathing hard in short, sharp breaths. "Give me some cover while I bust this door down."

"Forget it, Rock. You'll get us in all sorts of trouble."

"Then call the police. Call your girlfriend, Paula." Rock rattled the door knob.

"She is not my girlfriend. Will you get over it, already? Besides, what are we going to call the police and tell them? That we've got a hotel guest in his room with the door locked? That he won't talk to us no matter how much and how hard we threaten to kick in his door?"

Tony was relieved to see that the maid had gone into one of the open rooms with a cleaning bucket. He was also relieved to see that it wasn't Jim Stafford. "Face it, Rock, it's more likely that Butch is inside there right now calling the police on us."

Rock growled. He didn't admit it, but Tony was probably right. "What do we do?"

Tony fished his notebook out. He quickly wrote a short note and stuffed it under Butch's door.

"What's that all about?"

"When you're dealing with a dumb animal," explained Tony, "you've got to be direct if you want to get its attention."

"I thought I was doing that pretty well, myself," quipped Rock, giving the door an imaginary yet potentially savage kick which ended a hair's breadth from the door panel. Was it his imagination, or had he actually seen it flinch?

The door slowly opened.

Rock's eyebrows twisted into question marks. "What did you write on that note anyway?"

"I told him we knew what he'd done and that he could either talk to us or talk to the police, his choice."

"Clever."

Butch glared at them, his face large and flabby, like an out-of-shape pumpkin. He was unshaven.

Rock flashed a look of superiority and triumph. "Good choice, Butch." He shoved his way past Donald's manager and into the room, not bothering to wait for introductions or invitations.

Butch frowned and followed after him. Tony picked up the rear.

"What do you guys want?" Butch padded across the room and helped himself to a bottle of Jack Daniels that didn't have long to live.

"Little early in the day to be drinking, isn't it, Butch?" Rock looked disapproving.

He glowered at the big guy and downed his drink. "Who do you think you are, my nursemaid?" The glass slammed down on the bathroom counter with a jar that rattled Tony's teeth.

The room smelled of whiskey and cigars. Butch was a real class act. "Hardly," said Rock, "because if I was your nursemaid the first thing I'd do is put you on a diet. Ever hear of lettuce, Butch?"

Butch blustered and came at Rock with his open hand and it looked big enough to swat a watermelon. "Ever hear of a—"

"Try it," whispered Rock, unmoving and unblinking.

Tony jumped between them. "Don't mind Rock, Mr. Domino. He likes to make friends wherever he goes."

Tony's eyes bugged out in Rock's direction emitting 'Be nice' signals.

Butch backpedaled. "Talk fast," he said, turning to Tony. "I'm in a hurry."

"All packed, are you?" Tony noticed two overstuffed suitcases standing near the TV.

"That's right."

"I don't think the police want anyone leaving town just yet."

Rock picked up a briefcase lying on the nearer of the two double beds. "Nice leather."

Butch snatched it right out of his hands. "Leave that alone."

"State secrets?" asked Rock.

"Never you mind." Butch hoisted the briefcase and stuck it on the top shelf of the small closet beside the bath. The shelf was narrow and the valise stuck out like a sore thumb. "I don't like people touching my stuff." He turned and folded his arms across his chest. He directed his look at Tony once more. "You ain't talkin' fast enough."

Tony cleared his throat. "We're looking into the murder of B.A.D. Spike."

"Why?"

Butch stood as unmoving as a slab of marble. With a body like that, Tony feared it would take Hurricane Hugo to move him. Good thing he had Rock along in case things got ugly. "That's an odd question. B.A.D. was your boss, your friend, probably."

"You aren't cops."

"No," Tony said, "we're not, we—"

"You're nothing but a couple of musicians." Butch's nostrils flared.

If he'd been a bull, Tony would have figured Butch was about ready to charge them. He wasn't a bull and he half-feared it anyway. Kozol found himself stepping back. "That's right. We were hired by Nanci Dement to perform at Kewpiecon." Assuming they still had jobs.

Butch raised his hands. "Then why don't you go play dolls with the rest of those doll people? Stop messing around where you don't belong."

"Where *we* don't belong?" boomed Rock. "We have every right to take an interest in this case. I would think you would be interested, too, Butch."

"My interest in B.A.D. ended when he died. Time to move on. I suggest you all do the same."

"Jim has asked us to help look into this matter. Clear his name."

Butch snorted and Tony ignored it.

"Do you have any idea who might have wanted your boss dead, Mr. Domino?"

"Jim Stafford."

"Impossible," Rock said. "You can do better than that, Butch. Jim and B.A.D. were friends."

"You're crazy, buddy. They hated each other. The whole town knew." His eyes were thin and sharp as razors.

"But that was all an act," said Tony.

"Act?" Butch laughed. "I heard all about Stafford trying to spread that lie." He leaned into Tony. "That's all it is, a lie." Butch seemed to be enjoying himself. He had a real sadistic streak.

Tony had to admit, this guy was good. Good at getting under a person's skin, like a hungry and nasty little tick, and clinging there for the duration. A guy like Butch was bound to make enemies, some who'd probably have loved to shut him up, permanent like. Maybe Mr. Domino had simply beaten his adversaries to the punch. In this case, the deadly punch. "I hear B.A.D. owed you money."

"Lots of money," added Rock.

Butch's whole body shrugged as one. Tony feared a room-size earthquake.

"Yeah, B.A.D. he owed me some money, so what?" He wiped spittle from the corner of his mouth. "Him dead doesn't do me any good, does it? I mean, he can't pay me back from the grave." He bared his teeth. "If you guys know what's good for you, you'll give up this murder angle and get back to playing with Kewpie dolls."

Rock stifled the urge to swat the ugly man. "Big words for a little man."

This set Butch laughing.

Tony feared a fight coming on and moved to cut it off. "You don't care at all who killed B.A.D., do you?"

The laughter stopped. "Nope, Mr. Nosey, I don't. Dead is dead. What I care about is where my next job is coming from. Butch has to take care of Butch."

"Did you take care of yourself by planting listening devices in B.A.D.'s theater?" demanded Tony.

"You're nutty," retorted Butch. "I don't know what you're talking about."

Tony kicked the bedcovers that dragged to the floor, hoping to get a look under the bed. People kept all kinds of secrets under beds. "Someone planted several bugs in Donald's apartment."

"So that's how—" Butch hesitated. "It wasn't me. What do you think? You think I sat around listening in on B.A.D. when he was boinking his girlfriend or eating his breakfast? How's that gonna help me?"

Much to his chagrin, Tony couldn't come up with an answer.

Rock came to his rescue. "I'll bet a whole *mountain* of cash would go a long way towards helping Butch." Rock cocked his right eyebrow as if symbolically drawing a blade.

"How did you know about that?" His eyes darted to the briefcase full of cash he'd picked up at Merel Pearce's home, then narrowed and bored through the back of Rock's skull.

"It's not exactly a state secret, is it?" interjected Tony. "Even the local paper has reported the mountain missing."

"Huh? What's that supposed to mean?"

Rock explained. "It means whoever has the Kewpie Mountain stands to make himself a chunk of change."

Butch looked at Rock quite stupidly. "Kewpie Mountain? I thought you said those Kewpie things were dolls?"

"Right," said Rock, slowly. "Well, this is a mountain of dolls and it's worth a mountain of cash."

"How much cash?"

Was Tony mistaken or were those dollar signs flashing before Mr. Domino's eyes? Maybe he was only succumbing to the fetid blend of booze and cigars. Kozol was all for cutting this little interview short and getting a health-restoring dose of fresh air.

"One hundred thousand dollars," pronounced Rock, "maybe more."

"Really," drawled Butch. He grinned. "Now ain't that something." He moved to the door. "Time to go, boys. Go play dollhouse with your little friends. Butch has got some thinking to do."

"But—"

He slammed the door in their faces.

Chapter 26

"I wish you would talk to him."

Merel Pearce's daughter, Sherry, threw herself down at the breakfast table in the chair beside her mother's. She made a determined effort to appear most upset. It was a well and often rehearsed look.

Her mother looked sympathetic, but answered, "I'll try but you know it won't do any good. It never does any good." She poured a generous helping of artificial sweetener into her coffee and stirred. "Your daddy isn't real fond of Aaron. You know that, Sherry."

"He's never fond of any man I like. Why can't he let me alone instead of chasing everyone I ever care about off?" She reached into the vase in the center of the table and bent an unsuspecting tulip stem in half. "I hate him."

Mrs. Pearce admonished her daughter and told the cook, Sylvie, to fix Sherry some breakfast. "Have a bite to eat," coaxed Dolly. "You're tired. It's low blood sugar that's making you talk this way."

Sherry ignored the cold bran flakes that were suddenly and silently thrust upon her. "I really do hate him. He isn't even nice to you, Mother. I don't know why you stick with the man."

Dolly glanced awkwardly at Sylvie whose back was to them as she bent over the sink rinsing off breakfast plates. The sweet scent of the toast and orange-lemon marmalade on her plate no longer tempted her. "It isn't good, what you say, Sherry." And more softly she said, "And you shouldn't go around speaking that way about your daddy when there are others about."

"What? Sylvie? I don't care if she does hear me. I don't care who hears me."

In an about-face, Sherry rose and draped her arms over her mother's small shoulders. "Please, Mama. I'm in love with Aaron. I'm going to marry him whether you and Daddy like it or not."

"Sherry—"

"I am. And if Daddy doesn't like it, then that's simply too bad. If he won't be nice to Aaron, then me and Aaron are going to run off."

"Sherry, you don't mean it."

"I do, Mama. We've talked and talked about it."

"But what would you do? Where could you go?"

"I don't know and I don't care. We'll get in the car and drive as far away from Branson and Daddy as we can get." She removed her arms and stuffed her hands in her pockets. "Let's see how Daddy likes that."

Johnny Jones loped slowly and soundlessly into the kitchen where he said good morning to Sylvie and helped himself to the coffee pot. "Morning, ladies." He took a position between mother and daughter, effectively and neatly cutting the tension between them as professionally as if he were an obstetrician severing an umbilical cord. "What's up?"

"Daddy's what's up," moaned Sherry. "And I've had it up to here." She marked an imaginary point on her forehead with the side of her hand. "Can't you talk to him, Johnny?"

Johnny was like a kind, old uncle. He'd been around forever and never said anything derogatory or scolded Sherry in any way.

Johnny set down his coffee and glanced at Dolly Pearce before speaking. "You know I can't go doing that, Sherry." A person didn't stay with Merel Pearce thirty years talking back to him. And Johnny was too old a dog to start looking for a new owner.

"Of course not," said Mrs. Pearce.

"I think you're both cowards." Sherry's face was red with pent up frustration. She ran from the room and the sound of her footsteps carried up the stairs.

Even though she was expecting it, Dolly flinched when Sherry's door slammed shut with a bang like an audible exclamation point. "Sherry's talking about running off, Johnny."

He nodded and blew a head of water vapor across his coffee cup. "I know. I heard." He patted Dolly's hand. "Don't give it no mind, Mrs. Pearce. "Sherry's just letting off steam. She'd never leave home."

"I hope not," Mrs. Pearce said quietly. She looked out over the garden. "She's all I've got." Her home, her husband and her daughter, they were really all she had, all she wanted.

Sylvie left the room and Johnny said, "Did you hear

they found that body down at the old theater?"

Dolly Pearce's face sagged. "I heard."

Johnny sat silently a moment, sipping his coffee slowly. "Is there anything I can do?"

Dolly's shoulders twitched. "I don't know, Johnny. I just don't know." She turned to him. "What went wrong, Johnny? Life used to be so nice. Even when we didn't have all this money. We had good times, Merel and I. And now everything is so—" Her gaze wandered around the huge kitchen. A person could get lost in a house this big. Guests sometimes did. "So messed up."

Dolly sighed. She could hear the sounds of loud music leaking through the ceiling. Sherry was playing her stereo full blast. Rap music. That silly B.A.D. Spike man. Probably to annoy her. Sherry had ordered B.A.D. Spike's best-of collection right after he'd come to town and leased the theater.

Dolly often wondered what it was about her daughter that made her want to challenge her daddy so much. Merel hated that music and had forbidden his daughter to play it. "Sometimes I believe there is no making it right again."

Johnny rose. Merel was expecting him. It was nearly eleven o'clock. "I hate seeing you this way, Mrs. Pearce. Are you sure there isn't something I can do?"

Dolly almost imperceptibly shook her head. "I don't think so, Johnny. I don't think so."

Dolly listened to the echo of Johnny Jones' boots headed towards her husband's office. "Just pray," she said softly. "Just pray."

Chapter 27

"Chief, we got an ID on that corpse down at the Mongrel Theater."

"What body at the Mongrel Theater?"

Robinson stood at the door to Chief Schaum's office. "Sorry, I mean B.A.D. Spike's Crib, the old Mongrel Theater, not the new one. I get mixed up sometimes."

"Hard to get used to the changes around here, ain't it?" remarked the chief. "Sometimes I get confused myself and I've lived here all my life."

Robinson nodded but kept her mouth shut. She'd been with the force long enough to know when Chief Schaum did and did not expect a reply.

"You're not from here, Paula. Springfield, correct?"

Robinson said yes.

"I can remember when Highway 76 was a little old creek of a road compared to what it is now. A few motels and a couple of shows, like the Baldknobbers. We had Silver Dollar City, of course, and Shepherd Of The Hills. And the Owens Theater downtown has been there more than sixty years, but not all this."

"Yes, chief."

"And we sure didn't have a big, fancy new head-quarters like this either." Chief Schaum laid down his pen. "I can't say whether it's been good or bad."

"A little of both, I expect."

Chief Schaum's eyes twinkled. "I suspect you're right." He folded his hands. "Now, I can tell by the look on your face and that somber tone of your voice that there's something you're not telling me and," he drawled, "the truth is, I've been reminiscing here, putting off hearing what it is. So, spit it out, Paula. What have you got and why ain't I gonna like it?"

The captain motioned for Officer Robinson to sit and she did so. "To begin with, like I said, the lab came up with a positive ID on the John Doe that contractor dug up when he started remodeling the stage at Donald Milquist, aka B.A.D. Spike's theater. The ID using dental and medical records jibes with the driver's license found in the victim's wallet."

"His wallet was found?"

"Yes, sir, in cement a couple of feet from the body."

"Who was he?"

"A young man named Ned Ledbetter."

Chief Schaum scratched his head. "Sounds familiar. Why?"

"It should sound familiar," said Robinson. She had a pad in hand and looked through her notes. "Ned Ledbetter, age twenty, was last seen close to four years ago. Carvin interviewed his ma and pa. They live out near Forsythe."

"I remember now," Chief Schaum said. "A missing person case. That was before your time, wasn't it?"

"Yes, sir."

"Poor folks." Chief Schaum shook his head. "They must be mighty upset. I remember they took it pretty hard when Ned disappeared. I told them he'd probably run off somewhere. Some kids will do that, you know."

Robinson nodded.

The chief sighed. "Guess I was wrong." He thought about his own two daughters, now both married and settled down. Thank Heaven they'd both turned out all right. "So how did the boy die? I don't imagine he drowned in a pool of liquid concrete."

"No, sir, I'm sure he didn't. But no one has come up with a good explanation of how he did die or how he ended up at the bottom of that stage." Robinson cleared her throat and fidgeted. "We do have some promising leads, however."

Chief Schaum scowled. "Stop squirming around, girl, and spit it out, will you? I ain't no delicate flower. I'm a grown man and I've been on the police force since I was twenty years old, myself. Whatever you've got to say, say it." He leaned over his desk and waited impatiently.

"Carvin interviewed the Ledbetters—"

"You already told me that."

"Yes, sir. And the Ledbetters mentioned a couple of other folks who had given statements to the police back around the time that their son disappeared."

"So?"

"Did you know that Ned Ledbetter had been work-ing for Jim Stafford at the time he disappeared?"

Chief Schaum scratched his droopy jowls with the side of a finger. "Seems to me I remember something of the sort. What of it?"

Robinson laid the notebook in her lap and looked her boss in the eye. "According to those witnesses, chief, Ned Ledbetter had been seen in a heated argument with Mr. Stafford late in the afternoon of the day he is suspected to have disappeared."

Chief Schaum let out a long, low breath. "And you think Mr. Stafford, a pillar of our little community, might have had something to do with this Ledbetter's death?"

"Carvin and I have discussed the possibility."

"Impossible," said the chief. He was shaking his head.

"I know how you feel, chief, but let me explain. According to his folks and others, Ned Ledbetter was a sort of all around handyman for the Staffords. Worked at Stafford's theater and his house. Then one day, Mr. Stafford up and fires him. For no reason, according to Ledbetter's parents. We even found the remnants of Ned Ledbetter's last paycheck, his severance pay, dated the day he was last seen alive."

"Where did you find this?"

"It was in his billfold. A check for over eleven-hundred dollars. That's a lot of money to a kid like Ledbetter. I called on the bank and a teller there remembered Ned. She said Ledbetter normally cashed his checks the same day they were cut. He was always short on money, she said. And that check went uncashed."

Robinson paused a moment to let the news sink in, then added, "Because the boy never had time to deposit or cash it."

Chief Schaum whistled.

"It's signed by Jim Stafford."

Chief Schaum rose from his seat and paced his small office. "Tell me, Robinson, how did Ned Ledbetter end up in a cement coffin in B.A.D. Spike's Crib if, as you say, he was working for Mr. Stafford? I mean, I could see you might have something if the boy's body had been uncovered at the Jim Stafford Theater, but this is stretching things."

Robinson stayed seated. "In Mr. Stafford's original statement to the police four years ago, he stated that he had fired Ned Ledbetter while he was working in his home and then had given the boy a ride into town himself that evening as the boy didn't have a car of his own."

"Ledbetter wasn't living with his folks?"

"No, sir. He had an apartment on Fall Creek Road. But Mr. Stafford stated that the boy wanted to be dropped off on the Strip."

"Where on the Strip?"

"The Mongrel Theater."

The chief stopped pacing. His face displayed an evenly divided look of disbelief and shock. "You're saying that instead of dropping Ledbetter off at the theater, Jim Stafford killed the boy and hid the body in Pearce's theater?"

"It is a possibility."

The chief frowned, deep in thought. After a moment, he relaxed. "Wait just a minute. If Stafford had dropped Ledbetter off at Merel's theater in the evening, there'd have been plenty of witnesses. No, there's no way Jim Stafford could have dragged a dead body through a theater full of people."

Robinson was shaking her head. "The theater was empty."

"Empty?"

"It was a Monday night. Merel doesn't work on Mondays, remember?"

The chief did.

"And the theater was undergoing some renovations at the time, though Mr. Pearce was working around them, according to the contractor."

"Was that Andrew Jergen?"

"Yes, sir. According to Cyndi Parker, B.A.D. had hired him because he had worked on the theater previously. I guess he figured the work would go quicker that way."

The chief nodded. Jergen did good work and was always in demand around town. When folks found someone good, they kept him busy. He caught Robinson's eye and held it. "And you want me to arrest Jim Stafford?"

Robinson didn't say no. "What if Mr. Stafford killed B.A.D. because B.A.D. was going to dig up the theater? He might have had in mind to try and stop the work. Keep anybody from finding Ledbetter's body."

The chief held back a groan. He could see the headline already. And it wasn't pretty. He'd taken enough flak from the locals already for merely asking Jim to bring in that dang Kewpie doll. Stafford was a popular guy. He had done tons of good for the community, they said, as if he didn't know it.

The chief hadn't believed for a moment that Stafford had anything to do with stealing dolls. He was simply following regs when he questioned Mr. Stafford.

"It seems to me, in light of these new events, we should at least ask him a few questions. We owe it to the boy's family."

Chief Schaum closed his eyes and silently said a prayer. The occasional reckless driver, a drunk or two, maybe a car break-in, that was a crime wave in Branson. Suddenly he was hip deep in dead bodies when he ought to be hip deep in rainbow trout. "Fine," he said, "but we go easy on this. And we don't tell any reporters."

Chapter 28

Rock was simmering as Tony started up the car and cranked up the cold air. "That was pleasant."

"What did you expect from a guy like Butch? Tea and scones?" Tony scribbled some notes.

"Come to think of it, I am kind of hungry."

"You're always hungry."

"What are you writing?"

"Some thoughts. You know, Rock, I don't think Butch knew about the Kewpie Mountain."

"I don't want to hear it." Rock looked like he'd sunk his teeth into a lemon. "That slimeball is guilty of something. I just know it."

"Maybe," agreed Tony. "But what?"

"Killing B.A.D., I hope." Rock arched his back. "Maybe Butch took out an insurance policy on B.A.D. Trying to get some of his investment back." He still worried Jim might be guilty, but he was such a nice guy, he hoped it wouldn't prove to be true.

"That's possible." Tony closed his notepad and put the car in gear.

"Sure. Probably for a million bucks or so. But how are we going to prove it?" His fingers drummed against the window. "I know, why don't you ask your girlfriend, Paula?"

Tony held his tongue. His phone was ringing and he figured he'd ignore it. Rock dredged out from between the seats and pressed the send button. "It's Nanci," Rock said with some surprise. He pushed the phone to Tony's ear.

Tony tried vainly to push it away. "What are you giving it to me for?"

Rock squeezed himself into the corner of the car.

"Hello? Nanci?"

A string of vindictives flew out, filling the car with ire. "Where are you clowns? When are you going to get here? What am I paying you for?"

"You see, Miss Dement," Tony began, "we've been very busy. I know I promised we'd be there. It's just that something came up and—" She interrupted with another string of foul language. Tony had no idea folksingers could be so colorful. "We really are quite dependable."

"I'm in a meeting. You've got one hour. One hour," she said, slamming down the phone.

Tony blanched. "Yes, Miss Dement."

"What did she say" asked Rock, though he'd heard plain enough. "She want to see us?"

"Actually I think she wants to fry us in hot peanut oil."

Rock grabbed the phone. "You want me to talk to

her?"

"Oh, sure. Now you want to talk to her, Mr. Ladies Man."

Rock looked at Tony. "Well?"

Tony threw the car in gear. "We've got about an hour. Time to take the bull by the horns." No way he was going to let everybody run over him and his life. That had been happening too much already. "The way I see it, we smooth things over with Nanci, help Jim out of his jam and do a little story on Kewpie dolls and—"

"—And live happily ever after?"

"You got it."

"I'm buying," said Rock. "So where are we off to?"

"Merel Pearce's house."

"That arrogant son-of-a-gun? What for? Even if he's home, Merel isn't going to see us. He wouldn't throw either of us a life preserver if we were drowning in Lake Taneycomo and offered him twenty bucks to boot."

"You're probably right. That's why we're going to talk to Dolly."

"His wife?"

"That's right. You saw her at her husband's theater. She's a sweetheart. Plus, she thinks we're doing a nice story on her husband. She'll talk to us."

Rock grinned. "Unless Merel has talked to her first and told her who we really are."

Tony turned about and headed towards Table Rock Lake. "Something tells me that Merel Pearce is not the type of husband who shares a lot with his wife. If you ask me, he's the kind who keeps his cards close to his vest, to coin a phrase."

Rock laughed. "You're turning into a local, Tony.

Soon you and Paula will be settling down and raising a couple of fiddle players."

"Rats." Tony looked across Highway 265. He'd read in one of the Branson guidebooks that Merel Pearce had a home in the exclusive Trails' End Country Club but he hadn't considered that it might be a gated community. Tony studied his goal from a well-worn patch of hard dirt opposite the entrance.

Rock watched as the lanky uniformed guard routinely stopped each vehicle at the gatehouse before lifting the gate arm and allowing entry. It was a bright, hot afternoon and water from raised sprinklers rained happily down on the multicolored flower beds while a gardening crew worked diligently sprucing things up. "Now what?"

One of the gardeners had hopped over the gate arm with a weed whacker and was attacking the grass growing along the edge of the wall. Tony waited until the traffic thinned out then headed up the highway. He found a spot to cross and turned, coming to a stop behind a clump of trees on the same side of the highway as the Trail's End entrance.

"What exactly are we doing?" Rock followed Tony out of the car. "Going over the wall?"

Tony shushed him. "Follow me," he whispered. "Hurry."

He spotted a middle-aged, modestly paunchy, Latin-looking fellow with a lumpy briquet of hair heading for the pickup truck. He appeared to be the supervisor.

He was starting their way.

Tony put a foot up on the back of the trailer attached to the truck and hauled himself up.

Rock leapt in after him. He clutched the sides of a riding lawn mower as the truck and trailer lurched forward. "Give me a hand."

Tony grabbed Rock's arm and pulled him up and over. The big guy wasn't all that graceful. "Keep your head down, Rock." Tony scrunched himself up in a pile of grass shavings and tree limbs and motioned for Rock to do the same.

"What on earth are you thinking?" Rock said softly.

"You saw the kid with that weed whacker go behind the gate. The way I figure it, they're finishing up the outside and about to go in." Tony smiled. "And they're going to take us with them."

Rock thought about this for a moment. "And what if this guy's heading for the dump or an incinerator or something? Have you thought about that? I do not feel like having my limbs set fire to like these tree limbs."

"Quiet." Tony pushed Rock's head lower and covered herself with more grass. The back of the slat-sided trailer held the earthy scent of fresh-cut grass. "We won't have to worry about that. The driver's headed straight for the gate."

True enough, the truck pulled up from the edge of the road where it had been parked and came to a stop at the gate. The guard laid his hands on the open window frame. "Hey, George, you catch the Pistons last night?"

"Yeah, some game, eh?"

Tony stole a glance out the lowest slat, praying the guard wouldn't notice. Come on, come on. He sent out thought waves begging the guard to open the gate and let the driver on through. The longer they sat here the more likely they were to be exposed.

What if one of the workers came to the trailer looking for some piece of lawn equipment or a drink of water from the cooler attached to the back edge of the trailer?

A mower started up nearby, catching Tony off guard.

"What's going on?" asked Rock, who couldn't see a thing.

"Nothing, they're shooting the breeze. Don't worry about—" His phone went off with a loud trill. Tony's breath caught in his throat. He dug in his pocket, dove under cover and answered.

"Hey, your phone's ringing, George."

The driver picked his cell phone off the dash. "I don't think so."

"Hello?" whispered Tony.

"Hi, Tony. This is Paula."

"Oh, uh, Paula."

"Is everything all right? Are you okay?"

"Okay? Oh, yes. Just fine. But I'm kind of busy right now, Paula."

A shiny green Cadillac pulled up behind the trailer and its driver honked. Tony rolled himself up into a little ball. If the driver saw them, they were sunk.

"I heard a horn. Are you in your car?"

"Yes. Hard to talk when I'm driving." The pickup lurched forward pulling the trailer along with it. The guard was waving to the driver and the Cadillac was following on its heels. "Can I call you back later?"

The vibration of the trailer under motion was loosening his camouflage. The Cadillac's driver was right behind them. Tony was afraid to even try to improve his situation for fear of being spotted. "See you." Tony cut the connection and ripped the battery pack off the back of the phone.

The boys held their collective breath as the landscape vehicle passed the gate. They came to a stop in a smallish lot behind the gatehouse. They heard the pickup's door open and slam shut.

"Quick!" Tony said. He pushed himself free of the yard debris and crawled his way to the back of the trailer. Soundlessly, he fell to the ground with Rock right behind. They turned to the side of the trailer as George came up, grabbed a rake off the back end and joined his mates.

"That was close," whispered Rock.

Tony sneezed. All that grass and pollen, no doubt. "Come on," he said, straightening his knees and wiping himself free of yard debris. "Now all we have to do is find Pearce's house."

"What's the address?" Rock scanned the horizon. Trail's End was big. And like most of the Ozarks, it was anything but flat. They were in for a walk no matter how close Merel's home was to the entrance.

"I'm not sure. Something-lane. I saw a picture of the house in one of the guidebooks about Branson. Don't worry, I'll recognize it when I see it."

"Something lane?" Rock groaned. They were in for a long walk. A long, long walk.

Chapter 29

By the time Tony did find Merel Pearce's house, Rock was about ready to collapse. He considered his big legs to be built more for propping up atop a thick ottoman than hiking through the hills.

At least they had reached their destination. It was touch and go there for a while. And unlike anything Rock was expecting, the Pearce home was a large, pleasant-looking estate reminiscent of a Tuscan villa, where he had been expecting a rustic log cabin and plenty of bull horns. But instead of overlooking the Mediterranean, this villa was on a golf course looking out over Table Rock Lake.

There was a white van parked near the top of a circular drive. If that drive had been straightened out, it would have been long enough to land a Cessna on. According to the stenciling on the van's side, the vehicle belonged to a place called *Ozark Mountains*

Shoe Repair.

"Perfect," grumbled Rock. He had stopped and was leaning a sweaty palm against the Pearce's mailbox post for support. He pulled off his right shoe and massaged his foot with his free hand. "Because I've just about worn this pair of shoes out. Maybe these Ozark Mountain people can fix me up. Should've worn sneakers. Would have, if I'd known what you had in mind."

Tony wasn't waiting and was halfway up the long drive and heading for the main doors, two ten foot tall, intricately carved and burnished rectangles of wood with massive bronze door pulls. "Come on, will you, Rock?"

Rock groused some more, winced as he stuck his shoe back on, and hobbled up the drive. He was going to have blisters on the bottoms of his feet, he just knew it. Forget the sneakers. He should have worn hiking boots.

The doors opened as Tony took the first step up the raised threshold. A plump, round headed man with a receding hairline was coming out. His crisp, white shirt was embroidered with the name *Hal* above the name *Ozark Mountains Shoe Repair.*

Dolly Pearce stood in the doorway wearing a peach-colored house dress, yellow shoebox in hand. "Thank you so much for bringing these out to me, Hal." She held up the shoebox.

"You're welcome, ma'am. I'm only glad I could get a new heel for you on such short notice."

"Thank goodness for overnight delivery," chirped Mrs. Pearce.

Hal nodded and headed for his van. He rolled down

the passenger side window and waved.

Dolly had stepped out onto the front porch. "I'll be sure my husband gets you tickets for his show Thursday."

Hal shouted out a thank you and slowly curved away.

"Hello, boys," said Dolly. "This is a surprise."

At least she's smiling, thought Tony. That's a good sign.

"What are you doing here? If you're working on your story, I'm afraid Merel isn't in."

Tony couldn't have been happier and improvised accordingly. "Actually, we were hoping to have a word with you, Mrs. Pearce." Tony held his breath. Dolly Pearce seemed to mull this over. Was she going to ask how they'd gotten in the neighborhood?

"Yes, we wanted to get your perspective. Being the wife of a famous country star and all." Ignoring his aching feet, Rock hobbled up and placed an arm around Dolly's shoulders. "Perhaps you'd even allow me to take your picture for the magazine?"

"Picture?" Mrs. Pearce stuck the shoebox under her arm and fluffed up her hair. "What magazine did you say this story was for?"

"I didn't," said Tony.

"What my partner means," said Rock, "is that the agency we work for, the David Bowie Agency, sells our stories to many, many outlets. In fact, we're thinking Good Housekeeping or Ladies Home Journal on this one."

"Oooh," cooed Mrs. Pearce. "Really?"

Rock's head bobbed up and down. "Uh-huh." He pulled the shoebox from Dolly just as it was about to fall to the ground.

Sometimes Tony found Rock's ability to lie with such facility frightening.

"Thank you, dear," replied Mrs. Pearce. She stepped away from the door. "Come inside, won't you? It's quite warm today." She tugged at her dress. "And humid."

Rock rushed inside. Tony slowly followed.

"Come into the parlor, gentlemen." Mrs. Pearce rubbed the corner of her left eye.

"Are you all right, Mrs. Pearce?" Tony had noticed the woman's inflamed red eyes when he came to the door.

"Yes, fine, thank you."

They passed through a long hallway bisecting the center of the home. In the kitchen, Tony noticed a young woman slumped in a barstool at the island. She was minimally attired in denim short-shorts and a red halter top, twisted into a knot at the middle. The girl was crying and looked up as Tony and Rock entered.

"Who are they?" The girl's face was blotchy and her face all puffy. She was looking at Tony and Rock as if they were a couple of unwanted strays passing through her otherwise perfect home.

"These gentlemen are here to interview me for a magazine article, baby. Isn't that wonderful?"

"Yeah," said the girl, sniffling and wiping her nose with an already damp handkerchief. "Wonderful, Mother."

"This is my daughter, Sherry." She patted the girl on the arm. "She's a bit upset." Mrs. Pearce daubed her own eyes once more. "I'm afraid it's catching."

"Are you sure we aren't coming at a bad time, Mrs.

Pearce?" Tony asked once more.

Mrs. Pearce smiled bravely. "No, no. The bad times are when we need something to cheer us up. Perhaps you'd like to interview Sherry for your article?"

"Of course," Rock said quickly.

Sherry jumped off her stool and headed for the stairs. "No, thank you."

There was an awkward silence as Sherry Pearce's footsteps faded to nothing.

"I'm afraid Sherry's taking all this very hard," began Mrs. Pearce as she led the boys to the parlor and pointed them to a couple of comfortable looking recliners.

"All what?" Rock asked.

"Rock—" Tony shot her friend one of those, 'You idiot, that's none of our business' looks.

"That's all right." Mrs. Pearce settled down on the sofa beside a half-empty glass of something brown and bubbly. "It's all this murder business. So many dead bodies." She was shaking her head.

"Yeah," quipped Rock, "a real Branson bloodbath."

Tony rolled his eyes. Rock could be a bit insensitive at times.

But Mrs. Pearce only nodded in agreement. "Yes, and now this latest with the poor Ledbetter boy."

"Ledbetter boy?" Tony leaned forward. Had he missed something.

"That's the young man whose body was found at my husband's old theater. Can you imagine?"

"I knew there was a body found but I didn't know the authorities had identified it," Tony said softly. It seemed worse somehow, now that there was a name to go with the body.

"Yes." Mrs. Pearce sipped her drink. "Can I get you boys something? A soft drink?"

"No, thank you," Tony said.

"I'd like some ice water," Rock replied. Though a six-pack would have been perfect.

Mrs. Pearce called for Sylvie and relayed Rock's request. Sylvie returned moments later with a tall glass of water packed with ice. Rock, who'd all but forgotten he was carrying Dolly's shoes, set the box on the carpet. "Ceruccis," he commented, reading the box for the first time. "Nice."

"Yes, but quite delicate. The heels keep falling off."

"Hey, beautiful things are always high maintenance," Rock said. He ignored his ice water and opened the box. "Yeah, these babies are worth it."

"Did you know this Ledbetter boy, Mrs. Pearce?" Tony was looking out the big pane of glass which so neatly framed the woods and the lake below. A head with a white cap popped into view then disappeared from sight. How odd.

"No." Mrs. Pearce folded her hands. "I suppose I'd seen him around town. Branson is still a small town, you understand."

Tony nodded. The head at the window appeared and disappeared once more. The cap and dark sunglasses hid his face, but Tony had a horrible suspicion. He tried to get Rock's attention but he was too busy ogling Mrs. Pearce's shoes and swilling his ice water.

"Pardon me," Tony said. He rose. "Is that a bathroom I see over there?" There was an open door on the far side of the parlor and, with luck, there would be another door leading to the outside deck.

Mrs. Pearce said it was. "Please, help yourself."

"Thank you." Tony excused himself and hurried off. He had no doubt Rock would keep Mrs. Pearce occupied while he cornered Jim. Because Jim Stafford it had to be and Tony had to get him out of there.

What was that nut up to now? Didn't he realize how much danger he kept putting himself in going around undercover and spying on folks?

Sure enough, there was a glass door in the bathroom leading outside. He pressed his nose against the window but there was no sign of Jim. Slowly, he pushed open the door. A beep came from somewhere overhead. There must be a security system in place. His Aunt Louise had one at her house and every time you opened a door, the thing beeped.

Tony only hoped Mrs. Pearce didn't give it any thought. A big house like this, and with Sherry and the housekeeper and maybe others about as well, doors could go beeping all the time.

Leaving the door ajar, Tony stepped outside. The yard was huge. A golf course ran through a good fifty yards away with a low perimeter fence separating it from the Pearce yard. Somebody's errant golf ball had ended up half-buried beside the birdbath. Beyond that, the ground sloped down where the woods led up to the lake. There was a small dock visible at the edge.

A movement in the thick bushes at the nearest window caught Tony's attention. He tiptoed over, holding his breath and sneaked up on Jim from behind. He was costumed in a pair of white painter's pants, a white T-shirt and had that goofy cap on his head. He had a squeegee in one hand and a long, aluminum pole in the other.

Tony grabbed his elbow and spun him around.

"Jim, what on earth are you—"

He cried out, dropping his window washing equipment. He stepped back, pulling himself free. He lost his sunglasses in the flowerbed.

It wasn't Jim. It wasn't even a Jim Doppelgänger. And his eyes, which were very visible, being that they were bugging out in frightful surprise, were clearly green.

Tony went red. "Ooops. Sorry, I thought you were someone else."

The man puffed out his chest and blustered. "You want your windows washed or you don't want your windows washed?"

"Yes, please. I want the windows washed." Tony forced a smile. "Please, continue. I'm sorry."

The man bent over and retrieved his squeegee. Plucking a rag from his side pocket, he wiped the blade, leaving a track of brown on his cloth. "I cannot work like this. The blade is all dirty. The dirt can ruin the blade. Make tiny nicks. Ruin it completely."

He held the blade up to Tony's nose. "The blade must be clean and free of defects," he said, giving it a shake. "Otherwise the windows will be all streaky."

He leaned in, reeking of vinegar and added, "You want streaky windows, mister?"

Tony shook his head.

"I must rinse her now." The window washer sighed with gusto, picked up his extension pole and, muttering under his breath, marched across the patio leaving a trail of shadowy black footprints.

Tony ran back inside. Rock was alone and trying on Dolly's shoes. "Will you take those off? What if Mrs. Pearce catches you? What if you break them?" Rock was a size thirteen, quadruple E. He'd be lucky to squeeze his big toe in those delicate little things.

Rock stuck out his tongue, put the high-priced shoes back in their box.

"Where is Mrs. Pearce?"

"Dolly got a phone call. Don't worry, she'll be right back. What was all that going to the bathroom stuff about? You looked like you were about to explode, but not from needing a toilet."

Tony shook his head and sat. "I saw Stafford."

"You saw Jim?"

"I thought I did, but it turned out it was only a window washer."

"Then what was all the commotion I heard out there?" Rock looked towards the window.

"Nothing."

"I know I heard shouting. Come on, what happened?"

Tony tried explaining how he'd seen the head bobbing up and down outside the window. He'd been sure it was Jim Stafford and so he had excused himself to go and find out what he was up to. And to warn Stafford that he could be seen from the house. But it was tough explaining himself what with Rock laughing throughout his tale.

"And then his sunglasses fell off and his eyes were green and wide-set, like they belonged more on a pumpkin than a human head."

Rock covered his mouth and smothered his laughter.

Tony folded his arms. "He did have Jim's nose."

Rock snickered, "I hope you asked him to give it back."

Tony glowered. "Listen," he whispered hotly, "it could very well have been Jim. After all, you remember the first time we saw Dolly, Jim was there at her husband's theater, dressed like a temporally displaced Civil War soldier."

"That doesn't mean he's out here dressed like a window washer. Unless maybe you think poor Jim is moonlighting washing windows?"

Tony wasn't responding.

"Buddy, you were out in the sun too long. When we get back to town, I suggest a long nap."

"That's not the only time Jim's done something—" Tony hesitated, "wacky. How about when he was in Cyndi Parker's room, huh? How about that?"

Rock's brow furrowed. "What are you talking about, Tony?"

"Jim, when he was dressed up like that maid. You remember. You were there."

Rock's face went from blank to comprehending. "Oh, my God." His hands flattened his cheeks. "That was Jim?"

"Well, well, seems you don't know everything." Tony said smugly.

"That woman. . ." Rock thought a moment then snapped his fingers. "She said her name was Patty."

"Yippee-I-aaay—"

Rock finished the line, "Cow Patti." Rock snorted. "I thought that poor dear was one homely looking thing. I kind of felt sorry for her, especially with that Cyndi Parker giving her such a hard time. And to think, it was Jim all along. Why I—"

Tony shushed him. "Mrs. Pearce is coming back."

Mrs. Pearce was smiling brightly as she swept into

the room. "Good news, boys. That was my husband on the phone and when I told him the two of you were here he said he'd be right home." She rubbed her hands gleefully. "I'll tell Sylvie to prepare us something to eat."

Tony jumped to his feet. "Sorry, Mrs. Pearce. Our boss, Nanci Dement, called while you were off and said we need to get to rehearsal." Tony looked put out. "I'm afraid we'll have to pass on that meal."

"Yeah," concurred Rock. "I'm afraid Tony's right."

"What a shame. Merel will be so disappointed."

Tony smiled. "Yes, I'm sure he will." He was probably headed their way right now brandishing a six-shooter or, worse still, a sawed off shotgun. Tony started for the door.

"What about your story?"

Rock looked at Tony and shrugged. Tony said, "No problem. We'll call you later this afternoon and schedule it for another day. Tomorrow perhaps? You know, we really want your profile."

"And picture," insisted Rock as they made for the exit.

Tony stopped, knowing this was the last chance for answers. "About the murders, Mrs. Pearce, is there anyone you can think of that would want Donald, that is, B.A.D. Spike, dead?"

"No," she shook her head. "Not really. He was a nice enough young man."

Rock said, "Your husband didn't seem too fond of him."

"Merel can be gruff. And he wasn't happy with what B.A.D. was going to do with his old theater. But killing is not his way."

Tony was glad to hear it.

"He had his lawyers working on getting back the theater."

"And if B.A.D.'s show had failed, your husband would have gotten his theater back anyway."

Dolly said, "Exactly, so why kill the man? I'm no detective, but it seems to me that it was probably a burglar. This Mr. B.A.D. must have surprised the intruder and the intruder killed him. Unless. . ."

"Unless what?" demanded Rock.

"Unless Jim Stafford is your killer. Ned used to work for Jim, you know. Maybe Jim killed them both. Maybe he's finally gone mad." She looked tellingly at the boys. "Merel always said that might happen." She tapped her head. "Says Jim's got a screw loose."

Mrs. Pearce was definitely the stand-by-your man type, decided Tony. "Did you know Virginia Plat?"

"Who?"

"She was the ROSE president. She's been murdered. Ms. Plat, B.A.D. and now this Ned Ledbetter. I'm trying to figure out how these murders are related, what the victims had in common that got them each killed."

"I do recall hearing about her murder, now that you mention it, but I haven't been to this Kewpiecon. I'm sure my husband hasn't either. He's not much for Kewpie dolls. So I'm afraid I can't help you there." A tired sigh escaped her mouth. "These are sad times. Their families must be distraught."

"Yes, I'm sure they are," dittoed Tony.

"Have you tried talking to B.A.D.'s girlfriend?"

"You mean Cyndi Parker?" Rock asked.

"Yes, that's the one. I hear she and B.A.D. had

quite a stormy relationship."

"I believe it," said Tony. "We tried talking to her."

Rock said, "She wasn't very cooperative."

"Besides," said Tony, "the police interviewed her already. She has an alibi. She said she'd gone to a movie and one of the ushers at the theater recognized her."

"And Cyndi Parker is pretty hard to forget once you've laid eyes on her," added Rock. "Especially if you're a red-blooded male."

"If the theater was crowded, how would anyone know if Miss Parker had left?" wondered Mrs. Pearce aloud. "It wouldn't be the first relationship to end in violence. It's too bad you can't find out what movie Miss Parker took in and maybe find some witnesses who can place her there the entire time." She paused and added rather pointedly, "Or not."

Tony smiled. "Maybe you ought to be a detective, Mrs. Pearce."

Dolly smiled back. "Taking care of Merel and Sherry is my job. And, believe me, I've got my hands full."

Tony believed she did from what he'd seen of Merel and Sherry Pearce. And speaking of Merel, they really ought to be going before he showed up and called them out into the street for an old fashioned gunfight. *Gunfight At Trail's End.* Not to mention Nanci was expecting them.

"We'd better be going, Rock. You know, you ought to check out Kewpiecon, Mrs. Pearce. It's running a couple more days. It might cheer you up, your daughter, too." Tony pulled open the big door.

"Oh, yeah," Rock said, "all those dolls. It's pretty cool. And the window displays at the Ramada are unbelievable. They are worth seeing, if nothing else. Drive by and have a look see."

"I'll do that." Mrs. Pearce looked down the empty drive. "Where's your car?"

"We parked up the street," improvised Tony. The boys marched down the sidewalk until Mrs. Pearce disappeared inside.

"And just how do you propose we get out of here? Gonna call up another gardener and hitch a ride in the back of his truck?"

"Very funny. A little walk will do us good," said Tony. "Come on."

"A little walk? I've already had a little walk. A little walk is from hotel room to ice machine. This is a friggin' Lewis and Clark expedition and I'll bet they were better prepared than we are!"

Tony marched resolutely on, Rock's complaints barely denting his thin skin. An open red convertible hit the rise of the hill in front of them. "That looks like Merel Pearce!" hissed Tony. He grabbed Rock, quickened his step and leapt behind a scraggly clump of bushes along the edge of a neighbor's lawn.

"Ouch!" Rock fell into a bristly bush.

"Sorry," said Tony. "Would you rather Merel Pearce found us?"

"I'm beginning to think that might be preferable."

"Can you imagine what he might do to us if he finds us here? At the very least, he could have us arrested."

Rock rose, shaken but reasonably whole. "You made your point. Now call your girlfriend."

"Rock, our car isn't far. We only have to walk a little."

Rock took Tony's head in his hands and twisted. "You see those clouds?"

Dark clouds were piling up over the lake. They were in for a big one.

"Call your girlfriend. I'm not taking another step." To prove his point, Rock sat at the edge of the curb, legs crossed, arms folded.

Tony bit his lip. There was no moving the big guy when the big guy didn't want to move. "Fine." He reassembled his phone, found Paula Robinson's number on caller I.D. and pushed the send button. "What was all that about the shoes anyway? How do you know so much?"

"Worked in a shoe shop part-time in Nashville before landing my first full-time gig. Ladies high fashion shoes. Ceruccis are the best. Dolly's got good taste."

Maybe in shoes, but not in husbands, thought Tony.

Chapter 30

It was humiliating.

That's what it was, humiliating. And Rock said so. Paula Robinson sat in the front seat of the police cruiser chuckling while Tony fought to get the twigs and leaves out of his hair. Rock told him his head looked like a vacant bird's nest.

The boys had remained hidden in the bushes until Robinson showed up, slowly coming up the street in search of them. Until then, they'd held their breaths every time one of the community's own security vehicles cruised by.

The rain showed up before Paula did. To say they were a little damp was to say that Niagara was a little waterfall.

On sighting the squad car, they'd hurried into the back and, except for giving directions to their rental, had remained stubbornly silent despite the officer's attempts to draw them out.

"What? Not going to speak until you talk to your attorney?" chided Robinson. "I don't know what you guys were doing wandering around in Trail's End, but you could have gotten yourselves in a whole lot of trouble. You're lucky somebody didn't report you for trespassing."

She swung out onto the main road leading past the clubhouse towards the entrance on Highway 265. "There are a lot of wealthy and high profile folks in here. They can be skittish. Why, there are even a couple of celebrities." Paula stopped the cruiser and looked over her shoulder. Her voice hardened, her eyes narrowed. "Like Merel Pearce."

The boys remained mum.

She groaned. "Oh, don't tell me you went to see Merel again. The chief's already getting complaints about you two. Merel called Chief Schaum himself. And when a man like Merel Pearce calls, the chief listens."

Robinson was shaking her head. "You guys are going to get yourselves in a whole mess of trouble." Robinson lifted her foot from the brake and didn't stop again until she was beside the boys' vehicle.

"He's guilty," Tony said as Robinson let them out of the back.

"Who? Merel Pearce?"

Tony nodded.

"Forget it. Merel Pearce was onstage doing his own show in front of more than a thousand people the night B.A.D. was killed."

"During intermission," Rock suggested. "Merel stabbed B.A.D. during intermission, then went back and finished his own show."

"Merel's show is at eight o'clock," said Robinson. "That makes intermission about nine. Jim was at the theater after ten and B.A.D. was still alive. That means he'd just been attacked."

Rock fought back. "Maybe Merel's got a secret double. Or B.A.D. had been attacked earlier and passed out or something. Maybe he'd just come to again when Jim arrived?"

"Please," scoffed Robinson, "this is all too far-fetched. Even for you." She was looking at Rock. "Have you noticed the traffic around here? Merel's theater is miles from B.A.D.'s. He'd have to have had wings to get there and back in time."

"Then he paid somebody," suggested Rock.

"And what was his motive?"

"Money?" asked Tony.

"Don't think so. Merel was loaded and B.A.D. was practically broke." Robinson pushed open their door. "Follow me into town and see for yourself."

"What's that supposed to mean?"

"It means that Jim Stafford is up at headquarters right now."

"Jim? Why, Paula?" Tony asked. "What's happened?"

"One Ned Ledbetter was found buried under the stage at B.A.D.'s theater."

"We heard. What's that got to do with Jim?" Rock wondered if the police had made the connection between Ledbetter and Stafford.

"Ned Ledbetter was last seen arguing with Jim Stafford four years ago. Mr. Stafford fired the boy."

So they had heard. Rock fastened his seatbelt. "And

Ned Ledbetter winds up over his head in cement."

"Come on, Paula, you don't think Jim did it?"

"He looks like the best suspect."

"But, Paula—"

Robinson cut him off. "Suppose that Mr. Stafford had an argument with Ned Ledbetter. Oh, I'm not saying he's a crazed killer. But maybe the two of them fought. Maybe Ledbetter attacked him first—angry that he'd been canned. Maybe Mr. Stafford was only defending himself."

Rock picked it up from there. "And Jim accidently kills this Ledbetter and buries the body in Merel's old theater." He shook his head. Jim was looking guiltier by the minute.

"That part doesn't make sense."

"Back when Ledbetter disappeared, Jim was questioned. He admitted dropping the boy off near the theater."

"Wow," said Rock. "It doesn't look good for Jim. I wouldn't want to be in his shoes."

"And you think Jim killed B.A.D. because B.A.D. was going to remodel the stage and that was where the body was buried?" Tony was wet and shaking from the cold. This simply could not be. Not Jim Stafford.

Robinson was nodding. "They're interviewing him right now. That's where I was when you called me to rescue you. Follow me and let's see what's new."

Jim sat with his arms folded across his chest. He had on a yellow shirt and a wrinkled pair of blue jeans. Tony and Rock followed Paula Robinson to the glass and silently watched for a moment.

"He certainly looks calm enough," Tony opined. "I

recognize Det. Carvin, but who are the others in there with him?"

"Chief Schaum is the man sitting across the table from Mr. Stafford."

Rock asked, "Who's the old guy?" A lean man wearing a neat brown suit sat beside Jim. He had an angular chin and short brown hair streaked with white.

"That's Jim's lawyer. Finally showed up. In a two-thousand dollar suit and a secretary in tow. Name's Abraham Nelson."

Tony watched. Nelson was talking. "Is there any way we can hear what they're saying?"

Paula turned the knob on a small wall-mounted speaker and the lawyer's words came through loud and clear. He was rambling on about his client's rights and the lack of evidence.

Det. Carvin came through the door to the adjoining room and returned a couple of minutes later. With him were Butch Domino, Cyndi Parker and Rick Elf.

Tony nodded to them but they each shot back hard stares.

Det. Carvin led them up to the glass. They peered through. "You recognize anybody in that room?"

"What? Are you kidding, man?" Butch said.

Rick was pressing his face against the glass and Carvin pulled him back. "I know that guy, the one in the middle with the yellow shirt."

Cyndi Parker laughed. "Of course you do, fool. That's Jim Stafford."

"Jim Stafford?" Rick looked again. "No. That's the fellow I saw out at Bonniebrook the other day." He paused, then added quietly, "The day that Virginia Plat was found dead out there." He took a harder look. "Except, when I saw him his face was all stubbly."

Carvin's brow did a little dance of delight. "Well, well."

Tony couldn't believe what he was hearing. "You saw Jim Stafford out at Bonniebrook on the day Ms. Plat was murdered?"

"I'll ask the questions around here," Carvin said, gruffly. "If you don't mind?"

Tony knew that last bit wasn't intended to be a question as much as it had been disguised as one.

"Well?" said Carvin, looking at Elf. "You want to tell me what you saw?"

"I saw him." Rick was pointing directly through the glass at Jim. "Only he never said he was Jim Stafford. And he wasn't dressed like that."

"How was he dressed?"

"He had on some sort of dungarees and boots, a flannel shirt—red, I think—and one of those hunter's caps. A green one." Rick scratched his head. "I think he said his name was Clyde."

"Well, well. My, oh my." Det. Carvin was grinning and looking at Jim like he was some sort of soon to be swallowed prey.

"Have you seen Stafford anywhere else?"

Rick thought a moment. "No."

"He was at Kewpiecon the other day with his daughter," Carvin said. "You telling me you didn't see him there? At B.A.D.'s theater?"

"No, sorry."

"What about you two?"

Butch's voice came out like spilled gravel. "Why are you asking so many questions? That's Jim Stafford.

Sounds like he's your killer." Butch chewed his lip some. "You got him. Lock him up so's I can get out of this lousy town."

"Butch is right. If Stafford's guilty, put him away," said Cyndi. "This is a waste of time."

"We're only trying to ascertain if any of you have seen him lurking around B.A.D.'s theater before the murder. Maybe prowling around the site where we eventually found Mr. Ledbetter's corpse?"

"I've heard all about how Stafford and B.A.D. had cooked up this crazy publicity stunt, but like I said before, B.A.D. never told me about it and I never, ever saw Stafford at the theater. Not even at this Kewpie thing."

Butch grunted. "It's a fairy tale. Stafford and B.A.D. hated one another. B.A.D. was always telling me how he hated Stafford."

"That's a lie," said Rock.

Parker glared at the detective. "Can I go now?" She was savagely tapping her foot.

Carvin pointed to the door and Cyndi headed straight for it. Butch, without asking, followed her out.

"Nice lady," Carvin mumbled.

"I keep telling you you're a prince with the ladies," Robinson quipped. "Right, guys?"

"Oh, right." Rock's eyes practically rolled right out of his cranium.

"Yeah, yeah. They don't pay me to be nice." Carvin headed for the door to the interrogation room. "Wait until the chief hears what this fella just told us."

Rick stood there, hands in pockets, looking like he wished he were anywhere but where he stood. He took two steps sideways. Maybe he liked it better there.

"Can I go?" he asked Robinson.

"Better stay put," said Robinson. "We're going to want to get your statement in writing."

Rick groaned. "I've got things to do. I've got my booth to run."

"Sorry," said Robinson. She didn't sound like it.

Carvin waited until Chief Schaum stopped speaking and then whispered in his ear. The chief chewed on the detective's words and then questioned Jim.

"Yeah, I was there. I was trying to get some information on who might have killed Donald. I was trying to clear my name."

Chief Schaum looked perplexed. "Why the disguise, Mr. Stafford?"

"I didn't want anyone to recognize me. You know how it is, chief. I'm a celebrity. Nobody is going to take me serious when I'm trying to get questions answered. Heck, they're only going to ask me for autographs. And how am I supposed to do surveillance if everybody recognizes me? So, I thought I'd go undercover."

"I can't believe that Jim is guilty," Tony said softly, firmly.

"I can't believe he's still smiling," replied Rock. Would he still be smiling in prison? On Death Row?

Chief Schaum warned Jim about dressing up and playing detective and interfering with police investigations and Jim vowed he'd only done it the one time and further promised not to do it again. The questioning continued with the chief wanting to know what Jim had found out and if he had any other information that might be useful in their investigations. Despite his lawyer's objections, Jim told all he knew. It wasn't much.

The men all rose, except for Carvin who'd been standing to begin with. The chief shook Jim's hand and then the lawyer's and they all left like they were best buddies.

Jim looked surprised to see Tony and Rock. "Hi, men."

Rock laughed. "Sorry. I just had this flashback to you dressed in a maid's uniform, Jim."

Jim and Tony made subtle faces at Rock to shut up. The police were giving the big guy odd, suspicion-laced looks as well.

The lawyer grabbed his client by the arm and led him out quickly. "Come along, Jim." The chief followed after them.

"He's been let go?" Rock asked. "Hey, Robinson, I thought you said he was guilty of killing this Ned Ledbetter kid and maybe even B.A.D.?"

"I said it was a theory under official consideration."

Carvin said, "Mr. Stafford has been released on his own recognizance. He is a pillar of the community, after all." And he didn't look happy about it.

Over coffee in the police department's breakroom, Tony said, "I still can't believe Jim killed anybody."

Paula sat across the table from Tony. She dumped a packet of sugar in her coffee and didn't bother to stir it. To his unspoken question, she replied, "This way I get the sugar that I crave but so long as I don't stir it up, I figure I'm okay. There's always a gooey lump left at the bottom."

Tony still looked baffled.

"I'm a borderline diabetic. This is my way of controlling my blood sugar."

"I don't know anything about diabetes, Paula, but should you even be having sugar?"

Paula shrugged her shoulders and quickly got back on subject. "As for Stafford, people do funny things. Even in a small town like Branson."

"Murder is a pretty big thing. And I still don't see Jim's motive in killing Ned Ledbetter or B.A.D., at least not viable motives."

"You're too naive, Tony. People don't need good motives for half the things they do. You don't read the papers much, do you?"

"I suppose not. It's all bad news, anyway."

"Trust me. The first killing—of Ledbetter—could have been a simple case of manslaughter. Unpremeditated. Now killing B.A.D. with a knife to the back, that was a primitive act of desperation by a desperate man."

"Jim doesn't look desperate."

Paula wrapped her hands around her cup. "I agree. But what else do we have to go on?"

Tony said, "Whatever happened to good old-fashioned motives like greed and jealousy?"

Paula smiled. "That would lead us back to Merel Pearce, for one, but he's got a tight alibi. There's B.A.D.'s manager and his girlfriend, Cyndi Parker, but I don't see how either of them are better off. And there doesn't seem to be any other hanky-panky that we've been able to dredge up."

Robinson's phone rang. After listening a few moments, she said, "Be there in five." She apologized to Tony. "I'm afraid I'll have to cut our date short."

"Duty calls?"

She rose and tossed her cup in the trash. "How

about dinner tonight?"

"I don't know, Paula. I mean, I have to touch base with Nanci." They'd missed their last meeting as well and now she wasn't returning his phone calls. What Tony didn't add was that while Paula was awfully cute, he just wasn't ready for a relationship, especially a long distance one. "And then there's Rock."

"Bring him along. You like Italian?"

"Yes, only—" Tony still hesitated. Rock would probably have a fit if he even brought up the idea of dinner with Paula. He'd certainly refuse to go. "We may have a show to do. I'll see. But I'm not promising anything."

Paula's eyes blinked mischievously. "Neither am I."

Tony stood. "I'll let you know." It was only dinner. It didn't have to be anything more than that. It was nice to be chased. He wasn't used to being chased, but could get used to it easy.

Paula caught his arm at the door. She peeked out into the hall. "I shouldn't be telling you this, but if you promise not to tell a soul—"

"Tell me what?"

"You promise?"

"I suppose. But I don't like committing myself to something when I don't even know what that something is."

"It's about Duncan Daniels." Paula pulled Tony away from the door.

"I'm listening."

"Seems he's still missing. He didn't show up at his tables this morning."

"That is strange."

"We have a witness who saw him talking to Rick Elf

outside his room."

"What did Mr. Elf say?"

"He said we ought to be out looking for his Kewpie Mountain instead of harassing him and looking for a grown man who has every right to disappear if he wants to. Elf's right, of course. He also has an alibi for the night Duncan Daniels was murdered."

"That's true," said Tony. "He was at the banquet. I saw him there myself."

"You haven't seen Daniels around, have you?"

Tony said he hadn't. "Do you think anything has happened to him?"

"Maybe. He's left behind all his show pieces. And we've searched his hotel room. All his personal things are there. We're going through them now. He left a camera and a laptop."

Tony frowned.

"What's wrong, Tony?"

"None of this helps get Jim Stafford off the hook."

Paula agreed.

Chapter 31

Jim had his feet up on the small desk in his dressing room. He was fiddling with some futuristic looking pair of 3D glasses that he said were going to revolutionize his show.

Tony took his word for it. "What about Dewey Rood? I still think he may be involved in all this."

"Who?" asked Jim.

Rock, rummaging around uninvited in Jim's refrigerator, raised his head. "He's this big old boy who is a member of ROSE. Dewey and his mother both." The big guy ran his index finger along his neck like a blade.

"Mr. Rood is good with knives," explained Tony.

"Interesting." Jim shoved the 3D glasses up on his nose and was looking at his hands and wiggling his fingers. Tony didn't know if he was talking about Dewey Rood or whatever it was he was now seeing through his glasses.

"He and his mother, Cleo, have a small business selling Rose O'Neill related bric-a-brac," said Tony. "They make the stuff themselves."

Jim was looking at Tony through the big, dark glasses. "And you think he's got something to do with this mess we're in?"

"Could be," Tony opined. "I told Officer Robinson about the Roods. Yet, when we were at the police station yesterday, she didn't mention anything about them."

Rock pulled a bottle of spring water from the fridge and asked if anybody else wanted one. Jim said yes and he tossed one over the bar. He missed. The bottle skidded over the desk and landed at Tony's feet. He picked up the cold bottle and pushed it in Jim's direction. "Maybe you should take those glasses off, Jim."

"Oh, right." He dropped the glasses back in their shipping box. "I'll figure these out later. So, Dewey Rood is good with knives and he's on a killing spree. How do we catch him?"

Rock laughed.

Tony answered, "We're not certain it's Mr. Rood. And even if Mr. Rood killed Donald, it doesn't seem likely that he killed Ned Ledbetter four years ago as well."

"It's possible," said Rock. "Barely."

The others agreed.

"Is this Rood a local man?" asked Jim.

"No. I'm sure he's not. I don't remember where he said he was from." Tony turned in his seat.

"He and his mom live in Vegas," said Rock. "I

remember them saying so."

"Not very likely that they knew Ned then, is it?" agreed Stafford.

"What about Ned Ledbetter, Jim? We know that he worked for you, but why did you fire him?"

"Easy," said Stafford, "the boy was spying on me."

"Spying?" Rock looked skeptical.

"That's right. I caught him more than once listening in on my phone conversations. Sneaking around the business office here at the theater. That sort of thing."

"Why do you think he was doing that?"

"That's easy, too," Jim answered. "I found out he was working for Merel."

Tony stiffened. "Merel as in Merel Pearce?"

"That's right. Didn't surprise me none that after I fired his sneaky little behind that he wanted to be dropped off in front of Merel's theater. I'll bet Merel was upset that I'd caught on to his sneaking ways, too." Stafford chuckled.

"Yes," said Tony, "I'll bet he was. Maybe enough to kill."

"You think old Merel killed Ned?"

"Don't you?"

Jim swigged some water and screwed the lid back on tight. "Nah. And as I remember, Merel had an airtight alibi, as they say, the night Ned disappeared."

Rock sat on the edge of Jim's desk. "Airtight?"

"He was out of town."

"That doesn't mean anything," suggested Tony. "He might have only said he was out of town and then sneaked back and bumped off Ned."

"Nope." Jim shook his head. "Merel was performing at the White House."

"Doesn't get much more airtight than that." Rock slid off the desk and slammed a fist against the wall. "Rats." He spun. "Maybe this Ledbetter kid only slipped in some wet concrete? The end. Not a homicide at all."

"Even you realize how dumb that sounds, Rock." Merel just had to be mixed up in this somehow. Yet how could he be performing at the White House and bumping off Ned Ledbetter at the same time?

"Paula says the evidence, so far, shows Ned Ledbetter had no blunt head trauma, but there was a possible nicked rib. He may have been stabbed to death."

Tony pressed his hands against the sides of his temples and pushed. "All right. One thing at a time. Let's get back to Dewey Rood. He kills Virginia Plat—"

Rock snapped his fingers loudly. "—And Elf kills B.A.D." He was beaming. "They were in it together, don't you get it? Rick Elf and Dewey Rood. Dewey's mother, too, for all we know." He was proud as a peacock. "Yeah, Tony, that's it."

"I don't know. . ."

"Remember how we couldn't understand how Rick Elf could have killed Virginia?"

Tony nodded.

"Well, he couldn't. So Dewey kills Virginia and Elf kills B.A.D. Or vice versa, who knows?"

"But we saw Dewey and his mother at the banquet, remember? Rick Elf was there, too."

"But maybe one of them got there late. We don't know they didn't. One of them could have gone out to Bonniebrook beforehand. Heck, Rick Elf was already there." He shrugged. "Well?"

"Rick Elf, huh?" Jim dropped his feet to the floor. "I don't like that guy."

"Not surprising since he identified you as having been out at Bonniebrook the day Virginia disappeared, Jim."

"Yes, why didn't you tell us, Jim?"

"I tried to a couple of times. Like when I saw you men out at Merel's theater. I didn't get the chance. I saw Rick Elf and Virginia Plat. Even saw Dolly in the museum. I was in my disguise at the time. She didn't recognize me. I'm surprised this Elf fella did."

Jim scratched his jaw. "Sure wish I could have heard what those two were talking about out in the woods."

Rock snorted. "And what about that snooping you did in Cyndi's hotel room? That was cute."

Jim reddened.

"Did you find anything there?"

"No, nothing. Miss Parker stayed in the room the whole time. I didn't get a chance to search much. I didn't want to raise any suspicions."

Rock snorted once more.

Jim shot him a look and went on. "She was on the telephone a lot."

"Do you know who she was talking to?"

Jim shook his head. "No. But she was trying to raise money. That much was clear. Trying to save B.A.D.'s theater."

"Hmm," Tony found himself reaching for Stafford's 3D glasses. "That doesn't sound much like something a killer would do."

Jim had picked up a nylon string guitar and was picking out some impossible looking classical piece.

"You know, I saw him yesterday morning."

"Him? Him who?" Tony had the 3D glasses hooked over his ears. Everything looked darker but that was about it. He didn't see what the big deal was.

"Rick Elf. That Kewpie guy. The one that lost the mountain."

"You saw Mr. Elf yesterday morning? Where was this?" Tony saw a dark shadow cross the room. Was that Jim? Or some fourth dimensional ghost?

"Out at the house."

"What do mean, Jim?" asked Rock. "Elf was at your house yesterday?"

"No, not exactly." Jim explained. "You see, I live out by Table Rock Lake. Down past the bottom of my property, there's a small dock. There are a dozen or so boats tied up there."

The boys made enough noises to show they were listening.

Stafford rambled on. "I've got a little one myself. It was a present from the manufacturer. I did a show for them a year or so ago. They gave the boat to me in appreciation. Don't use it much, though. Never enough time."

Tony urged him to get back to the point of his story. He adjusted the glasses behind his ears. The things were heavy and he didn't know how anyone would be able to stand them for more than short periods of time.

"Oh, sorry." He leaned the guitar against the bar. "Anyway, I saw this Elf guy down there yesterday at his boat."

Rock said, "Elf has a boat?"

"I guess so."

Tony ripped the glasses off his face. "No," he said, triumphantly, "Elf does not, but Daniels does. And the police are looking for him. I wondered what the heck he was doing dragging his boat all the way up here from Arizona to Missouri.

"And I don't recall seeing it in the parking lot out at the Ramada lately. Not in the last couple of days, anyway. You remember, Rock, Daniels' boat was sitting on its trailer out back behind the hotel."

Rock found Tony's smile to be contagious. "Booze or Gas—"

Tony completed the expression, "—Nobody rides for free."

Chapter 32

"Look," whispered Tony, "it's Mr. Rood."

"What's he doing here?" Rock fidgeted uncomfortably in the hot sandy soil. Once again he was ill-prepared for sleuthing and marching. But Jim had insisted on leaving his car up by the road and they'd traveled the remaining distance to the lake on foot. The three of them were huddling behind a small stand of trees and withering bushes.

Dewey Rood, walking stick in hand, was waddling across the wooden dock. A small olive green, flat-bottomed fishing boat with a dark outboard motor was chugging away across the still lake. Dewey's hands were otherwise empty. But there was no missing the knife strapped to his thick belt, as always. Tony had no doubt that Mr. Rood could easily dispatch a couple of victims with his knife skills.

"He's coming this way," said Tony. "Let's wait until

he's gone and then search the boat." He'd left half a dozen messages on Nanci's voicemail stating they'd had an emergency and would meet up with her soon. Rock left a message of his own saying that she was cuter than an upright bass and that she was driving him to distraction.

None of their calls were returned.

Staying low and out of sight, Stafford and the boys watched as Dewey tramped heavily through the soft ground to his car, a small white vehicle with Nevada plates.

"No trailer hitch," noted Tony.

Jim rose and dusted off his jeans. "So Dewey doesn't have a boat."

Tony asked, "What's a man without a boat doing at a boatdock?"

"I told you he and Elf were partners. Why do people never believe me?" Rock rose majestically. He leaned against a pine and slowly poured hot brown sand out of his shoes. "Let's check Duncan's boat."

Jim leapt up on the dock. "This boat's mine," he said, proudly pointing to a modest fishing boat nearest the shore.

"Nice," said Tony.

Rock looked unimpressed. "Played with bigger boats in my bathtub."

They continued on to Duncan Daniel's boat. It was tied up at the berth near the tip of the dock that extended into the lake like a tentative finger testing the water temperature. Tony hesitated, watching the boat sway lightly side to side.

"What are you waiting for?" Jim was already aboard.

"I don't know. I feel a little funny climbing on somebody's boat without permission." Not to mention he wasn't keen on boats.

"Duncan Daniels isn't around to give us permission," Rock said, inching his way past Tony and onto the boat. But he understood Tony's reluctance. "You want to wait outside? Keep watch?"

"No," said Tony. He reluctantly took the plunge and all three were aboard. Except for them, the dock area was now deserted. A couple of geese waded in and out of the pilings.

"Not bad," said Jim, stepping up to the helm and twisting the wheel.

"You know much about boats, Jim?"

"Not a whole lot, Tony. But this one's pretty fine. Oh, she's a little run down, but with a bit of work, she could be real fine. This here is a twenty-six foot Sea Ray. Probably about eight to ten years old by the looks of her. Sleeps four, I'll bet." He twisted the handle on the hatch leading belowdecks. It was locked. Jim jiggled it again just in case it was only stuck. "Locked up tight."

"Let me try," Rock shouldered up to the door and turned the handle. "Rats."

"Let's look around on deck, then get out of here," Tony said. "We're awfully exposed." He was getting nervous. He was also getting queasy.

Rock started opening storage compartments and tossing cushions. Jim was opening up the compartment to the engines.

Five minutes of labor produced no results, except for the wrench that Rock was now slapping against his palm. He'd found it in a small tool kit tucked under the captain's chair. "Time to get up close and personal with that lock."

"Rock, you can't break—"

Clink! Rock brought the edge of the wrench down on the handle. It collapsed in the first round much like a journeyman featherweight boxer in the ring with a super heavyweight champion. Rock smiled and pulled open the hatch. "Nice. There's room in here to sleep four easy, like you said, Jim. More if you like to get cozy and maybe a little kinky."

Tony poked his nose inside. The air was stale and hot. A sickly, sweat aroma filled the air. Still, it was better than being on deck.

"Something stinks," said Rock, pinching his nose.

What little light penetrated leaked through the white curtains over the portholes. Despite all this, the interior of the cabin was roomy and well-outfitted with a wide berth, stove, microwave—more than the bare necessities Tony had expected.

"All the comforts of home," said Stafford, pulling open the narrow door to the head. He looked up and down. "Nothing in here." He even popped up the lid to the toilet and looked inside.

Now that's dedication to the job, thought Rock. "If there's a Kewpie Mountain on this boat, it's bound to be in here."

"I hope so," said Tony.

"Me, too," said Jim. "The police can arrest Rick Elf and the rest of us can get on with our lives." He lifted the mattress and the boys looked under it. "See anything?" he asked.

"Nothing," said Tony. "This is ridiculous. There's nothing here. Did either of you hear something?"

Jim and Rock said they hadn't.

"I was sure I heard something. Never mind. We're wasting our time. There's nothing on this boat that doesn't belong here." Tony was sweating. It was hot and steamy inside. The boat had been shut up so long it was like walking around inside a pizza oven.

"Except you all."

Tony and Rock spun around. Standing in the hatch was Detective Carvin and he didn't look happy. The gun on his belt looked even less happy.

"Oh, hello, officer." Jim waved.

Det. Carvin's eyes narrowed ever so slightly. "That's detective." He took the few steps leading into the cabin, banging his feet heavily on each step. "What are you all doing here?"

There was an awkward silence which Rock broke. "Going fishing?"

"That's right," said Jim. "Me and the boys were heading out to do some fishing."

"What are you fishing for?" Det. Carvin inspected the tousled bed.

"Rainbow trout."

"Right." The detective sounded like he believed that as much as he believed in Santa Claus. He stopped in front of Tony, looked him up and down, then repeated the process with Rock and finally Jim. "Is this your boat, Mr. Stafford?"

Jim looked shocked. He spun around the cabin. "Why, come to think of it," he banged his palm against his temple, "this doesn't look like my boat at all. I mean, the colors are all wrong. I'm so embarrassed. My boat doesn't look a thing like this one."

Jim shook his head. "What was I thinking? Come

on, men, I think I made a wrong turn somewhere."

Stafford headed for the steps with Rock close behind, but Det. Carvin beat him to the punch and blocked the exit. They went through another of those awful, awkward silence routines.

The spell was broken when Det. Carvin said, "So, do you, any of you, want to tell me what you're really doing here?" He folded his arms and puffed out his chest. "Or shall we just head on uptown and you can tell your stories to Chief Schaum?"

Tony cleared his throat. Det. Carvin turned his attention back to him. "It's about Duncan Daniels," he began, "and the Kewpie Mountain."

"What about them?"

"We thought the Kewpie Mountain might be on board."

"What makes you think that the Kewpie Mountain is on this boat, Kozol? We've been looking all over for that crazy mountain. Do you honestly think you know better than the police do where to find it?"

Tony stammered. "We have this theory—"

Carvin laughed. "Oh, great. The guitar player has a theory." Beads of sweat had formed like a thunderstorm on his forehead. He wiped his brow with the back of his sleeve.

"Let me tell you, Kozol," he yanked open the door to the little refrigerator hoping to find a cold drink, "I have a theory of my own." He poked a finger in Rock's direction. "My theory is that you're all going to end up behind bars."

Carvin bent over and inspected the refrigerator. There was a half-empty plastic water bottle in the door side pocket. "Pitiful."

A large cardboard box took up the entire bottom shelf. It was heavy with a Ramada towel draped over the open top. There was something wrapped inside. He was hoping for a six-pack, or at least a bird, maybe chicken. He'd missed lunch. Carvin pulled. "What the—"

The towel hit the deck with a thunk, then fell open.

Tony recognized the tumbling object from a picture he'd viewed in a book on Kewpie collectibles. "The Kewpie Mountain!"

Carvin's mouth hung open and no words escaped. His hands were frozen at his sides.

A smile slowly appeared on Rock's face. "Gee, I sure hope you didn't break it, detective. I'll bet even a police officer could find himself in a good bit of trouble for damaging a hundred thousand dollar work of art."

Carvin said nothing. Tony noticed his left eyelid twitching nervously.

Jim stooped and inspected the merchandise. "Looks okay to me."

"Thank goodness," sighed Tony. This was his first look at the Kewpie Mountain that he'd heard so much about. It was magnificent. And with only two of them known to exist in the world, he could see why it was worth so much money.

Det. Carvin broke free of his trance. He picked up the white towel. "Let's wrap it back up."

Jim held the Kewpie Mountain and the detective gently wrapped the towel around it. Carvin held the covered object protectively to his chest. "Let's go."

"Hey," said Rock, bent over a small compartment along the floor, "that smell's coming from in here."

"What's in there?" asked Tony.

"Forget it," said Carvin. "Only a storage compart-ment. Probably full of trout. This is the prize I've been looking for."

Rock sniffed the opening. "Maybe." He pulled off the cover.

There was something large wrapped in black plastic within. Carvin inched closer. "I know that smell." He pulled out a small knife and cut away the edge.

The red hair was a dead give away. The boys knew exactly who that was.

Duncan Daniels.

Chapter 33

Det. Carvin ordered them all off the boat.

Rock was the last to debark. "How'd Daniels' body get there? And what were you doing following us, anyway, Carvin?"

"I wasn't following you." Carvin cradled the Kewpie Mountain against his belly and started up the dirt track. "Now shut up. I've got to phone this in."

"If you weren't tailing us, Detective Carvin," Tony said, "then why are you here?"

"I was doing what I was told to do." Carvin was not one for long answers.

"What was that?" inquired Jim.

Carvin scowled. "If you must know, I was following Dewey Rood."

"A-ha!" cried Rock.

Carvin gave him an extra strength scowl. "A waste of time, if you ask me. But," he sighed, "Chief Schaum told me to keep an eye on Rood and see if he was up to anything suspicious. Robinson told the chief what you boys had said about him and I guess that got the chief's interest up."

"You followed Dewey out here, to the dock?" Rock asked.

"That's right. Then the three of you showed up. At first, I thought the four of you were up to something. I waited a bit and saw how the three of you were watching Rood. He left and you all didn't."

Carvin smiled. "I figured I'd see what you did next thinking it might prove interesting." He hefted the Kewpie Mountain. "I figured right. Got me a prize and a dead guy."

Carvin called in the troops. Jim and the boys were told to go straight to the station. Chief Schaum wanted a word with them pronto. When they didn't show up, Officer Robinson was sent out looking.

The chief popped a couple of Hawaiian Punch flavored Tums in his mouth and chewed. Things were not going well. He'd had reporters on his back for days, calling about Jim Stafford and wanting to know if he was still considered a suspect in the murder of that dang rap singer.

Now they wanted to know whether or not he had anything to do with the death of these Kewpie people as the newspapers were calling the recently deceased Virginia Plat and Duncan Daniels.

How long could he say nothing? How long could he keep from locking Mr. Stafford behind bars?

The chief had put in a call to Stafford's lawyer who claimed he hadn't heard from his client. Was he lying?

Chief Schaum pressed his fingers against his forehead and squeezed. The Advil he'd taken an hour ago hadn't kicked in yet. The Kewpie Mountain was on full display, lying atop the white towel on the middle of the table. All those little critters seemed to be looking at him and they had these peculiar smiles on their faces. The bitty creatures made him uneasy and, for the life of him, he didn't know why.

Chief Schaum squeezed some more and looked at his watch. He was waiting for Robinson to arrive with Mr. Stafford. And hoped that would ease his pain, if not his mind.

Robinson had no real trouble finding the boys and Jim once she'd gotten the word and was underway. The call had taken her by surprise. Sunday was her day off and she and her brother and the boys were up at Silver Dollar City. She got the call while riding high, hanging upside down, on Wildfire, a highspeed, multiloop rollercoaster that runs at better than sixty-six miles per hour.

Heading into Branson, eyes on the alert, Robinson recalled the chief's words. Locate Jim Stafford, Tony Kozol and Rock Bottom. Get them to the station. Robinson chuckled when Chief Schaum had told him what happened. Carvin must have been furious and not a little embarrassed when Jim and the boys hadn't shown up at headquarters like Carvin had ordered them to.

Carvin didn't have much of a sense of humor and no patience whatsoever.

Robinson had told Chief Schaum that it would be no problem. And it wouldn't. All she had to do was to look at the big picture, think about where Tony, Rock and Jim Stafford could cause the most trouble and start there.

Because that was where they would be.

And they were.

Chapter 34

A lumbering, white Ride The Ducks amphibious vehicle stuck out in the Ramada's parking lot like a football on a basketball court.

Conceived and built quickly to aid the war effort, the swimming trucks were originally used to cart soldiers and supplies from ship to shore during World War II. The acronym DUKW was derived from the General Motors manufacturing code. D stood for the year of manufacture, 1942. U stood for utility amphibious truck. K was for front-wheel drive and W for dual rear-drive axles. On D-Day alone more than two thousand of the sturdy DUKWs had hit the beaches of Normandy.

Nowadays, the big, awkward looking, World War II DUKWs were major tourist attractions in towns like Branson and the ubiquitous 'ducks' as they had become known were seen on a daily basis plying sightseers through town and out to Table Rock Lake where they unblinkingly plunged in for a swim. One of their drivers was known to dress up like Santa. Go figure.

Robinson got out of her squad car. This duck must have gotten lost from the flock. She rapped the side with her knuckles as she walked along and heard a stifled cry. "What the—" She stepped back to get a better look over the rail. "Somebody in there?"

Only the crickets responded. Robinson scratched her head. She was sure she'd heard something. Walking around to the back, she climbed the ladder.

Robinson tiptoed aboard. The duck creaked. She heard scuffling sounds and her hand went to her gun. She caught a flash of red movement between the seats towards the front, on the side parallel to the Ramada. "This is the police. Come out slowly with your hands open and arms extended over your head."

A dirty brown head shot up. "Quiet, Paula. He might hear you."

"Tony?"

"And get down for Pete's sake."

Paula grimaced. That was a second man's voice. "Tony, what are you doing here? And who is that with you?"

Tony's voice rose over the seat. "Just squat down and come over here and I'll tell you. Please."

Reluctantly, Robinson dropped to her knees and crawled up to where Tony and the man were hiding, bumping her knees and scraping her elbows along the way, mouthing several oaths that were not part of any pledge. "Mr. Stafford? Rock?"

Jim and the boys were scrunched together between

two rows of seats. Jim nodded.

"What are you all doing here?"

"Keep your voice down, Paula." Tony poked her in the ribs. "You want to spook him?"

Robinson held her temper, only barely. "Spook who? You mind telling me what you all are up to? Chief Schaum sent me out to find you. You were found on a vessel with a missing valuable and a dead body."

Rock grumbled. "Tell us something we don't know."

She glared at him. "You all were supposed to be going back to HQ like Carvin ordered you. I can't tell you how mad he is. Not to mention the chief."

Rock said, "We were coming into town when Jim spotted Dewey Rood in the parking lot at B.A.D.'s theater."

Jim added, "He was carrying a big old box."

"So we decided to follow him out here and see what he was up to," said Tony. "He'd been out at the boat."

"Where Duncan Daniels' body had been stashed," added Rock.

"He put the box in his car and carried it up to his room," Jim said.

"So, Rood was carrying a big box and he brought it back to his room?" Paula was shaking her head like they were a couple of school children.

"Don't you think that's suspicious, Paula?"

"I think you boys and Jim Stafford hiding out in a duck is suspicious. A man carrying a box, not so much. No."

Paula put her hands on a seat and pushed herself up. A grunt of relief accompanied her. "Let's get to the station before the chief decides to put out an APB on the three of you. And he may just make that 'shoot to kill'."

Tony pulled Paula back down. "Look."

Paula banged her shin on the edge of the seat, biting her lip to keep from screaming. Getting hit in the shins was always a killer. Not to mention the ugly bruise it was going to leave.

"It's Dewey." Jim was peeking over the edge of the duck. "He's got something under his arm."

"Hey!" Rock whispered loudly. "That's the Kewpie Mountain!" He'd risen further than he had meant to and it was Paula's pleasure to push him back down. He complained at the rough treatment.

"Sorry," she said, but she was grinning. "How can that be the Kewpie Mountain? Chief Schaum told me Carvin found it out at Duncan Daniel's boat."

"Carvin found it?" Rock said angrily. "How do you like that? We do all the work, figure out what's going on, and Carvin takes all the credit."

"That's right," complained Stafford. "We were the ones who knew where to look. I saw Rick Elf out at the dock and Tony here is the one who got the idea to search the boat. Carvin was only looking for a bite to eat."

"Never mind who gets the credit," interrupted Paula. "Explain to me how Rood has gotten a hold of the Kewpie Mountain when Chief Schaum tells me he's got it at the police station?"

Tony told her to watch. Rood was taking the stairs now and ascended to the top floor. He stopped several doors up and leaned on his walking stick. "That's Rick Elf's room."

Robinson sidled up beside him and followed his gaze. "Are you sure?" Her eyes flattened.

Tony felt the light warmth of her breath on his ear. His shoulder touched hers and he felt a tiny spark. For a moment, he forgot the question.

"I said, are you sure?"

"Oh, yes." Tony looked Paula in the eyes. The woman had beautiful eyes. The kind of eyes that a girl he once knew had. He forced himself back from the precipice of unhappy memories. It was a dangerous place to be. "Rock and I have been through all these rooms. I'm certain that's Mr. Elf's."

Dewey Rood knocked on the door. After many seconds, the door opened. Elf stepped aside and Rood entered.

"What the devil are they up to?" Robinson found she was biting the inside of her cheek and stopped. Her brother was always telling her how ugly it made her look and now she'd been doing it in front of Tony. Had he noticed? No, he was still watching the hotel.

"He's coming out again," Jim said, continuing the play-by-play. "And he's empty handed."

Tony snapped his fingers. "I've got it! It's the second Kewpie Mountain."

Robinson demanded an explanation and Tony gave it to her. He explained how there were two and only two Kewpie Mountains known to exist in the entire world. "And that must be the second," he said triumphantly.

Paula was skeptical. "Elf never said anything about owning that second Kewpie Mountain."

"He never mentioned it to Rock or myself either. In fact, Mr. Daniels told Rock that the other Kewpie Mountain was owned by a woman in New Jersey or something like that."

Four heads bobbed above the side of the duck watching Dewey as he descended and made his way back to his car. "Are you going to let him get away?" demanded Rock.

"For the moment," answered Paula. "Right now, I'm more interested in Rick Elf and that Kewpie Mountain."

"Imagine," said Tony, "owning both Kewpie Mountains."

"That's some serious money," noted Stafford.

"Yes, it is," agreed Robinson. Dewey Rood drove off in his car and the officer rose. "It's time to find out what the devil is going on." She dusted herself off and leveled a finger at Jim and the boys. "The three of you stay put."

Tony looked pained. "But, Paula, we could—"

Robinson waggled her finger. "No buts. Stay put."

Jim looked at Tony and shrugged. "Come on, men, why don't we see if we can catch up with Dewey."

Tony quickly agreed.

"I'll bet he's headed back to the trade show. We can keep an eye on him there." Jim and the boys stood.

Robinson was blocking the aisle. "Oh no you don't. I said stay put and I meant stay put." She was dangling a shiny pair of handcuffs. "Now, do you promise or am I finally going to get the chance to use these?"

Jim and the boys were looking unsure of their next move so Robinson added, "You know, I've only got the one pair of cuffs, but I can still lock the three of you up. But it won't be comfortable. I can promise you that."

Rock dropped into the seat nearest the aisle and snarled, "Fine." Jim joined him, *sans* snarl. Tony frowned.

Robinson took the steps two at a time and knocked on Rick Elf's door. There was no answer and Robinson knocked again. Tony thought he saw the curtain part a fraction of an inch then shut again and wished he could tell Paula about it.

Jim rubbed his nose. "You think this Dewey Rood character could possibly have had something to do with Ned's death, Tony?"

"It seems like a long shot, Jim. You never did explain real clearly about Ned and Merel. You said Ned was spying on you, but there must be more to it than that. I can't help but think that all these murders tie together." Tony squeezed his eyes. "Somehow."

"There is." Jim frowned at the memory. "Did I tell you Ned was working for Merel?"

"Yes, you told us. But how could he be working for Merel Pearce if he was working for you?" asked Rock.

"Exactly. You see," explained Jim, as Robinson turned the door handle and found it locked, "Merel had paid Ned to plant listening devices in my office."

Bugs again. So here was the connection Tony was searching for. Merel Pearce had bugged Jim Stafford and he was bugging Donald's theater as well.

"And in my dressing room."

"But why?"

"That's Merel for you, always spying on everyone. Trying to stay one step ahead of the competition. I caught Ned planting a bug in my wife's office up at the house. Caught him red-handed."

"So you fired him. Did you know that the police found bugs in Donald's theater, too?" asked Rock.

"That doesn't surprise me any," replied Jim. "The

old dog's up to his old tricks."

Tony watched intently as Robinson looked over the rail and called to a maid working on the floor below. A minute later, she joined the officer and handed her a swipe card. She knocked a third and final time and after again getting no answer, inserted the card in the lock and inched open the door using her foot. Her hand was on her gun.

"There she goes," whispered Rock. He did a double take. As Robinson went into Elf's room and disappeared, the door to the room next door opened narrowly and Elf's head appeared. He took one look out onto the passageway then darted out and around the corner.

A second later, he was running down the stairs.

"What do you know," remarked Jim.

"He's getting away!" cried Tony. "We've got to do something." He stood and waved, hollering for Paula. But she was inside and couldn't see or hear him.

"He's getting in that SUV," Jim said.

"We've got to stop him. Come on!" They jumped off the duck and planted themselves in the SUV's path. Jim and the boys flapped their arms for Rick to stop. The SUV was only ten yards away now and closing fast.

He was close enough that Tony could see the look of grim determination on Elf's face as he quickly closed the distance between them.

"Stop!" Tony hollered.

Rock pulled Tony out of the way as the black SUV sped past, then squealed out onto Highway 76, ignoring cars left and right. Tony was all for running after him, but Rock tightened his grip on Tony's arm.

"Come on," Jim said, "I've got an idea!" He waved Tony and Rock back up into the duck and planted himself in the driver's seat. Rock pulled up the ladder.

"What are you doing?" Tony said. "Mr. Elf is getting away."

"A-ha!" Jim started up the duck. "I knew I saw the key hanging in this thing. A lot of the duck operators stop here for lunch afternoons. They don't bother to take the keys with them."

"You're kidding?"

"Nah. Lots of folks here don't lock up even when they leave their homes." Stafford pounded on the gas pedal and the duck shot forward. Tony landed in the aisle.

"Don't worry," shouted Jim, "we'll catch him. This thing is faster than it looks!"

Tony was being tossed around like a cucumber in a spinning salad shooter. He fought his way to his knees as the duck bounced out of the parking lot and up onto the main road.

Paula was coming out of Elf's room. The maid was talking and pointing her finger. Tony called Paula's name but wasn't sure if she'd heard him.

Then he lost sight of Paula completely as Jim put the duck in high gear.

They were in hot pursuit of Rick Elf.

Chapter 35

This duck wasn't built for speed and Jim wasn't an experienced operator, but he did know Branson better than Rick Elf.

He was also more accustomed to the traffic and guided the over-sized vehicle deftly in and out of the thick afternoon traffic.

Tony and Rock kept their eyes on Elf's SUV and exhorted Jim to keep his eyes on the road. "He's turning up ahead!" shouted Rock.

Jim nodded and crossed the center lane. The startled cries of a family in a station wagon could be heard a mile away.

"He's turned left up there by the Dairy Queen, Jim."

"I've got him in my sights," rumbled Stafford. He deftly twisted the duck around the corner. If it had been a real duck, she'd have been squawking and losing feathers left and right.

Tony smelled burning rubber and wondered how the tires on this tub would hold up. "I've lost him."

Rock stood on his tiptoes, his hands gripping the top rail of the duck as he peered over the sea of cars in the Radisson's lot. They were on the side street running past the Grand Palace on one side and Andy William's Moon River Theater on the other.

"I see the old boy." Stafford laughed. "He's gone into the lot over there on the right." He pointed. "I'll bet he thought it would take him around the hotel but it won't. Lots of folks make that mistake. He's stuck now. We've got him, men." Jim pumped the gas pedal and flew up into the parking lot.

Tony fell back in his seat. He saw the SUV hit the sloping embankment at the back edge of the parking lot. "He's going to go over the top. He'll get away for sure."

But the SUV's tires spun and slid backwards. Elf turned around and was heading straight for them.

Rock swallowed. Hard. Rick Elf had gone crazy. He was going to ram them!

It was going to be truck against duck.

Who would win?

Tony heard shouting, then realized it was coming out his mouth. Jim had no idea what he was saying. Neither did he. Jim threw the duck in reverse. At the last moment, the SUV shot past them. The duck did a one-eighty and Jim was on Elf's tail. Rick crossed to the right side, hit a parking bumper. The duck teetered on its right wheels before correcting itself.

Jim caught up with the SUV. He gave the duck a sharp turn, slamming into the SUV hard enough to rattle Tony's teeth. Duck and truck tore through the fancy landscaping surrounding Andy Williams' theater like a wild storm. Plants and earth flew out in every direction. The SUV was a black blur, a fast, low flying thundercloud.

Rock yelled for Jim to slow down. But Jim wasn't hearing or wasn't listening.

Tony caught a quick glimpse of Rick's face through the window of his SUV—he looked more surprised than terrified, but it wasn't by much—before he closed his eyes and screamed.

The duck was airborne.

So was Rick Elf.

When Tony opened his eyes, the duck was floating. They'd all landed in the drink—the artificial river that was the namesake of the Andy Williams Moon River Theater. The SUV was on its side and sinking like a four-wheel drive rock. Rock was clutching his sides. Jim was holding the wheel of the duck, crooning *Moon River*.

Jim looked at Tony and shook his head. "Andy's gonna just kill me."

A tourist, on his way to the Moon River box office to buy tickets to the Glen Campbell/Andy Williams show, spotted Jim. The startled tourist called to his wife, a rotund little woman in a green dress. As she ran up, he pulled a throwaway camera from his pants' pocket and snapped a picture standing in front of Branson's newest attraction—Disaster at Moon River—while Jim smiled and waved.

The three of them waded to shore. Elf's door was jammed and Tony had to go back in after him before he drowned. Elf didn't put up a struggle. In fact, he seemed almost grateful.

A wailing siren caught Tony's attention. A cruiser came coursing at him. Paula jumped out. Weapon in hand.

Tony smiled at her. "You saw me."

There were cars everywhere now, including half a dozen police cars, two fire trucks and a news van. An ambulance stood nearby, its back doors wide open and waiting.

"Yeah," Paula chuckled. "I saw you." She put her weapon away and took charge of Elf, slapping the cuffs on him. "And I saw Mr. Stafford driving that duck like it was a Formula One racing car. That was real dumb. You men could have gotten yourselves killed." She handed Elf over to a cohort. "Everybody okay here?"

Tony nodded. "Feel a little wobbly is all. Are you sure you're okay?"

"Yes. I'm all right. Excuse me a minute." She pulled away and walked over to Chief Schaum who was barking orders to his officers.

Jim was talking to a police officer standing near the shore so Tony knew he was okay. Rock was wrapped in a blanket, smiling wanly. Paula returned. Tony asked, "How's Elf?"

"A little banged up." Paula shot a look at the man in question. "But he'll live."

"We saw him come out of the room next door to his at the Ramada and tried to get your attention."

"Turns out he went out through the adjoining room. That's one slippery fellow. He'll have to be twice as slippery if he wants to slide through the metal bars that he'll be looking at the world through next."

Tony watched as Rick Elf's soggy form was placed

in a squad car. The car sped away, lights flashing.

"Come on," Paula said. "I'll follow you to the hospital." She gestured to the open ambulance.

"I don't need a hospital. I'm okay."

Paula looked skeptical.

"Really."

"You know, Tony Kozol," she said, crossing her arms, "it's okay to be vulnerable. It's okay to need somebody."

Tony opened his mouth to reply. Paula would make some lucky man a wonderful wife—it just wasn't him. But how could he tell her this without hurting her feelings? Would she understand that he wasn't ready for a serious relationship?

Paula didn't seem the type to take dating lightly. She seemed the type to fall in love and adore you, take care of you, stay by your side.

So why wasn't he ready to let himself be adored? And heaven knew he needed taking care of.

Too bad Rock wasn't here. He'd have plenty of answers. To questions Tony wasn't even asking.

"Hey, Tony, some ride, huh?" Stafford strode up. He waved to Paula. "What do you say we head up to the police station and see what they squeeze out of Elf?" He winked at them. "Besides a hundred gallons of Moon River, that is."

Chapter 36

According to the TV weather woman, it was supposed to be raining.

It was not.

Oh, maybe it was raining cats and dogs or maybe hogs in Kansas City or someplace hundreds of miles from here, but not in Branson, Missouri. Not this morning. Not at Ned Ledbetter's funeral. Despite the ongoing police investigation, Ned Ledbetter was being buried that morning at his parents' insistence and no one, not even the authorities, had felt like standing up to them.

The murder investigation hung over their heads like the nonexistent rain clouds, however. Rick Elf wasn't talking and Dewey Rood was protesting his innocence.

Tony and Rock stood under the canopy near the grave. A very small group was gathered, the grieving parents, a sister, and a few distant relatives. A number of Ned's buddies huddled together like a school of upright fish. A priest held a Bible and said a few words meant to comfort those left behind and hasten the Departed on his way to Heaven.

Tony hated funerals. They made him uncomfortable and fidgety. Maybe it was all that stuff about mortality. Maybe it was memories of his own parents' funeral flooding back. Rock nudged him. Sherry Pearce had emerged from a yellow Miata wearing a simple calf-length black dress. Even from a distance, it was clear she'd been crying.

Tony nodded in Sherry's direction but the country star's daughter ignored him and concentrated her attentions on the casket as it was being lowered into the ground. The first shovelful of earth was ceremonially tossed by Audie Ledbetter, the boy's father. His wife broke down at this point. He laid an arm around her shoulders and led her away.

A few moments later, Sherry Pearce drove off as well. She had said a word to no one. With her, she'd taken a single red rose from the small floral arrangement placed at the grave site.

"What do you suppose she was doing here?" Rock said.

"Beats me." Tony watched the Miata bounce along the dirt road that dissected the small, rural cemetery. "Want to see where she goes?"

Rock beamed. "Now you're talking, Tony." They had little else to do anyway. There'd been a message waiting for them at their hotel. Nanci had fired them. Rock had complained that he couldn't understand why. But that was just like the big guy. Reality was always just out of reach.

Now their time was their own. But if the boys were looking for some excitement, this wasn't going to be it. That much was clear the minute Sherry Pearce pulled into the parking lot at B.A.D. Spike's Crib.

"She's going to the Kewpiecon trade show," said Rock, feeling let down.

"Yeah." Tony parked and grabbed his notebook off the backseat. "We might as well go ourselves. Get some last minute stuff." Maybe they could still sell some kind of Kewpie piece to one of the papers and go home with at least a few dollars in their pockets.

Though it would never be enough to cover the expenses they'd racked up getting to and staying in Branson. Nanci Dement had left town in a huff and refused to pick up any of their tab. Rock was livid, but Tony figured she was justified. He only hoped they weren't blackballed in the biz because of this one aberrant incident.

"Okay, I'll get some pics."

Tony spotted Dolly Pearce inside, thumbing through a box of Rose O'Neill prints at a dealer's table and tapped her on the shoulder.

Dolly turned. "Oh, it's you. I thought it was Sherry."

"Hello, Mrs. Pearce."

"Hello, dear. I took your advice and came to check out Kewpiecon for myself." Mrs. Pearce's eyes scanned the crowd. "I don't know where my daughter is. She'd dropped me off earlier and is supposed to be picking me up."

"I think I saw her parking about the same time as Rock and I arrived. We saw her at the funeral for the

Ledbetter boy."

"She must be looking for you right now," added Rock. "I'm sure she'll find you soon enough."

The dealer, who had returned to his table with a cup of coffee and a donut, nodded. "Good to see you again."

"Pardon me?" said Tony, but the dealer was looking at Mrs. Pearce.

"You're with the Arkansas chapter of ROSE, aren't you, ma'am? Always good to see a regular. We've got to keep up the ranks."

Mrs. Pearce looked confused. "I'm afraid you've got me mixed up with someone else."

"Yeah," said Rock, "this is Dolly Pearce. Merel Pearce's wife."

The dealer whistled. "Well, I'll be." He scratched his head. "I'm sorry, ma'am. I must be having a senior moment."

Mrs. Pearce smiled. "No need to apologize. I've had several of those myself."

"I was surprised to see Sherry at Ned's funeral," Tony said. "Did she and Ned know one another?"

"What?" Mrs. Pearce ran a thin hand through her hair. "I believe they may have been classmates." Something caught her attention and she turned. "That's my daughter." She waved, bid a quick farewell, and was off. Mother and daughter hugged and left the room arm in arm.

Tony bumped Rock's arm. "Did you see the look on Sherry's face?"

"What about it?"

"She didn't look happy."

Rock's eyebrows shot up. He laid a hand on Tony's

forehead. "The girl just came from a funeral for Heaven's sake. Speaking of which, did you get heat stroke out there, Tony?"

Tony ignored Rock's sarcasm. "Come on. They went down that corridor." Tony quietly opened the door leading into the vestibule running along the main room. He held a finger to his lips when Rock opened his mouth to speak. Tony whispered, "I hear voices. They're probably behind the curtain. Come on."

Rock allowed Tony to drag him up the hall.

"He killed him, Mama, he killed him."

"Shush, child. He did no such thing." That was Mrs. Pearce.

"Yes, he did." Sherry Pearce's fierce voice penetrated the curtain like an arrowhead.

"No, baby."

"Don't 'no, baby' me. I'm a grown woman." There were sobs. "I went to the funeral."

"Sherry, you shouldn't have done that. I told you not to go. I told you you'd only get hurt more."

"I had to. I had to say goodbye to Neddy."

"Sherry—"

"Don't you understand, Mama? I loved Neddy. I loved him and Daddy killed him—"

Rock coughed and Tony slapped a hand over his mouth.

"—and I hate him. I hate him. I hate him. I hate him."

"You don't know what you're saying, Sherry. You're upset. That's only natural. But your father didn't have anything to do with Ned's death."

Sherry snorted. "I don't believe it."

"Well, you'd better believe it."

"Why should I? What makes you so sure he didn't murder Ned?"

There was a short pause. "Because," said Mrs. Pearce, "because I know your father. He's a good man. He would never do any such thing."

"Daddy hates every boy that I ever fall for. He's always trying to bust up my relationships. He's doing the same thing with Aaron even now. What's he going to do, kill him, too?"

"You're being ridiculous. Your Daddy is looking out for you. If you didn't go running around indiscriminately with so many fellows, boys who are too old for you and getting yourself in trouble like you're nothing but a cheap floozy instead of the daughter of Merel Pearce—"

The sharp crack of a slap filled the air. An unintelligible and primal scream rocked Tony and Rock off their feet.

Sherry shouted. "I hate you, too!"

The curtains shook. Tony and Rock raced back to the trade room. Sherry raced through the crowd while Tony and Rock leaned against the far wall, panting and out of breath. Sherry reappeared from the vestibule, cheek fiery red, then disappeared out the front door.

"What was *that* all about?" Tony wondered.

Rock slapped Tony on the back. "*That*, Tony, was the key to Pandora's box."

"What do you mean 'the key to Pandora's box?' Pandora's box is a source of unforeseen and unpredictable troubles. Are you trying to tell me that what we just witnessed is only the beginning of our problems? I mean, we need answers not more questions."

"That's what I mean, Tony."

"But the key to Pandora's box only opens up a box of troubles—"

"Forget Pandora's box. Forget I said it at all. What I meant was the lock to Pandora's key or—" Rock slapped himself in the head. "Listen to me, will you?"

Tony tapped his foot.

"Oh, great," muttered Rock, "the tapdance routine again. You ought to be in vaudeville."

"You want to talk vaudeville or tell me what's on your mind?"

Rock went for option number two. Option number one was a joke. Vaudeville was dead. Option number three would have been to sock Tony in his smug, jutting jaw, but the guy was his bestfriend, and it went against the code. So option number two it had to be. "Don't you get it, Tony?"

Tony stood there with that look on his face.

"Jim's innocent. Merel did it. Merel killed everybody. Ned was obviously Sherry's boyfriend and Merel didn't like it. Didn't like it one teeny bit. Merel offed him." Rock snapped his fingers. "Merel wants his theater back." Another snap. "He kills B.A.D."

"What about Duncan Daniels and Virginia Plat? Have you forgotten about them?"

Rock nodded. Drats, he *had* forgotten all about them. "No, I haven't forgotten about them. It was all that killing. You know how it is. The old coot just snapped. Went berserk. Went on a killing spree."

Tony was smirking.

"What? Don't look at me like that. What?"

"And I suppose Merel Pearce did all this while he was performing in his own show?"

Rock looked cornered for a moment, but the wheels

were spinning. "He wasn't working the night Ned Ledbetter disappeared. Remember? According to the police, Ned was last seen on a Monday and the theater was closed that night." It was his turn to smirk. "So it could have been Merel, after all."

"Forget it, Rock," Tony stated flatly. "Mr. Pearce was performing at the White House, remember? And even if that turns out to be wrong, that still doesn't explain how he could have murdered B.A.D. the other night. Let's face it, Rock, it's impossible."

"So who do you think is responsible for all these murders, Mr. Detective?"

"My money is still on Rick Elf," said Tony. "He ran from the police. He probably stole the Kewpie Mountain in collusion with Duncan Daniels and Dewey Rood. They stole all the collectibles, including their own, to throw off suspicion.

"The Kewpie Jim found in the parking lot was probably dropped in their getaway. That's sloppy. They've been sloppy from the start. Amateurs. Merel Pearce is too slick to make such a mess. Elf, Daniels and Rood."

"The three stooges. What were they trying to do? Corner the market on Kewpie Mountains?" Rock resented the way Daniels had apparently suckered him. He had seemed like a nice guy. Rock wondered how he could have been so wrong about him.

"Why not?" answered Tony. "Imagine, if they had both Kewpie Mountains. They could name their price."

"So why did Duncan end up dead?"

Tony thought a moment. "Greed. Mr. Elf and Mr. Rood wanted a fifty-fifty split. Neater that way."

"And Virginia Plat?"

Tony shook his head.

"And B.A.D.? I rather doubt he had anything to do with Kewpies, dolls or mountains. And then there's Ned Ledbetter—"

Tony squeezed his eyes shut. He was getting a three pill headache. "I don't know."

Tony paced. "We're missing something." He turned and looked at his friend. "I can feel it. We're close, but we're missing something." Something crucial.

Rock rubbed his wrist and checked his pocket watch. "Right now, we're missing lunch and I'm famished. It's nearly noon and you made me skip breakfast to go to Ned's funeral."

"Noon?" cried Tony. "We were supposed to be at the police station giving our statements concerning yesterday's chase." He had a stiff neck from that crazy duck ride and his hair smelled funny after shampooing once and conditioning twice. What was in that Moon River, anyway?

Tony headed for the door, then stopped mid-step. "Say, where do you suppose Mrs. Pearce is?"

"I don't know," Rock said, "left with her daughter, I suppose."

Tony's brow scrunched up. "No. Sherry came out alone. Remember?"

"Yeah," drawled Rock, "I guess so. So what?"

"Well," Tony said slowly, "they were fighting back there. There was that scream. And that sound of somebody being hit."

"You're not suggesting that Sherry Pearce killed her mother, are you, Tony?"

"I don't know," said Tony. "Am I? I mean, is it possible? Could Sherry Pearce be our killer?"

Rock groaned "Why are you always doing this to me?"

They ran through the vestibule and up the hall. Rock said, "If there's a dead body in there, I'm leaving on the next plane."

The hall was deserted. "They were right around here," whispered Tony. He wasn't sure why he was whispering.

Rock nodded and began fiddling with the dark red curtain that filled half the left side. He found an opening and both boys stuck their heads out the other side.

Dolly Pearce was on her knees.

Tony rushed over. "Are you all right, Mrs. Pearce? Are you hurt?" The poor dear looked like she was in deep shock. Had that horrible daughter of hers beaten her?

The boys helped Mrs. Pearce to her feet. "Don't worry," said Rock, "everything's going to be all right now, ma'am."

"What?"

"Poor dear," Rock said, "she's been hit so hard it's addled her brains."

Mrs. Pearce shook herself free of the boys' grip. "I am not addled," she said harshly. "I dropped my car keys. I was looking for them."

Rock whistled. He twirled his finger around his ear, the universal signal for scrambled brains. Fortunately, Tony was the only one to see it.

"You weren't driving, remember, Mrs. Pearce?" Tony's voice was soft, soothing and nurse-like. "Your daughter drove you."

"Oh, my." Mrs. Pearce brought her hands to her

cheeks. "Silly me."

"Come on, Dolly." Rock took Mrs. Pearce's hand. "We'll call you a cab." Dolly Pearce was one nutty lady. Could have stuck her picture on a jar of *Planters Peanuts*.

Chapter 37

The station door opened and Officer Robinson escorted the boys into the back. "You're just in time. Rick Elf is spilling his guts. What's left of them, that is, after that crazy chase you and Mr. Stafford had him on yesterday, Tony."

"Don't remind me."

"I'm looking forward to the DVD," said Rock. "Killer Ducks From Branson."

They followed Paula down the now familiar corridors. She stopped outside a closed door. "Elf's in there now with his lawyer, giving his story."

"He's confessing to everything?" Rock asked. "That lets Jim off the hook."

Robinson smiled. "He's admitted to conspiring to steal his own Kewpie Mountain along with the rest of the missing property."

"Why?" Tony asked. "Did he say why he did it?"

"Money, why else? And Elf wanted the money for himself. He and Duncan Daniels had a buyer all lined up."

"Not Dewey Rood?"

"Nope. But greed caught up with our Mr. Elf and he didn't feel like sharing the proceeds with his partner."

"And so he faked the theft." Tony stared at the door.

"That's right."

"He's the murderer?"

"He's admitted to murdering Duncan Daniels," Robinson said. "And to the grand theft. We found some of Mr. Elf's hairs on the towel the Kewpie Mountain was wrapped in when you found it out on Daniels' boat. More traces on Daniels' body.

"With the evidence mounting against him, Elf has decided to come clean. Elf was planning on disposing of Daniel's body and scuttling the boat when Kewpiecon was over and the police lost interest."

Paula laid a hand on Tony's arm. "He's hoping his cooperation will get him a lighter sentence."

Tony looked at Paula's hand and made no comment. "What about the others?"

"What do you mean?"

"He means what about Virginia Plat and Ned Ledbetter," put in Rock. Tony nodded. "And B.A.D. Did Elf kill B.A.D.?"

Robinson shook her head. "He says no."

"And you believe him?" Rock looked incredulous.

"It's not a question of what we believe," Robinson said. "The fact of the matter is that it would have been impossible for Elf to have killed Duncan Daniels and Virginia Plat at the same time.

"As for Ned Ledbetter, Elf was not at Kewpiecon that year. We already checked. His employer's records clearly show he was working that year, not in Branson. Nowhere near here."

"What about B.A.D.?" pressed Rock. "That doesn't mean he didn't kill B.A.D."

"He swears he didn't do it," Officer Robinson explained. "In fact, I think it was his fear that he'd be nailed for all the killings that led him to confess to murdering Daniels."

"If he killed Duncan, then he could just as easily have killed B.A.D." Like a dog with a meaty bone, Rock was not about to let go. And he liked to see things wrapped up nice and neat.

Paula looked at Tony, then Rock. Her eyes softened. "I'm sorry, Rock, I know you'd like to find somebody to blame besides Mr. Stafford. But it isn't Rick Elf."

Rock fumed. "What makes you so sure, Robinson?"

An unexpected voice answered from behind. "Because Rick has an alibi."

Tony and Rock spun around. It was Susie Garcia, incoming ROSE president, dressed in a white blouse, black wool skirt, dark nylon stockings and one-inch black heels. Her eyes were tinged pink. She filled the hall with the scent of Chanel Number 5.

"What are you talking about?" shot Rock.

"Rick was with me when that rapper, B.A.D. Spike, was killed."

"All night?"

Susie looked at the ground and said, "All night."

Robinson cleared her throat. "That was Mrs. Garcia's room that Rick went through when he got away from me at the Ramada yesterday, boys. Rick Elf and

Mrs. Garcia here had adjoining rooms."

"When Rick came through my room yesterday looking scared, I had no idea what was going on. I never imagined that he was involved in any sort of thefts." A sob shook her body. "And I never dreamed he might have killed anyone."

Susie Garcia looked imploringly at Tony. "He's a good man. He said he only wanted the money so we could be together."

Sure, thought Tony. A good man. That's why the married Mr. Elf was having an affair with the equally married Mrs. Garcia. Remnants of his conversation with Evie and Becky at the dinner table the night of the banquet came to mind. There had been insinuations. Something about how Elf always came when Garcia did?

The naughty ladies had snickered about Rick Elf and Susie Garcia; knowing and furtive glances had been exchanged. It must have been common knowledge that the two of them were carrying on an annual affair under cover of Kewpiecon. Tony should have caught on to that earlier and he silently kicked himself for having missed it.

Elf wanted the money he'd make on the Kewpie Mountains so he and Susie could run away together.

"Why don't you boys have a seat in my office, Tony." Paula took Mrs. Garcia's arm. "Det. Winston will take your statement, Mrs. Garcia. Follow me, please."

"How do you like that?" Rock said with wonder. He helped himself to a fat, sugar-free candy bar sticking out between two sheets of paper on Robinson's desk. The big guy tore open the wrapper and bit into the dark, rich chocolate. So what if it wasn't nutritious, this was the closest thing he was going to get to a lunch and he was going to indulge himself. "It has to be Dewey. He's the only one left."

Robinson stepped into the office. "What has to be Dewey?" She saw Rock wipe a line of chocolate from his lips. His hand clutched a candy bar wrapper and a glance at her desk told the story. Her bar was missing. Paula held out her hand, palm up. "Mind if I have a bite of that?"

Rock broke off a chunk. "Sure. Share and share alike, I always say."

Robinson lifted Rock from her chair and planted herself in his place. "What has to be Dewey?"

"The killer." Rock took a seat across from Robinson and pluckily popped the rest of the chocolate in his mouth before she could demand more.

The grin on Robinson's face was as big as a double-wide.

"What did I say that's so funny?"

"Dewey didn't kill anybody."

Tony leaned forward. "He didn't?"

Robinson shook her head. "No. He didn't." She inspected the meager chunk of chocolate that Rock had relegated her and offered it in Tony's direction. Tony shook his head. Paula shrugged and lowered the tidbit onto her tongue. Heaven. So much for watching her sugar.

Tony looked at her disapprovingly. She felt bad, but not that bad. Everyone needs chocolate once in a while, don't they?

"He had that second Kewpie Mountain so he must be guilty of something."

"If Dewey Rood is guilty of anything," said Robinson, wiping her mouth with a finger, "it's of being one hell of a craftsman."

Rock was getting annoyed. All of this chit-chat was getting them nowhere, most specifically nowhere nearer to finding B.A.D. killer. "What's that supposed to mean?"

"It means that the Kewpie Mountain that Tony and Mr. Stafford saw Dewey Rood take to Rick was a fake."

"A fake?" gasped Tony.

"That's right."

"I don't believe it," said Rock, refusing to give up what appeared to be his last good suspect.

"That Kewpie Mountain wasn't even porcelain. It was wood."

"Wood?" Tony hadn't expected this at all. "I was sure that they, Rick Elf, Duncan Daniels and Dewey Rood were all in on this together."

Paula was shaking her head. "Nope. It seems Dewey felt bad about Elf having his Kewpie Mountain stolen. Turned out he'd been working on this Kewpie Mountain reproduction for the past couple of years. Brought it with him to Branson.

"He was going to sell it at auction, but instead gave it to Rick Elf as some sort of consolation for the one he'd supposedly lost. You should see it, we've got it down in the evidence room. All painted up, it looks real nice."

"Is it that good?" inquired Tony.

"From a distance, like you first saw it, it looks like the genuine article. But when you see his reproduction next to the real one, you can tell them apart easy." She folded her hands. "Still, it's a mighty fine reproduction.

Like you said, Tony."

"What's that?" he asked.

"Dewey Rood is good with a knife."

Tony nodded.

Rock's mouth thinned out. "If Dewey is so innocent, what was he doing out at Duncan's boat? You want to explain that, Robinson?"

She pushed back her chair and tucked one foot under her rear. "Sure. He was delivering some lures he'd made to a fishing buddy of his that has a cottage out that way. Brings him some every year."

Tony rolled his eyes. "The man in the fishing boat. We saw him motor off as we were arriving."

Rock groaned. "You mean he wasn't up to no good on Duncan's boat?"

Robinson shook her head. "He didn't even know Duncan had a boat, let alone that it happened to be at that dock." She dropped her feet. "You want to see it?"

"See what?" Tony wondered.

"Dewey's replica of the Kewpie Mountain. It really is impressive."

"Sure," shrugged Tony, "why not."

"Why bother?" Rock asked. "It's a waste of time."

"We can get a shot of it for our article, Rock. Think about it. Lots of folks are interested in arts and crafts."

"And they buy newspapers and magazines," replied Rock. "Fine. Lucky for you I've got my camera."

Paula escorted Tony and Rock to a small locked storeroom not much bigger than a walk-in closet. She scanned the dusty shelves and pulled down Dewey's masterpiece. The real Kewpie Mountain was on the shelf beside it. She handed the copy to Tony.

"Can I hold the real Kewpie Mountain?" Rock

asked.

"I don't think so," Robinson replied. "Can't take any chances."

"You afraid I might drop it?"

She said yes.

"What's all this?" Rock was shaking an open box marked *Evidence: B.A.D. Spike's Crib*.

Robinson looked over Rock's shoulder. Tony did the same. "That's some stuff that turned up at the theater. Mostly garbage. Even though B.A.D.'s theater wasn't open yet, hundreds of people were in and out of that building—construction workers, business people, B.A.D.'s employees. Some of the Kewpie folk were even seen wandering around for a look. And there wasn't any sort of regular cleaning service in place.

"It hasn't all been sorted through too closely. But it's not likely to yield much in the way of clues or evidence."

"I'll say," muttered Rock. "Not unless the lazy janitor did it." His nose wrinkled up. "A rusty wrench, two nails, gum wrappers, a couple of old brochures, a heel from a shoe, half a page from a newspaper dated two weeks ago, a pair of flimsy looking sunglasses. And those are only the highlights." He stuffed the box back on the shelf and wiped his hands on his shirt. "So, what happens now?"

"How do you mean?" asked Robinson, her eyes narrowing.

"I mean, if all the good suspects are gone—and unless B.A.D. stabbed himself in his kitchen and Virginia committed suicide plunging a knife in her chest in that hidey-hole and Ned Ledbetter, well, maybe he went wading in a pool of concrete and forgot how to swim—unless that's what happened to all these dead people suddenly appearing around here, then that only leaves Jim Stafford."

"Looks that way," said Robinson.

"Good thing Jim can play the harmonica. I hear that's practically required in prison."

"I don't think Jim's going to be needing that harmonica just yet."

"Why's that?" asked Rock.

Tony put aside Dewey's wooden Kewpie Mountain replica and reached into the evidence box. "Remember what you said before about not wanting to be in Jim's shoes?"

"So?"

"So there's one more suspect."

Chapter 38

"If you ask me," grumbled Det. Carvin, "this is nuts."

"I didn't hear you telling Chief Schaum that when we went over this little plan." Rock elbowed Carvin in the ribs. They were squeezed tight, side to side, along the back of the kitchen. Why did he always end up in tight spots with the difficult ones?

Stafford sat cross-legged on the floor, breathing slowly. Said it was part of a new yoga ritual he was trying.

It was pitch black and smelled of rotten fruit. Jim said he recalled seeing a basket of fruit on the counter that night—the night he saw Donald for the last time. He hoped Tony was right about this hunch of his, because if Tony was wrong he'd be doing a variety show at the state pen.

"Stop pushing." Carvin shoved Rock back. Rock

punched him in the arm and he squawked.

"Will you two shut up?" Paula said. "You're worse than an old married couple."

Tony squeezed Paula's arm and whispered in her ear. "How are you doing?"

"Okay. You worried?"

Tony said yes. He was having second thoughts and said so. "I hope this works."

"It was a good idea you had, Tony. It will work." She squeezed him back.

"That's right," said Jim. "It's a good plan, Tony."

Tony hoped Paula and Jim were right almost as much as he hoped he was wrong. He was about to express his doubts when the tiny but unmistakable sound of a key being inserted in a lock came from the back door. His breath caught in his chest like a jagged rock. He pushed himself back against the wall, one hand deep in his pocket.

"Quiet," cautioned Rock. They drew their collective breaths.

The door opened slowly. A dim shaft of light spilled in before the door closed once more casting them all in darkness. Tony heard shuffling footsteps and the sound of a clasp clicking open followed by rummaging sounds.

A moment later a weak flashlight sputtered then went out. Tony heard the sounds of a hand slapping the flashlight in frustration. The beam responded to the beating, flashed on and stayed on.

The beam of light scanned the wall at waist height then fell to the floor. Methodically, the flashlight's beam worked its way around the kitchen table and chairs. The intruder was muttering barely audible curses and searching closer to the ground now, pushing the chairs out of the way one by one.

Tony was about to whisper to Paula when the back door was flung open and the lights flashed on.

"Dolly!"

"Merel!"

"Mr. Pearce!"

Dolly Pearce jumped, banging her head on the underside of the table. She was wearing a long black coat and low-heeled black shoes. The hand holding the now pointless flashlight fell to her side.

Merel strode into the room and dragged his wife out from under the table. "Dolly, what in tarnation are you doing under there?" He aimed a finger at Stafford. "What's going on, Stafford? What kind of trouble you causing now?"

"Catching a killer is what," said Jim.

Dolly quivered. Her eyes had grown and she looked like a possum caught in a crossfire. "M-Merel—what are you doing here?"

"Johnny told me you were in my dressing room this afternoon and ran out at the end looking all upset. I figured something was going on, so I asked him to keep an eye on you. He's been tailing you and called me as soon as you pulled up here. What the devil are you up to, honey?"

Paula and Tony had come to their feet. Rock and Det. Carvin rose as well. Det. Carvin had his hand on his gun but had yet to draw it.

Merel swirled in agitation and looked at the whole lot of them. "What the hell is going on here? Why are you all here? Does somebody want to explain?" His gaze stopped on his wife but she refused to meet it.

Tony stepped forward. He pulled his hand from his pocket and extended his arm. His fingers held something as treasured as a jewel. "Looking for this, Mrs. Pearce?"

Mrs. Pearce said nothing.

"What the devil is that?" snapped Merel. He took a step towards Tony. "Have you all lost your minds?" He turned to Stafford. "This nut's rubbing off on y'all. You're all looney."

"It's a shoe heel, Mr. Pearce," explained Tony. "A Cerucci, to be precise."

"A whatchee?" Merel scratched his forehead.

"A Cerucci. Says so right on the inside of the heel. It's a brand of designer shoes that your wife favors."

Merel took a closer look and shrugged. "So?"

"So your wife killed B.A.D.," said Jim with more tenderness than Rock would have been capable of. He turned to Dolly. "That funny little sound I kept hearing the night Donald was killed. That was you," he shook his head sadly, "walking on your broken heel. If it wasn't for Tony here, I never would have remembered."

"Your wife lost this heel in the theater the night she stabbed B.A.D., Mr. Pearce," Tony stated. "We were at your house when the cobbler brought out the repaired shoe with a new heel."

"That's why Dolly's here now. Searching for it," Jim said.

Tony said, "The other day, when you had that confrontation with your daughter, we thought you were confused, Mrs. Pearce. We even thought that maybe your daughter had struck you."

Rock sneered. "You told us you lost your car keys."

"Instead you were looking for this." The Cerucci

heel sat in the palm of Tony's hand. Mrs. Pearce couldn't take her eyes off it.

"That's nutty," said Merel. "So my wife likes Ceruttis, or whatever you called them, that don't make her no killer."

"That's a very rare brand of shoe here in Branson," said Robinson. "In fact, no local store carries them."

"And we've checked with Hal at Ozark Mountain Shoe Repair, Mr. Pearce," put in Det. Carvin. "He's confirmed that your wife brought in the broken left shoe for a new heel the very morning after B.A.D. Spike was found dead."

"That still doesn't mean—"

"Oh, do be quiet, Merel. Just once, please." Mrs. Pearce stepped forward. "How did you catch me?"

Tony squirmed. Mrs. Pearce was so close he could smell her perfume, feel her breath.

Dolly was smiling. "You naughty, clever boys. You set me up, didn't you?"

Tony nodded ever so slightly. Tony, Rock and Jim had had a clever little contrived conversation in B.A.D.'s apartment earlier, laying out a plan to urge the police to search the place for a shoe heel. Hoping that Dolly would hear.

"What is she talking about?" Merel glared at Tony. "I think you and I had better go home, honey." He reached for Dolly's hand. "You're not feeling well. We'll get you a doctor, honey. You're not yourself."

"Yes, I am!" Dolly stamped her foot. "I am finally being myself. That's what I'm doing. I killed Ned." She turned to her husband. "I killed Ned. I hated him and I killed him." She was shaking like a coconut palm in a hurricane. Her face was riddled with red blotches and the area around her lips was white, as if drained of all blood.

Merel stepped toward Det. Carvin and Officer Robinson. "I don't know what you've done to her, but my wife is clearly having a nervous breakdown. I'll call Chief Schaum. I'll call the mayor. I will not let my wife be treated this way."

"It's all right, Merel." She patted her husband's hand. "It's better this way. The boys played a little trick on me. You knew about the bugs all along, didn't you?"

"Yes, Mrs. Pearce," admitted Tony. "We knew about the bugs."

Merel looked uneasy now.

"They are your listening devices, aren't they, Mr. Pearce?" said Paula.

Merel looked unhappy as he replied, "This is my theater. I have a right to do what I want with it."

"You and your bugs, again. It's those bugs that got Ned fired in the first place, Merel," scolded Jim.

"You were listening in on B.A.D. and Dolly here knew all about it," explained Tony. "We caught her with a tape in her hand the first time we met her in your dressing room. We didn't think anything of it at the time, but once we figured out what was really going on, it all made sense."

Tony paused for dramatic effect. "I'll bet if the police look, they'll find a tape recorder setup hidden in that desk of yours in your theater, Mr. Pearce."

Rock said, "I'll bet you didn't know that she was listening to those secret recordings you made?"

"No, I didn't." Merel's strong voice for once was barely audible. "Dolly, what were you thinking? You had no business going through my desk and listening to those tapes. You've got to let me handle things." He draped an arm around her waist. "I've always taken care of you, haven't I?"

Dolly shook him off. "No, you haven't."

He looked hurt.

"It's not your fault, Merel. Don't take it that way. You're a star. You're busy. You didn't always know what was going on." She was looking at Tony now as if he was the only person in the room who might understand. "That Ned Ledbetter boy. He ruined my daughter. He was too old for her. She was only a child and he-he—" She sobbed, unable to continue.

"He got Sherry pregnant, didn't he?" Tony said softly.

Mrs. Pearce nodded. "I sent her off for an abortion and—"

"An abortion?" Merel Pearce's face lit up in shock. "What abortion?"

"When she went to California that time, Merel."

Merel's voice was getting weaker and weaker. He looked like a marionette with one good string. "You told me she was visiting your mother."

"You wouldn't have understood." Dolly Pearce took a deep breath. Her eyes focused on someplace far away. "Merel wasn't home the night that Ned called and said that Mr. Stafford had found out he was bugging his office and fired him. I told Ned to meet me here at the theater. With all the construction going on, I knew this would be a good place to get rid of him for good."

"Don't say anything more, Dolly," urged her husband, "not until I get that darn lawyer of mine,

Slootsky, out here."

"No, dear. That won't be necessary. Let me finish. I killed Ned. Bashed him on the head when he wasn't watching and dropped him in a hole that I knew was going to be filled up. With all the work going on, I knew no one would notice. Anybody that did would merely think someone else had poured the concrete."

"What about B.A.D.?" Paula asked. "Why did you kill B.A.D.?"

"My husband was recording all Mr. Milquist's conversations. I knew that they'd be digging up Ned soon enough what with all the renovations Mr. Milquist was planning. I thought that if I could stop Mr. Milquist, the poor dear, from opening then I could stop them from digging up Ned."

"And what better way to stop the show from opening than to kill its star." Tony shook his head, wondering if Dolly Pearce would ever be deemed sane enough to stand trial.

Det. Carvin added, "And you knew that your husband would get the theater back."

"Yes. I figured I could talk him out of letting anyone else dig up the stage area and that Ned Ledbetter would stay buried forever." The broken woman turned to Rock. "I'm sorry."

Rock averted his eyes. He'd expected this moment to be triumphant and now appeared sorry. The big guy looked ready to cry.

"And Virginia Plat?" asked Tony. "How does she fit into all this?"

"I do feel badly about that," Dolly confessed. "The poor, dear woman."

"You mean, you—" Tony shot a glance at Merel who

was leaning forward, hands on his knees. A tear was running down his cheek. The man who always thought himself in control had suddenly lost it all.

"I didn't want to kill her, you know. But she had seen me here the night I went to see Mr. Milquist. I was out in the parking lot. Sitting in my car. I wasn't sure I could go through with it. I was sitting there. Trying to steel my nerves. Ms. Plat drove by. I was so surprised, I didn't even think to duck." She shook her head. "I should have ducked."

"Miss Plat pulled up beside me and asked me if I was all right. I told her I was only getting out of the traffic for a few minutes. She drove by the trade show door. She was looking for someone judging by the way she behaved."

Dolly's shoulders shook. "Then she drove off. But I knew it was only a matter of time until she put two and two together as they say. I couldn't let her tell the police about me."

"But she might never have been able to identify you," replied Tony. "Why kill her?"

Dolly Pearce drew herself up. "I am the wife of a celebrity," she explained. "Sooner or later she would have realized that. My picture is in all the brochures for my husband's show. Me and Sherry are even in Merel's commercials.

"No," said Dolly, with a shake of the head, "I'm afraid she had to go. I followed her out to Bonniebrook and arranged to 'accidently' bump into her. It was nearly dark. We talked.

"She remembered me from the night before. I had no choice in the matter. No choice at all." Mrs. Pearce laced her fingers and squeezed. "The poor woman didn't suspect a thing."

"Why, Dolly? Why?" Merel's eyes peeked out from behind his hands. It was as if he was afraid of what he might see.

"To protect you," Dolly replied. "And Sherry. You couldn't do it. Oh, you gave her things, me too. Money, clothes, cars, jewelry. But you were always so busy with your career. You didn't have the time to be a real father. And Sherry needed to be protected, from boys as much as from herself."

Mrs. Pearce turned to Tony. "Sherry *is* a good girl, but she has bad tendencies. That's what the pastor calls them, anyway."

She turned back to Merel. "So I had to protect her and you. It's my job as a wife and a mother." Dolly clasped her hands. "My duty."

Thoughts raced through Tony's head, yet none formed into words. And though Jim suddenly found himself out from under a murder rap, he looked more saddened than relieved.

Chapter 39

"What do you think he wants?" Rock rubbed some minty-scented gel through his stubbly hair and examined himself in the mirror for the hundredth time.

"Maybe he wants to thank us for clearing his name." Tony looked at the clock between the double beds. "Come on, already, Rock. Jim said we were supposed to meet him downstairs at eleven. It's eleven-fifteen now."

"Hold your horses, Tony." Rock pulled on a fresh T-shirt. "You know, last night was the best night's sleep I've had in a week. Maybe all year. We should do good deeds more often."

"I'm glad to hear it. Can we leave now?" Personally, he'd had enough of solving mysteries and murders. From now on, he was determined to stick to playing guitars. Maybe take up a nice quiet hobby, like collecting Kewpie Dolls.

Something was different about Rock and he'd just figured out what it was. "A *white* T-shirt?"

"Okay, okay." Rock tugged at his shirt. "Got it from Jim. Some girl that works for him sent over a whole bag full of booty. T-shirts, CDs, autographed photos. Even some foam cow patties." He jerked a finger. "It's all over there on the bed. See for yourself."

Tony raised the bag open with his finger. "Sure enough. Cow patties." He turned his attention to the muttering TV. "Anything about Dolly?"

"Same old thing. I expect the newspapers will be carrying the full story. You want to get a paper?"

"No."

Poor Mrs. Pearce. Tony couldn't help but feel sorry for the woman to a certain degree, despite all the evil she'd done. She'd be locked up a long time. Hopefully, she'd get some help there.

She needed it.

As for poor Virginia Plat, the woman had the unfortunate fate of being in the wrong place at the wrong time. More than once. And this fate had cost Ms. Plat her life.

On further interrogation, Rick Elf had confessed that it was he and Daniels who had planted the missing Kewpie items, minus the Kewpie Mountain, in Virginia's room after her death. They knew the police would find the merchandise once they searched her room. The two men had been hoping to make the conveniently dead Virginia Plat their scapegoat. They figured the sacrifice of the smaller items was a small price to pay for this. Then Elf got rid of his partner, Daniels.

Elf wasn't going to be meeting up with Susie Garcia

at next year's Kewpiecon, that was for sure. Susie was going to have to find herself some new diversion.

Rock opened the door and was leaning over the railing. He held a hand over his eyes, blocking the bright late morning sun. "What the—"

"What is it?" Tony turned off the television. "And who's honking? It's driving me crazy." Somewhere below a horn was blaring to the tune of 'shave and a haircut, two bits.'

Rock was grinning. "It's Jim."

"Jim?" Tony gripped the rail and looked down. A long, red, twenty-thousand pound, turn-of-the-century looking trolley was double-parked in the Ramada's parking lot. "Jim Stafford's Jolly Trolley Company, Fun Sightseeing Tours," Tony read aloud. The name was emblazoned in big letters on the side, in the shape of a banner.

Jim was at the wheel. Of course he'd be the one honking. He gave it one more 'shave and a haircut' before knocking it off. He looked up at the boys and waved. "Come on, men! Tour's about to start!"

The trolley was filled with tourists, nearly thirty of them in all. And they were all looking up at Tony and Rock. The big guy waved.

Rock pulled Tony away from the rail. "Come on, Tony. You heard Jim. This ought to be a blast!"

Tony was forced to run as Rock dragged him down the stairs at near light-speed.

Approaching the Jolly Trolley, Tony noticed Paula was riding shotgun. She was wearing civilian clothes, too. A pale green shirt and knee-length skirt in a slightly darker shade. She looked gorgeous. Very.

She said good morning. "Mr. Stafford has offered to

personally take us on the grand tour of Branson and its environs."

"Terrific," said Rock. The boys climbed aboard. Two spots had been saved for them right up front.

Jim held out his hand. "I want to thank you men again for saving my neck."

"It was nothing." Tony shook Jim's extended hand.

"No, no. I was in a mess of trouble. Thought I might go to jail for a crime I never committed."

"We always knew you were innocent, Jim." Rock pumped Jim's arm up and down like he was trying to restart a dry well.

"Oh, please." Tony rolled his eyes and muttered. How many times had Rock given up on Jim in the past few days? He'd lost count. "I do feel bad about Mrs. Pearce though."

"Don't you worry about her none. I hear Merel's got her a whole ton of doctors and lawyers. I'm sure she'll get proper care, though she's done a horrible thing and she's going to pay a heavy price."

"I'll say." Tony smiled at Paula. "How about if we change the subject? Did I ever tell you how beautiful you are, Paula?"

She smiled sheepishly.

Rock groaned. "Just a minute, Tony. First things first." Rock laid his hand on Jim's shoulder. " We're really glad we could help you, Jim," he said. "Now don't forget our deal."

"Deal?" Jim scratched his head. "Oh, right. Your story. I promised you an exclusive interview, didn't I?"

Rock nodded.

"You got it." Jim winked at Tony. "And I'm going to do you one better."

"Better?" asked Rock suspiciously.

"That's right. How's about if you boys come work for me in my show?"

Tony answered for the two of them. "Thanks, Jim. That's very generous of you, but I don't think I'm ready to leave Florida just yet."

"Yeah, me, too," said Rock, though he sounded disappointed. "I guess." He looked at Tony but Tony shook his head in the negative.

"Okay, I can understand that." Jim snapped his fingers. "Here's a thought then. Next album I record I want you both in the studio."

"Now that's a deal," Tony replied, "we can accept."

"Terrific. Enough business now," said Jim, rubbing his hands together with glee. "We've got places to go and things to see!" He motioned for Tony and Rock to sit.

As soon as they hit their seats, Jim grabbed the wheel, circled the Ramada and headed for the exit onto Highway 76. He had a microphone in one hand and, with boyish enthusiasm, was explaining all the fun they were going to have.

Jim stopped at the edge of the road a moment waiting for a gap in the traffic. A line of cars went by, Jim found his opening and the trolley lunged into the street.

The image of a high speed chase ending in an icy plunge in Andy Williams' Moon River ran wildly through Tony's thoughts. He gripped the edges of his seat, expecting the worst. Did this tub float?

Jim turned his head, rose up in his seat and said with one hand on the microphone and the other on the wheel, "Hey, everybody, I've got an idea. What do you say?" There was a mischievous glint in those blue eyes of his. And neither eye was on the road.

Tony held his breath and started praying.

"As we drive past his theater, let's all drop our pants and moon Mickey Gilley!"

Afterword

I need to thank a lot of people for their help in this book's creation. Firstly, thanks go out to the kind and helpful members of the International Rose O'Neill Society. In her day, the gifted Rose O'Neill was probably the most famous female artist in the world and, one of her creations, the Kewpie, was as adored and ubiquitous as anything today. If you'd like more information about Rose O'Neill, Kewpie dolls or the IROC, a good place to start would be to check out www:kewpieroseoneillclub.com.

Thanks to Chief of Police Steve Mefford and Asst. Chief Carroll W. McCullough and the entire Branson Police Department for not locking me up and other courtesies. I hope these courtesies, especially that 'not locking me up' one, still exist after the reading of this novel (it's only fiction, boys and girls).

Thanks to Mark Schaum and his family for their very generous contribution to the A.D. Henderson School in exchange for my including him in this story. I think he made a great chief.

And many thanks to Jim Stafford for being incredibly foolish, I mean generous, in offering to be portrayed as a murder suspect in one of my novels. I only hope he doesn't turn out to be guilty because he's a really nice guy.

That said, as I was in Branson working on this novel, I'd mention to persons curious as to what I was up to that Jim was going to be playing himself as a character in this murder mystery. Every time I mentioned this (and I do mean *every* time) the person I was speaking with, whether they knew Jim personally or not, always replied with a laugh, "That Jim Stafford, he is a character!" And they're right.

Thanks also to Jim's wife, Ann, and children, G.G. and Shea, for putting up with me. Without giving away the story, I can safely say that the three of them are completely innocent. Thanks also to Jim's staff.

For more information about Branson, Kewpies and further points of interest, useful websites include the following: Bransonchamber.com, ExploreBranson.com, Springfield.org, Missouritourism.com, as well as Kewpie-museum.com and JimStafford.com.

And if you'd like to see Jim's show for free while you're in town, just tell him I sent you. . .And he'll point you to the ticket window. Have your purses and wallets ready, folks.